About the Author

MICHELLE VERNAL LIVES in Christchurch, New Zealand with her husband, two teenage sons and attention seeking tabby cats, Humphrey and Savannah. Before she started writing novels, she had a variety of jobs:

Pharmacy shop assistant, girl who sold dried up chips and sausages at a hot food stand in a British pub, girl who sold nuts (for 2 hours) on a British market stall, receptionist, P.A...Her favourite job though is the one she has now – writing stories she hopes leave her readers with a satisfied smile on their face.

If you'd like to know when Michelle's next book is coming out you can visit her website at www.michellevernalbooks.com[1].

To say thank you, you'll receive a short New Year's Eve O'Mara family story.

---

1.   http://www.michellevernalbooks.com

Also by Michelle Vernal

The Cooking School on the Bay
Second-hand Jane
Staying at Eleni's
The Traveller's Daughter
Sweet Home Summer
Series
Isabel's Story
The Promise
The Dancer
The Guesthouse on the Green
O'Mara's
Moira Lisa Smile
What goes on Tour
Rosi's Regrets
Christmas at O'Mara's
A Wedding at O'Mara's
Maureen's Song
The O'Maras in LaLa Land
Due in March
A Baby at O'Mara's out 28 May, 2021
And... Brand New Series fiction, Liverpool Brides
The Autumn Posy
The Winter Posy
Book 3, The Spring Posy out 28 August 2021

Compendum of Liverpudlian words

A ntwacky
      Old fashioned or out of date

Queen

A woman

Cob on

To feel angry, agitated or irritated

Baltic

It's freezing

Brassic

No money

Woollybacks

People who come from outside Liverpool

Moggies

Cats

The Dancers

Upstairs on a double decker bus

Part One

Chapter One

Liverpool, 1952

Patty

IT WASN'T THE DAMP and the rats that scuttled about the walls that killed her, Patty Hamilton thought, watching as her dear mother's body was carried from the squalid room they occupied in Osbourne Court, Toxteth. No, it was despair.

She was certain if there'd been a glimmer of hope their circumstances would improve then her mam would've found the strength to shake off the rumbling cough that had turned sinister as the winter months stretched long and the cold crept into all their bones.

Patty, who was ten and her eight-year-old brother, Davey were sitting at the table that had come with the room. The tea things were still laid out because their mam liked things to be nice. Aside from the two mattresses she'd insisted they drag into the middle of the room of a night to be away from the scratching sounds and rising damp in the walls, it was the only furniture in the room. The one-ring cooker pushed into the corner didn't count as furniture in Patty's opinion. It was as useless for cooking as it was for heating.

Patty's blue eyes, which were mirror images of her mam's, had once shone brightly. Now they were dull as she looked at her mam's mattress where she could see the indent her body had made in it along with the damp patches left behind by her feverish sweats. Her breath caught and her throat tightened to the point where she felt as if it were closing over as the reality of what was happening hit her.

She'd never see her mam again. Geraldine Hamilton who'd left Ireland with her family as a fourteen-year-old girl for a brighter future in Liverpool had not lived to see in her thirty-third birthday.

The unfairness of it all weighed down on Patty but she knew thinking like that would get them nowhere and grieving was a luxury she couldn't afford. There'd be time for that later once she and Davey were safely settled. She'd made her mam a promise so she could pass peacefully and she intended to keep it.

Now, she needed to gather their things and go. Mam had told her what she was to do. She'd mustered what strength she'd had left to clutch Patty's hand as she rasped, they weren't to linger after she'd gone or she'd find herself in a children's home, likely separated from Davey. She'd made Patty promise they'd stick together and that she'd look after her brother come what may. Then, she'd pressed a piece of paper with an address she said they were to make their way to.

It was their father's.

Mrs Maher from next door had poked her head around the door to give a sanctimonious tut when Mr Maher and kind Mr Finnegan, who lived downstairs, had come to take their mam away not fifteen minutes earlier.

She'd no right, Patty had thought, with a scowl at the hard-faced woman who was known for being quarrelsome. She was no better than them. Her flat, while marginally larger and with more in the way of homely furnishings, was no palace and it reeked of onions. She was slovenly.

Mam had done her best by her and Davey but it was hard when you had nothing; even harder when you had no hope.

Patty didn't like Mrs Maher and this feeling was cemented as the woman's eyes, pushed into a fleshy face like currants in a bun, had feigned concern over where'd they go now they were orphans.

'We're not orphans, Mrs Maher,' Davey had replied indignantly. He was the spitting image of his father with his brown hair and grey-green eyes. He shared the same ski ramp nose as his mam and sister though. 'We've a father and that's where we'll be going.'

Mrs Maher had raised a disbelieving eyebrow, her dimpled hands resting on fat hips, 'And what makes you think he'd want you? He hasn't done much for you up to now has he, young Davey? Leaving your poor mam to fend for youse both on her own, like.'

It was a good point, Patty had thought with a stab of uncertainty at what lay ahead but Mam had assured her the man she'd married wouldn't turn his own flesh and blood away. Not when he heard what had befallen them. He was a weak and arrogant fella she'd said but he wasn't cold-heart-ed.

'Because he's our daddy,' Davey replied simply.

With the speed Mrs Maher had thudded down the stairs after that, Patty surmised the meddling woman had decided to hotfoot it around to the powers that be to notify them the Hamilton children from Osbourne Court were orphans and what were they going to do about it?

It was with this in mind she told Davey to gather up his things and not to mess about doing so as she retrieved the battered case with which they'd arrived. Back then, Mam had assured them it was only for a little while as she'd surveyed their grim surroundings. Patty shook that memory away and scooped up her own scant belongings depositing them in the suitcase.

There'd been no wake for their mam but she and Davey had said their goodbyes and that was what mattered. Patty had sung to her as she'd done to soothe her when she was alive and the pain got bad. Mam had always said she'd the voice of an angel. It was a gift she'd said and she must be sure to use it. She hoped her mam was with the angels now.

There was no family to contact because she'd been estranged from them since before Patty was born. There was nothing of hers to keep either. The engagement ring with its red-pink ruby Patty used to enjoy gazing at had been pawned long ago to pay the rent. It was still at the shop and would have to stay there. She'd have liked that ring as a keepsake.

The children's mother hadn't been fit to work at Cadbury's where she'd worked on the factory floor for some months now. Patty had wanted to leave school to help out but Geraldine Hamilton wouldn't hear of it.

'You'll finish your schooling, Patty, and find yourself a decent job. Don't leave yourself beholden to a man like I did,' she'd choked out. 'You must make your own way in the world.'

It was the closest she came to talking about their daddy, who'd gone to apply for a job one morning and never come back.

They weren't to worry about what would happen to their mam now, Mr Finnegan had said, giving them a reassuring smile as he'd wrapped their mother's body carefully in the sheet she'd lain on. Father Sean would look after her. She'd not have to suffer anymore.

He was cut from the same cloth as his wife, Patty had thought, grateful for his kindness. Mrs Finnegan had a soft heart too. She'd often sent up an extra bowl of whatever she'd cooked for dinner, stretching it out somehow because she'd known the Hamilton children were in dire straits with their poor mam not fit for earning.

Patty pulled herself back to the here and now. 'Have you got teddy?'

Davey sat down cross-legged on the floor by the case pushing his thumb in his mouth. Their mam had told him he was far too old for that sort of carry-on and he'd catch germs putting his thumb in his mouth like so but Patty figured if it gave him comfort so be it.

The little boy nodded and pointed to where the grubby worn toy he refused to sleep without was nestled between their meagre assortment of clothes.

Patty scanned the room once more, reassuring herself there was nothing more to go in the case. Then, she closed it. The click echoed in the empty space that no longer felt like any sort of home now their mother was gone.

She'd not miss this place, she thought, casting her eyes about one last time. It didn't hold happy memories and she doubted she'd ever get the smell of damp and decay from her nostrils.

The Hamilton family hadn't always lived hand to mouth picking their way through the parts of the city still pock-marked by bombsites. Once they'd lived in a terrace house with a front room, a proper kitchen, and a bathroom on Lowry Lane. It hadn't been the smartest of addresses but so far as houses went it had been happy and it had been home.

Patty and Davey had shared one of the two upstairs bed-rooms. The wallpaper had not been hanging off the wall and they'd had a proper front door to come and go through. They'd not been cold and they'd not gone to bed hungry either.

Patty had thought she'd live in that house until she was old enough to get married but then one evening their father stormed in waving his P45. She'd only been eight at the time but she remembered him spouting off about having told that bunch of woollybacks he worked under at the English Elec-tric he'd had enough. 'Anthony Hamilton won't be told what to do by the likes of them,' he roared in a manner that made Patty and Davey's eyes pop. He was a senior salesman who knew his domestic appliances better than any of the others on the payroll he went on to lament, saying it was their loss.

He'd seen his children watching on from the doorway wide-eyed and had given them a wink telling them not to worry he'd be moving on to bigger, better things.

Even at her young age, Patty would never forget the way the light had seemed to go out in her mam's pretty blue eyes that evening.

Patty couldn't understand why because she'd believed every word her daddy said but then he was her hero. She worshipped the ground her handsome father walked on and if he said not to worry, well then she wouldn't. Davey was too young to know what was going on and so long as he was fed and watered he was a happy lad.

The weeks had ticked by though and with each day that passed without their father walking through the door with a spring in his step and news of his new job, the atmosphere in the house shifted. It became oppressive and their mam always seemed to be crying.

Patty had been told often enough she was a sensitive child but the evidence that things had changed was stark. The reminder was there each evening in the lack of meat in the stew and the watery soups Mam was presenting them with.

Patty had asked her mam when Daddy would find work and to her surprise and horror she'd set her mam off on a fresh bout of crying.

Geraldine had sniffed out that Patty's father was a dreamer and she should have seen beyond his good looks and listened to her auld mam because dreams were all well and good but they didn't put food on the table and provide a roof over the head.

'He came from wealth,' she sniffed. 'He thinks he's destined for grander things than selling on the shop floor. Your daddy,' she carried on, her mouth forming a hard flat line, 'sees himself at the top of the ladder. He wants to sit up there lording it over all those below without doing any climbing first. It's not the first job he's thrown to the wind, Pats. Selfish is what he is. He doesn't think about what he's doing to me or you and Davey.'

She'd gestured to the stack of letters that had been pushed through the letter box at a steady rate of knots these last few weeks. All had big red angry letters jumping off them.

Patty had wanted to put her hands over her ears. She didn't want to hear any of this but her mam had kept going wiping her hands on her pinny.

'Your father thinks he knows it all you see. It's not a good trait to have and if I ever see it in youse children I'll be snuffing it out.'

Patty didn't like her mam talking to her like she was an adult. Nor did she like hearing her talk about her daddy like this. The sun rose and set over him where she was concerned and her bottom lip had trembled with the urge to bite back but she wasn't a child to give cheek by answering back and anyone could see her mam was on the edge.

Geraldine had sighed, picking up the knife once more to return to the spuds. 'I was like you once, luv. I believed all his pie in the sky big talk and let my head be turned by a handsome face but my dreams died the day your dad walked out of English Electric. I should have listened to me mam,' she repeated, half to herself and half to Patty.

'He'll find something else, Mam. You'll see.'

'He won't, Pats. He's marked his cards. The word's spread he's difficult.' She'd begun to peel the potatoes then and the set in her shoulders had told Patty she wasn't about to say anymore. The conversation had left Patty, feeling unsettled as though her life as she knew it was an eggshell that had cracked.

Things had gone from bad to worse after that, and one day she and Davey had arrived home from school to find Mam and Daddy waiting on the front path, suitcases by their side. Their father's expression frightened Patty. It was one she'd never seen before. It was of defeat.

The two Hamilton children were bewildered by what was happening but their mam had jollied them along with how it was a big adventure going to live somewhere else.

'Will I have to go to a new school, Mam?' Patty had asked, clambering aboard the bus behind her.

'You will.'

'But what about my friends? I haven't said goodbye to any of them.'

'Now, now none of that. You'll soon make new friends. You can't dwell on the past, Pats. You must look forward.'

Patty's head was spinning as she sat down on the seat and the bus pootled away from the street she'd called home.

Their new home was a flat above a newsagent with no front entrance. Patty and Davey hadn't liked it. Davey found the boys his age who played in the street rough and Patty had come home from school crying to her mam that she was scared the nit nurse would shave her head like some of the other girls.

Their daddy had found temporary work in a menswear shop but he wasn't happy with the wages and they'd hear their parents hushed whispers as Mam told him he'd have to put it up with it and he hit back that he deserved more. The hushed voices had grown louder in intensity each evening and Davey would ask Patty to sing to him to block out their arguing. Then, one morning, their daddy set off for work and never came back.

That had been over three years ago now and they'd had to move again to the room in Osbourne Court and their mam had found work in the Cadbury factory.

She'd never offered an explanation as to where he'd gone or what had happened despite her children's confusion and tears over his disappearance. It was only when she knew she'd not long left that she'd pressed the handwritten address near the sea into Patty's hand and made her promise to go there with Davey when she passed.

Now, Patty felt in her pocket for the fare Mam had put away for them. She closed the door on their old life and hefted the case down the stairs, holding Davey's hand with her spare hand. It was time to go.

Chapter Two

Liverpool, Autumn, 1981

Sabrina

Sabrina pinched herself just to be sure she was really there in the room seated across from her dear friend Jane, and not dreaming. The fire ticking over in the grate, which had brought a pink flush to Jane's cheeks, and the aroma of baking seemed real enough though as did the radio softly playing a song she didn't recognise. Jane catching sight of Sabrina plucking at the skin on her arm laughed.

'I'm quite real, Sabrina. Not a mirage.'

It was a laugh Sabrina remembered well. It was unchanged and it made her feel warm inside. A precious laugh to be treasured because poor Jane hadn't been given much to laugh about in the short time they'd been friends. All the events that had unfolded whilst they'd known one another had been ever such a long time ago for Jane but had unfolded only weeks ago for Sabrina.

It was still surreal this business of having stepped back in time to 1928 when Jane had lost her parents in a terrible accident and been separated from her younger sisters. She'd been cast out by Magnolia Muldoon, the lady of the big house on

Allerton Road where she and Sabrina had toiled, only to find out she was pregnant to Magnolia's son, Sidney.

Jane had nearly lost Sidney too, but they'd found their way back to each other on Liverpool's Bold Street. Just as Sabrina had somehow found her way back through the portal or whatever the strange frisson of time slipping through that peculiar pocket of Bold Street to 1981 where she belonged was. That was then though and this was now.

It was the now she'd come to find out about.

Sabrina had come here to the house on Terryborough Street with its immaculate front garden and shiny brass knocker to hear about all that had happened to Jane and Sidney in the fifty years since they'd last seen each other. She hoped theirs had been a happy life because there'd been too much sadness in Jane's younger years. She deserved to have had a life filled with laughter and joy.

She soaked her friend in as she was now. Her hair, once a mass of golden curls, was still curly but worn short so that it sat around her face a little like a halo. The colour had faded to sand and her face was crinkled in a manner that suggested there'd been lots of laughter over the years. Her eyes were unchanged though, still as blue as the sapphire engagement ring she'd chosen and with just as many hidden depths.

She was dressed for comfort in a sweater to match her eyes and trousers made of soft cotton with slippers on her feet. Age had ensured she filled her clothes out in a much cuddlier manner than the waif she'd once been.

'Am I very changed?' Jane asked, her eyes dancing from where she'd sat down opposite Sabrina.

'No,' Sabrina shook her head. 'I'd have known you any-where.'

'Fibber,' Jane giggled. 'I was only a girl of eighteen when you last saw me I'm a great-grandmother over seventy now. And, look at you still twenty-one! It's a mysterious world ahright, Sabrina luv. I gave up trying to understand what happened a long time ago. There are some things for which there's no explanation.' Jane shrugged and then drank in the sight of her friend in her modern clothes.

Gone was the mob cap and servant dress. The reddish-gold hair, no longer pulled back into a bun, was worn long and hung curtain-straight just past her shoulders. Her un-usual brandy eyes seemed even deeper made up with mascara and eyeshadow. The freckles still danced across her nose though and her smile still lit her face. She was still her Sabri-na.

Sabrina shook her head in wonder, hearing Jane was now a great-grandmother and then smiled, 'A great-grandmother you may well be but you're still my friend Jane.'

Jane stretched her arm over from where she was perched and patted Sabrina's thigh. The glow from the remembered sapphire ring reassured her. She'd been with Jane when Sid-ney had asked her to marry him. She probably remembered the details of that day better than Jane or Sidney, given for her it was recent history.

'That, I am, Sabrina,' she said, her smile equally warm be-fore she straightened and slapped her hands down on her knees. 'Right-ho, I'll put the kettle on and then we can have a good old natter over a brew. We've a lorra catching up to do, you and me, over fifty years' worth by my count.'

She got to her feet and took herself off to the kitchen leaving Sabrina free to inspect the cosy front room Jane had ushered her into when she'd arrived. It was filled with antiques as you'd expect but the walls beneath the floral print paper paid homage to hers and Sidney's family.

Photographs vied for attention giving clues as to the life the couple had led since Sabrina had last seen them. She was pleased to see there were lots of smiles beaming down at her. It felt like a room filled with love.

She shuddered, recalling the Muldoon house where she and Jane had both been in the employ of Magnolia Muldoon. The dining room had been adorned with portraits, not photographs and had made her feel as though she were being disapproved of by Magnolia's gilt-framed ancestors. What had happened to Magnolia she wondered? She and Sidney had become estranged when he'd married Jane. Had she wound up an embittered, lonely old woman?

She stared at one picture and fancied she might have been looking at Jane as a young woman once more but the clothes and quality of the photography were all wrong and so she surmised she must be looking at a grandchild. She scanned the pictures for a clue as to the baby Jane had been carrying when she'd left. Her brain did the sums, he or she would be fifty-two now.

There were two women who didn't look far apart in age and who definitely took after their mother and pictures of a man a few years younger. He was handsome. A mix of both his parents, Jane thought, as she spied a sepia-toned, silver-framed photograph on the sideboard. Her heart leapt and she got up and crossed the room for a closer look, picking the frame up as she stared at the Jane and Sidney she remembered. It had been taken on their wedding day.

There they were, frozen in time on the steps of the stone church in Wigan. Jane a beautiful bride clutching her autumn posy, her brother Frank and his wife Marie standing next to Sidney. She was alongside Jane. Aunt Evie had done such a wonderful job with Jane's dress. It had hidden her bump beautifully to ensure no tongues wagged in the village she'd grown up in.

Sabrina recalled the pain and frustration she'd felt at seeing Aunt Evie and her not knowing who she was. Her story, that she'd stepped back in time from 1981 to 1928, implausible even to her own ears. She couldn't blame her aunt for refusing to believe her but it had hurt.

'You caught the bouquet,' Jane said from the doorway where she stood with a silver tray and tea service in her hands, a smile on her face. 'Dare I ask how things are with your young man? I hope he is your young man, Sabrina?'

'Ah, Jane, don't say that. He's my fella, not my young man!' Sabrina laughed as she put the photo down and tucked the memories away before sitting down. 'You sound just like Aunt Evie.'

Jane set the tray down on the table and Sabrina's tummy rumbled at the sight of the thick slabs of fruit cake with white icing drizzled on top. 'Well, that's because I'm the same age as your Aunt Evie, Sabrina. I've looked in the window of the shop many a time, you know. I've seen you growing up and I wanted to come in and say hello but it wasn't the right time, was it?'

Sabrina shook her head. She wouldn't have known Jane just like Aunt Evie hadn't known her. She watched as Jane sat down on the edge of the pale green velvet sofa once more. The highly varnished legs, Sabrina noted, were Queen Anne style. She didn't know how she knew this, she just did. She was guessing it would have come from Muldoon's Antiquities, the business Sidney's father had handed down to him on Bold Street.

It wasn't there anymore. It had saddened Sabrina to walk past the antique shop after she'd come back from what she'd decided to think of as her 1920s' sabbatical to find it was now a photography gallery.

Black and white arty photographs of Liverpool's street life had stared down at her from austere white walls in a space which had once been an Aladdin's cave of antiques.

'Adam is, well, he's—'

'Perfect? That's how I felt about my Sidney.'

Sabrina nodded, not picking up on her use of the past tense. 'And he's very tasty.'

Jane laughed. 'That's a new expression for me.'

'Aunt Evie's not keen on him riding a motorbike, though.' She closed her eyes. She'd have confided to the Jane she'd known back in 1928 that he'd kissed her. She'd have told her everything just as Jane had her. She reminded herself this woman who was indeed close to her aunt's age was still her Jane, just an older, wiser version as she blurted, 'He kissed me on Everton Brow and again at the back entrance to the shop on Wood Street and it was gorgeous.'

Jane put the pot down and clapped her hands delightedly. 'Luvly,' she declared settling herself against the studded back of the sofa, a strangely wistful expression on her face as she said, 'I've had to wait ever such a long time for that news, you know.'

Sabrina smiled, knowing it was the same goofy, lovelorn grin Flo kept telling her she got on her face whenever she talked about Adam.

Jane picked up a cup and saucer to pass to Sabrina.

'Sabrina, I'm afraid I've some sad news to tell you.'

'Oh?'

'I lost Sidney two years ago.'

Sabrina's mouth formed an O and the teacup shook in the saucer. She'd assumed Sidney was out and about and so hadn't questioned Jane as to where he was. She'd hoped he'd be back shortly keen to reminisce with him. It was hard to take in the fact that the young man whose wedding she'd attended was gone.

'He dropped dead doing the garden. It was a heart attack.'

'Jane, I'm so sorry.' She put the cup and saucer down and got up, hugging her old friend, and a tear slipped down her cheek as she did so. She was sorry she'd missed him. She'd have liked the opportunity to get to know him in later life.

Jane patted her on the back and her voice was muffled as she said, 'It was sudden, he'd have known nothing about it but it was ever so hard to reconcile him being there talking about trimming the roses for winter one minute and gone the next.'

Sabrina sniffed.

'Now, now, no tears. I won't have it. This is a happy re-union. Sidney wouldn't have wanted tears. I still talk to him you know. I like to think he's up there watching over me.'

'I'm sure he is.'

She released Sabrina and mustered up a smile. 'Drink your tea before it gets cold and you'll be wanting a slice of my fruit cake too. It's Mrs Brown's recipe. I never forgot it. And I never found one better.'

Mrs Brown was the cook both girls had worked under at the Muldoon residence. She'd been a marvel in the kitchen and Sabrina helped herself to a slice, sitting back down to drink her tea. The hot drink she sipped at settled her shock at the news of Sidney's death.

'It's delicious,' Sabrina mumbled a moment later through the mouthful of cake she'd attacked. As she swallowed and washed it down with tea she decided the time had come to pluck out one of her burning questions, 'Was it a daughter you had first then, Jane?'

'A baby girl, yes. We called her Sabrina,' Jane said, an amused glint in her eyes as she looked over the rim of her teacup at Sabrina's reaction to this news.

'Sabrina,' Sabrina echoed in wonder, her cake momentarily forgotten.

'Well now, sweetheart, what else would we have called her?'

'I don't know what to say, Jane. I'm honoured.' Sabrina blinked back the sudden tears that threatened.

Jane smiled but her story wasn't finished yet. 'We had three children, two girls and our late surprise John Henry. He came five years after Ciara who's three years younger than our Sabrina. He lives in Canada now. Sidney and I have visited him and his family several times since he emigrated. It's a wonderful country but it's not for me. Far too cold and too many bears for my liking. I'm a home bird, me. Sidney hoped John Henry would follow him into the family business but he'd his own path to carve. Sidney accepted that. He was a good father and he doted on the girls.'

Sabrina's head whirled with the names. Ciara had been their dear friend at the lodging house on Parliament Street and as for John Henry, she recalled Jane having had two brothers who'd been killed in the great war. They'd named their son for both of them.

'And don't get me started on my grandchildren and great-grandson,' Jane sailed on. 'There's seven of the rascals and I do miss John Henry and his brood but I get plenty of letters and photographs telling me what they're up to.'

'What about Magnolia, Jane? What became of her.' Despite her being an arrogant woman with both feet firmly planted in a dying class system, it was sad to think of her all alone in that echoing house on Allerton Road. What a shame it would be if she'd missed out on all this, she thought, her eyes flitting over the family photographs once more.

'I insisted Sidney go to see his mother after our Sabrina was born. If you could have seen her face when she came here to visit for the time. It was a picture! She played the dowager duchess right up to the end but she was a part of our life here in Terryborough Street. She tried to get us to go and live with her but we'd no desire to go back. We were happy here. It was our home. She died twenty-odd years ago and left the house to us. We sold it to a fella with deep pockets. It was beginning to fall down around her ears by then. We were glad to see the back of it and it meant we had the funds to travel out to Canada to see our lad.'

Sabrina smiled across at her friend. 'You've had a lovely life, haven't you?'

'I have Sabrina. I've been blessed and I'm even more blessed now you're back in it.'

Sabrina got up then and hugged her dear friend with whom she'd gone through so much.

'But tell me,' Jane said when Sabrina had sat back down. 'What of your mam?'

Sabrina shook her head. 'I haven't found her but I will.'

Chapter Three

Liverpool, 1952

Patty

P atty stepped off the bus when they reached the stop for Blundellsands, Davey following behind. She stood there on the pavement next to her brother who was peering out from under his cap as the bus chugged off and, despite his proximity, felt very alone.

The air had a fresh, salty flavour that overrode the fumes the bus was belching and she gulped in lungfuls, of it. It calmed her and she tried not to shiver inside her coat as the bracing wind blowing in from the Merseyside coastline cut through her. She fancied she could hear the roar of the sea over the passing traffic but couldn't be sure whether she was imagining it or not.

Patty remembered the long-ago trip to the seaside with the mams and children from the street they lived on before their father lost his job. He'd stayed behind to do the garden as had the other fathers and she, Mam, and Davey, a curious toddler, had caught the bus here just as they had now.

Everybody was carrying something that day and off they'd trooped over the green parkland with its glimpses to the blue water beyond. Down the jigger past paint-peeled doors, beyond which were the tiny backyards of the cottages where the brown pots of tea were to be had. Then, there it was. The beach!

The children's chatter at the anticipation of a dip in the sea had grown louder as the cobbled jigger gave way to sand. The excitement over potted meat sandwiches, a dip in the ocean, and the sandcastle building that lay ahead reaching fever point.

Before they'd a chance to discard their shoes and socks and run down to the water's edge though she and the other youngsters, each clasping a few coppers, had been sent back up to knock on the back doors of the cottages. They were under strict instructions as to which numbers made a good strong brew leaving their mams to open deckchairs, sort the smaller children and unpack the sandwiches.

Patty could almost taste the potted meat in the sandwiches she'd dined on that afternoon. They were the best she'd ever tasted. It was funny how food could taste different depending on where you were and what you were doing.

A flash of her mam with her blonde hair whipping about her face, her head thrown back as she laughed at Davey's antics dancing on the sand, made her yearn for her so badly it hurt her stomach.

There was no time for standing about dwelling on the past though. It was far too chilly for that. Mam had trusted her to look after Davey and that was what she planned to do. She'd need to ask someone where they'd find the street their father lived on now.

She tried not to think of him living his life without them here while they'd struggled daily in Toxteth as their mam had fallen sicker.

He'd be pleased of this chance to make things right by them, Patty assured herself, looking about and seeing there were plenty of people milling around the shops. Someone was bound to be able to direct them to Elton Avenue.

She pulled Davey out the way of a woman who was pushing a pram with a well-wrapped up baby sitting up watching the world go by. The baby flashed her a gummy smile and she mustered a smile back before her gaze settled on the tearooms across the way. A smartly dressed young man with a paper tucked under his arm exited it.

Oh, what she'd give for a warming cup of tea and a slice of cake she thought, looking longingly at the warm glow emanating through its windows. She'd no money for frivolities like tea and cake though.

'Can we go and see the water first, Patty? Please.' Her brother's eyes which had been dull since their mam had passed had a gleam of light in them at the thought of the sea.

Patty was torn, feeling they should go straight to the address on Elton Avenue. The sooner they got there then the sooner she could see how the land lay and get them both settled in. It would be a shock to their father to find them on his doorstep but Davey's pleading expression tugged at her heart.

There'd been so little in the way of joy in his life this last while. What harm would it do?

'Come on then. Just for half an hour mind. It's far too cold to be hanging about.'

She retraced the path she remembered from that long-ago outing, with her brother stooping to pick up a spindly stick broken off a tree by the wind. He gave an excited yelp as he spied the sand ahead at the bottom of the jigger and charged off. She called after him, 'Don't go getting wet!' She needn't have worried; as she drew closer she could see the tide was a long way out.

It was quiet, apart from the screeching of gulls and whistling wind, no chatter of mammies or squeals from children.

She placed the suitcase down in the dunes and sat on it not willing to risk a damp backside. The spikey blades of grass prickled her calves through her tights.

Davey, his cheeks reddened from the bracing sea air, was using his stick to draw pictures in the soft sand and she watched him forget his worries as a gust threatened to whip his cap off. The sight made her smile.

She allowed herself to think about her mam and without knowing she was doing so began humming the Vera Lynn hit she'd loved, Auf Wiedersehen, Sweetheart. She'd sung it to calm her in between the spasms of coughing. Mam always loved to hear her sing. A tear trickled down her cheek, salty like the sea way off in the distance and she wiped it away not wanting Davey to see her cry.

She sat there until the cold began to make her cramp and getting up cupped her hands either side of her mouth to call her brother back. He pretended not to hear her for a minute or two and then gave in, dragging his stick behind him to where she was waiting.

'C'mon on, you,' she said brusquely wanting to get moving. 'I'm freezin'.'

'Just think, Pats, we'll be able to come here every single day if we want from now on.' His eyes, so like their mam's, danced.

'Well, if the weather's like this for the rest of winter you'll be coming on your own,' Patty replied tartly.

Once they were back on the main road again, she took charge asking the first passer-by, a woman with a scarf knotted tightly under her chin and a shopping bag slung over her arm, if she knew the way to Elton Avenue.

She looked annoyed at being stopped and waved her arm about as she said, 'Left onto Downhills Road, follow it down a way, and you'll come to Elton Avenue on your right.' Her eyes flicked to the suitcase Patty was holding and then she looked at Davey. 'It's a funny time of year to be on your holidays if you ask me. Where's your mother?'

Patty didn't like the sharp look in the woman's eyes and made up a story on the spot. 'She's not well so we're going to stay with our gran for a few days.' She elbowed Davey to be quiet.

She eyed them a moment longer then muttered something about getting to the butchers before it was only the scrag ends left and carrying on her way.

Patty exhaled.

'Why did you lie, Pats?' Davey asked as she set off at a clip despite the weight of the case.

'Because she looked the sort who'd make trouble for us if she was so inclined. Besides, it was only a half-lie,' Patty replied. 'We've a gran. Two of them, in fact. We're just not going to stay with either of them.'

'We've never met them,' Davey said, then he came to a halt, a frown embedded between his fair eyebrows. 'Why haven't we?'

Patty knew her brother well enough to know he wouldn't get moving again until he had his answer and so with a sigh she said, 'Mam told me it's down to church.'

'But we're Catholic.'

'I know that. Mam was Catholic but Daddy was the other and when they married neither family wanted anything more to do with them.'

Mam had confided this to her once, telling her Dad's side of the family had their own furniture business and pots of money. Patty had wanted to know why they hadn't helped them then when things got tough. Her mam had made a sniffing sort of a sound but hadn't answered.

Patty hadn't been able to see the logic in either set of grandparents thinking because so far as she was concerned God was supposed to love everybody. It didn't seem very Christian to her, cutting off your children. She told her mam this but she'd said it wasn't as simple as that shaking her head when Patty had retorted that it should be.

'Is that why Daddy left us then? Because we're Catholic and he missed living in a big house.'

'Stop talking and start walking,' Patty said, not wanting to answer that. She didn't know why he'd left them. Not really. Mam had told her he'd gone home to his parents because he wasn't man enough to stand by his family but she'd not wanted to hear that. Not about her beloved daddy.

Davey's eyes were out like organ stoppers as he took note of the houses decorating the road they were walking down. 'Look at the size of them. Do you think we'll live in one like that, Pats?' He was pointing to a semi-detached, two-storey home with an enormous front garden. 'It's got six chimneys,' he stated in awe. 'Does that mean they've got six fires?'

'I expect so.'

'It would be like summer all year round with six fires roaring.'

It wasn't long before they'd reached Elton Avenue. It was quieter again down here with only a handful of cars parked on the street. The brick walls separating the front gardens from the street were low and the houses as large as the one Davey had ogled. She dug around in her pocket and pulled out the crumpled piece of paper with the street number on it. 'That's it there,' she said, coming to such an abrupt halt, her brother nearly walked into her.

They both stood and took stock of their new home.

Chapter Four

Liverpool, Winter,1981

Sabrina

'Ouch, flamin' pin!' Sabrina dropped the mound of charmeuse fabric she was in the process of stitching pearl beads onto and stared at the red globule oozing from her thumb.

'You're not Sleeping Beauty, Sabrina, even if your hair could do with a trim,' Evelyn Flooks tutted above the Radio Merseyside, DJ's chatter as she eyed Sabrina's ends. 'They start looking like you've been chewing on them if you let it get too long. And if you get blood on that charmeuse, you'll never get it out or hear the end of it from me, gorrit?'

Sabrina stuck her thumb in her mouth and glowered over at her Aunt Evie who was looking like a canary in Tuesday's yellow shop coat. She'd never been one for tea and sympathy. Scratch that, she thought, her eyes flitting to the china cup with the telltale tannin stain inside on the cutting-out table, tea yes, sympathy no.

'You're muddling your fairy tales. It's Rapunzel with the long hair,' she retorted once she'd removed her thumb and was satisfied there'd be no more blood. The thought of getting a rusty print on Stephanie Byrne's wedding dress was

one that didn't bear thinking about. She was putting the finishing touches on the girl who hailed from Speke's gown
which was a relief because she'd proven a most demanding
bride-to-be and Sabrina was looking forward to her coming
to collect the dress on Friday.

Evelyn had muttered more than once she was glad it was
Sabrina who dealt with her because she'd not have the pa-
tience for her contrariness. As it was, Sabrina only managed
to keep her cool with their prima donna client's ever-chang-
ing demands when it came to her dress by focusing on the
fact she was soon to be Stephanie Shufflebottom. She only
had to put up with Stephanie for a few months. Stephanie
would have a lifetime of being a Shufflebottom! The thought
made her smile.

The two women were seated in the workroom of Brides
of Bold Street where they spent their week cutting out,
sewing, and fitting wedding and bridesmaid dresses. A roll of
brown paper stood to attention and a mannequin was currently posed in a calico toile awaiting a fitting.

They were partially hidden from the shop as they set
to the practicalities of dressmaking by a wall behind the
counter. A rack of dresses protected by plastic sheaths waited
to be collected by their namesakes—Sabrina and Evelyn
named all their bespoke dresses after their brides-to-be because each dress was a reflection of the girl who would be
wearing it, their dresses a part of them.

The shelves were laden with every item a seamstress
could possibly need and, to the uninitiated, would appear a
chaotic mess but both women could have located the spool
of cotton, roll of ribbon or bolt of lace they were after with

their eyes shut and hands tied behind their backs for that matter!

The shop, longer than it was wide, was located on Bold Street in the heart of Liverpool and they lived in the flat upstairs. Bold Street itself was an eclectic mish-mash of olde-worlde buildings, home to shops and businesses that came and went, unlike the bridal shop which was a stalwart of the street.

Evelyn Flooks had opened her doors in the late 1920s when she was still a slip of a girl and against the odds had built herself a thriving bridal business. She maintained she'd be carried out of the building in a box. Sabrina didn't doubt it for a moment.

She'd been an eager apprentice learning the art of wedding dress making at the woman she called her aunt's knee. There was nothing else in the world she'd rather do than stitch together the dresses of her clients' dreams and as such it had been a given that she'd work in the shop once she'd left school. These days she was in charge of the running of the business while her Aunt Evie still enjoyed toiling at her trusty Singer sewing machine in the workroom out the back.

The Singer she was seated at was as old as Evelyn and sometimes Sabrina fancied her aunt's foot was welded to the treadle and that when she eventually did decide to retire they'd have to get it surgically removed!

'Less time daydreaming about that lad of yours and more time thinking about what you're doing is the order of the day,' Evelyn said primly before dipping her silvery head once more to rearrange the swathe of alabaster satin she'd been in the process of feeding through the machine.

Sabrina couldn't say much to that. She *had* been thinking about Adam. He occupied her thoughts a great deal these days! In particular, she'd been thinking about the way his hair had flopped into his sooty eyes giving her licence to reach over and brush it away as they'd shared a fish 'n' chip supper the night before. They'd been seeing each other a few months now and she'd been smitten with him from the moment she'd seen him walk into her local pub, the Swan Inn for the first time.

So much had happened since that night she thought, reaching into her pocket for the Opal Fruit sweets she always had to hand. Adam's accident, her decision to search for her mother, meeting Jane. Her brain hurt with trying to sort it all out in her mind because it was hard to make sense of something that made no sense at all.

'Oh, I forgot to tell you, your friend, Ray Taylor was asking after you last night,' Sabrina said popping a sweet in her mouth.

'That wide boy is an acquaintance, not a friend, Sabrina.' Evelyn sniffed in a manner that said why should she care. She didn't look up either but her foot faltered on the treadle and Sabrina saw the girlish pink flush rise in her cheeks at the mention of the local property developer.

In a 'the world's a small place' way she'd unwittingly been dating Ray Taylor's son. It was something Sabrina had only just figured out, the penny dropping when Adam told her about his job working alongside his father in their property developing business. She'd tentatively asked him what his father's name was and her suspicions were confirmed when he'd replied, Ray.

She'd yet to mention the connection to Adam or her aunt for that matter. She didn't want Aunt Evelyn taking against him for no reason other than he was the son of that 'wide boy'. She was unsure why she hadn't shared this new-found knowledge with Adam. Wondering if perhaps it was because she sensed Adam held his late mam on a pedestal and might find it unsettling were he to know his father, who'd known her aunt since she was a girl, had a soft spot for Evelyn Flooks.

It was a soft spot however that didn't appear to be rec-iprocated because Aunt Evie was always brusque with the property developer when he ducked his head in the shop to see how she was. And, if he was bold enough to suggest an outing she turned him down flat. He'd take it on the chin though and a few weeks later, in he'd swagger once more.

Sabrina picked up her needle and thread again. She was making something out of nothing she told herself, vowing to tell Adam how she knew his father next time she saw him. Small things could become big things if they were kept se-cret, she thought. A little like whatever the shared history be-tween her aunt and Ray really was. She'd get to the bottom of it one of these days. She glanced at her aunt who was beavering away once more.

She'd often wondered why Aunt Evie had never married and it niggled at her that it may have something to do with Ray Taylor but Aunt Evie's response when she'd asked her outright had been most unsatisfactory.

'I'm married to my shop, aren't I?'

'Keep your mind on the job, Sabrina,' Evelyn said now, not pausing in her task.

She'd an uncanny way of reading her mind Sabrina thought as her aunt added, 'Or you're liable to sew one of those pearls onto your trousers.'

Sabrina smiled at the not-so-subtle attempt to get her off the subject of the property developer. Aunt Evie was right, she thought, chewing what was left of her sweet and turning her attention to the tray of pearl beads. Her mind began to play over what had been bothering her more and more with each passing day and by the time she'd sewn another five of the iridescent beads onto the bodice of Stephanie's dress she couldn't keep it to herself any longer. 'I want to see if I can go back again, Aunt Evie,' she blurted.

There, she'd said it. She'd been feeling guilty over even thinking about disappearing again but the urge to make sense of what had happened between her and her mother would not let her be. She needed to know how they'd come to be separated.

The machine continued to whir away and the only clue Evelyn had heard what she'd said was in the puckered lips and frown on her face.

Evelyn's emotions batted off one another. She was torn because on the one hand she could understand why Sabrina needed answers but on the other, the business of a timeslip on Bold Street terrified her. She'd heard it said it was something to do with the tunnels that ran under their part of Liverpool. Whatever caused it to happen, it wasn't natural and shouldn't be deliberately meddled with the way Sabrina had.

She'd been lucky once insomuch as she'd come back to them but she might not be so lucky a second time and that was something that didn't bear thinking about.

'Aunt Evie?'

'I don't think it's a good idea.' Evelyn's reply was tarter than a gooseberry and even as she said it she knew she was wasting her breath. Sabrina had a mind of her own. She always had. If she wanted to try to step back in time once more there was not a thing Evelyn could do to stop her. Her inner voice whispered, 'It's inevitable, Evelyn, because it's already happened, you know it has.' Sabrina hadn't just visited her in 1928 she'd come to see her again in 1962.

Chapter Five

Liverpool, 1952

Patty

'It's only got two chimneys,' Davey said, staring at the house they'd found themselves in front of.

'Any more's greedy,' Patty stated as she took in the white house with its red roof upon which a cockerel weathervane was twirling madly. The trim front lawn was encased within a matching low wall as were the rest of the houses they'd walked past. Two big picture windows on either side of the front door looked out to the street. It could have been plucked from the pages of a storybook, Patty decided, thinking it very pretty.

'It's a big house for one person,' Davey said dubiously.

Patty had been thinking the same and she hadn't liked the squirmy feeling it gave her to think of their daddy living here while they were in the horrid Courts. She banished the thought that mam would still be with them had she been living in a house like the one they were stood gawping at now.

She saw the net curtain twitch in the window to the left of the front door and wondered if perhaps it was a housekeeper. It was the sort of house that would have a housekeeper, she decided. Perhaps she'd make them tea and get them something to eat while they waited for their father to get home from work. The thought cheered her.

He must be working to afford a house like this, she thought, wondering why he'd not sent money for them. She wished with all her heart Mam hadn't shouted at him the way she had because maybe if she hadn't nagged at him he wouldn't have left. They could have all been living here in that house then happily ever after.

Instead, it was as if Mam, her and Davey had ceased to exist the day he'd walked out on them. Her breathing was shallow and her palms suddenly clammy as she wondered what his reaction to seeing them both after all this time would be. It wasn't her and Davey he'd been mad at, she re-assured herself. It was Mam.

It was no good standing out here making herself ill wondering, she thought, steeling her resolve and unlatching the front gate. She tilted her head indicating Davey should follow her as she marched up the brick path with a confidence she didn't feel. She reached up and rapped the shiny knocker before she could change her mind and run away.

They glanced at one another as footsteps sounded and the door swung open a minute later. Patty found herself staring up at a pretty woman with her hair set in soft brown fashionable waves. She'd very red lips, she thought, as her eyes strayed to the navy dress with a lace collar, overtop of which she had an apron with bright yellow sunflowers decorating it. She smelled of baking and flowers and a fragment from the children's rhyme flitted absently to mind *sugar and spice and all things nice.*

'I saw you standing out there on the street staring at the house. What do you want?'

It wasn't the greeting Patty had hoped for and she took a step backwards nearly tumbling off the step. She regained her composure. They'd come too far for her not to stand her ground.

'We've come to see Anthony Hamilton, please.'

'*Mr* Hamilton isn't home he's at work.'

It dawned on Patty then she hadn't asked who they were. She'd not opened the door any wider either and there was no warm smile on those red lips.

'Listen,' the woman said breathing peppermint on Patty as she leaned toward her. 'I know who you are. You're that woman's bastard children and I don't know why you've come—'

Patty blanched as if she'd been slapped, not understanding what the woman was talking about. 'We've come to see our father because our mam told us to, she died and we've nowhere else to go.'

There was no softening of her expression upon hearing this despite her words. 'Well, I'm sorry to hear that for your sakes but I really don't know what you expect from me.' Her eyes flicked over to the suitcase and back to Patty.

Davey fidgeted behind her and she could sense his anxiousness. You promised Mam you'd look after him, she reminded herself. She squared her shoulders and planted her feet firmly on the doorstep her hands clenched at her sides. 'We'd like to see our daddy please and we won't be leaving until we have.'

The woman flinched as Patty said the word 'daddy'. 'I hope you're not threatening me, young lady.'

'Are you a housekeeper?' Davey interrupted, peering around the side of his sister. Patty bit her bottom lip. She was fairly certain from the way the woman was twisting the ring on her finger beneath which was a gold band that she was not the housekeeper.

'No, I'm not.' She drew herself up straight. 'I'm Mrs Hamilton, thank you very much. I'm married to your father.'

Patty shook her head confused.

'But he's married to our mam,' Davey piped up and Patty wanted to kick him to be quiet. He wasn't helping matters. 'He can't be married to you as well.'

'He was never married to your mother.' She sniffed dismissively.

'But Mam had an engagement ring and a wedding ring,' Patty spoke up not wanting this woman telling lies about her mam when she wasn't here any longer to defend herself.

She sighed huffily. 'It's not my place to talk about it. The past should stay where it belongs, in the past.'

Patty decided right there and then she didn't like this woman. She sensed a cold, selfish heart beneath her pretty frock. And, she didn't believe for a moment her parents hadn't been married. Perhaps their father had told her this was the case. She knew there was a name for men who married more than one woman though she didn't know what it was. Maybe he was one of those.

Had he told this awful woman he was divorced or his wife was dead? It didn't change the fact they were his children though. You couldn't divorce your children and they most certainly weren't dead.

'Do you think we could come inside and wait for him, please? It's cold outside today.'

'It's not very convenient,' this interloper who'd replaced their mother said as a baby's wail sounded from within. She gave Sabrina a withering stare that said she'd like her to disappear off to wherever it was she'd come from before turning to glance back over her shoulder.

Patty would not be swayed. 'We've nowhere else to go. It's cold and my brother's only eight.'

The new Mrs Hamilton swung her attention back to the two waifs on her doorstep. 'Well, I can't very well have you sitting on the front wall until Anthony gets home. What would the neighbours think?'

She took a step forward and glanced to her left and right as if expecting to see them gathered on their front doorsteps gossiping as to what was going on.

Her eyes swept their clothes and Patty felt grubby beneath her gaze.

'Leave your shoes outside. You can wait in the kitchen and you're not to sit on the chairs or touch anything. Do you understand me?'

Both children nodded, slipping out of their shoes and lining them up to the side of the door. Patty reached behind her for her brother's hand. He took it and she gave it a reassuring squeeze as the door was opened further. Their stepmother or whatever she was stepped aside allowing them to pass before closing the door with a firm click.

Patty and Davey stood in the hallway, hearing the baby's cries growing louder as its demands weren't met.

'The kitchen's down the end of the hall there. And don't touch anything!'

She took to the stairs following the direction of the wailing.

Patty and Davey barely dared look around as they crept through to the kitchen which opened up at the back of the house. They were unsure where to put themselves and stood with their backs to the worktop as though awaiting inspection.

It was very modern, Patty thought, using the opportunity to glance about the tidy kitchen which smelled warm and inviting but felt anything but. A large, south-facing garden could be seen through the window. Her mouth watered and her stomach rumbled loudly as she spied freshly baked biscuits sitting on top of the stove.

'I'm hungry, Pats,' Davey whispered. 'And thirsty.'

Would it be noticed if they helped themselves to a couple of biscuits? She knew the answer and wasn't willing to get caught out.

'I'm sure we'll be given something to eat and drink soon while we wait for Daddy.' She wasn't sure at all. They'd hardly been welcomed into the house.

They heard a creaking on the stairs and she elbowed Davey to be quiet. The woman appeared with a pretty, plump baby girl on her hip. She was like a doll, Patty thought, taking in the squidgy rolls of fat on her arms and legs which were wrapped around her mother. She blinked at

Patty and Davey but didn't seem concerned in the least that there were two strange children in the kitchen.

'This is Amelia, our daughter, and you can call me Mrs Hamilton.'

Patty nodded, transfixed by the baby. 'Hello, Amelia.' She looked at Mrs Hamilton. 'She's luvly.'

Mrs Hamilton didn't say anything but Amelia gurgled happily as though aware she'd been paid a compliment. She stared at her half-sister, her enormous eyes unblinking, and Patty thought she could see her daddy in those eyes of hers.

Mrs Hamilton dislodged her daughter to slide her into the high chair by the table.

Patty itched with the urge to hold her sister but didn't dare ask. She'd have loved to have been allowed to feed her too she thought a moment later as Mrs Hamilton set about heating her food. Sometimes she'd helped Mrs Finnegan with her little ones and she said Patty had a way with children.

Amelia picked up the rattle from the tray and banged it like she was playing the drums, making both Patty and Davey laugh. When she dropped it on the floor, Davey shot forward to pick it up for her.

'Leave it,' their father's new wife barked, turning her attention from whatever she was heating in the pot to Davey. He placed the rattle down on the tray before moving to stand by his sister's side once more. Quick as a flash Mrs Hamilton whipped the rattle off the tray and ran it under the tap while her daughter began to grizzle at having her toy taken from her. She wiped it down and placed it back in her pudgy hand.

She thought they were dirty, Patty realised, putting her arm protectively around her brother. The next time Amelia flung the rattle over the side of the chair neither made a move to pick it up. Not even when she began to shriek.

Her mother shushed her by sliding a bib over her head and, sitting down at the table, she began spooning what looked like stewed apple into her mouth.

Amelia reminded Patty of a fish coming up for air the way her little mouth was opening and closing as she made short work of her meal. Their mam's replacement wiped her baby daughter's face down with the bib when she'd finished and deftly pulled it over her head without getting apple stuck in the downy blonde hair.

It would seem they weren't going to be offered so much as a biscuit from the batch by the oven let alone a glass of water, Patty thought, chewing her lip as Amelia was lifted from the chair.

'Don't touch anything,' Mrs Hamilton reiterated before hoisting her daughter on her hip and fixing them both with a steely gaze.

Patty's mouth opened to ask whether they could perhaps have a drink and something to eat but the words died on her tongue as the woman swept from the room with her child.

Just like in the stories she'd devoured at school, their evil stepmother had left her and Davey thirsty and hungry loitering in the corner of the room.

Patty wondered if, like in her favourite book *Cinderella*, they'd be made to sleep by the hearth.

'Daddy will be home soon, Davey. It'll all be alright then. She'll have to be nice to us,' Patty said to her brother trying to put conviction into her voice. She could sense tears were close to the surface and knew he was trying his best to stop them spilling over. 'He won't let her be horrible to us.'

They could hear the odd squeal coming from nearer the front of the house but didn't know where Mrs Hamilton and Amelia had disappeared to.

Both children's feet were beginning to ache and Davey jiggled from one to the other as he asked his sister to sing to him. 'Sing the song you used to sing to Mam.' His face looked up at hers imploringly before he gazed longingly at the cooker as if by staring at the tray of baking he could will a biscuit into his hand.

It wasn't fair, Patty thought, pushing down the anger at the way they'd been treated by their father's wife. She took a deep breath and began to croon the Vera Lynn song hoping to soothe her brother just as she had her mam.

Davey leaned into her and she tried to keep her voice steady as she sang about teardrops and meeting again. Her voice broke off as they heard a door closing and a voice neither of them had heard in a very long time call out, 'I'm home, girls.'

Patty's body stiffened and she tried to relax as Davey stared anxiously up at her but her stomach was lurching and she swallowed hard as bile rose in her throat. She knew she wouldn't be sick as such because there was nothing in her stomach for her to throw up.

They strained to hear what was being said but couldn't make out the words, only the hushed angry tone of his wife. Patty bit down on her lip, wincing as pain shot through her but at least it served to distract from the churning in her belly. She tightened her grip on her brother's shoulder as they heard footsteps heading down the hall. The door to the kitchen swung open and there he was. Their father.

Chapter Six

Liverpool, 1981

Sabrina

Sabrina wasn't even aware she was singing along to Olivia Newton John's new song which had come on the radio until Evelyn took her foot off the treadle and said, 'What's she warbling on about getting physical?' She didn't expect Sabrina to answer. 'She's not a patch on our Cilla. Now she could belt out a tune.'

The shop door jangled open sparing Sabrina from Evelyn's views on Olivia's new song which Sabrina happened to love. She and her best mate Flo had seen her film, Xanadu the year before and had thought the songstress lovely. They'd also had an urge to go roller skating afterwards but while Flo was busy showing off by skating backwards and executing a few fancy moves, Sabrina had been clutching the side inching her way around. She'd told Flo, never again.

Stephanie soon-to-be Shufflebottom's bodice was the bane of her life but she was nearly there. She'd lost count of how many pearl beads she'd stitched onto the bodice. She'd be glad to see the back of this particular dress she thought, gathering it up and draping it carefully across the worktop, out of harm's way, before smoothing her sweater. There were no appointments today so she was guessing it was a walk-in. She always enjoyed meeting prospective new customers. She'd see the shop through their eyes as they soaked in her carefully chosen romantic palette of white, grey and pink, full of the romance of getting married.

She arranged her mouth into what she liked to think of as her professional saleswoman smile, not too smarmy but friendly and welcoming, and stepped through into the shop.

'Hello there,' Sabrina greeted the young woman standing in the middle of the shop floor. She was staring bewilderedly at the racks of ready-made wedding and bridesmaid's dresses on offer near the fitting room. The plush pink velvet drape which Sabrina would pull to for their clients to try on their dress in private was currently pushed to one side and hooked over the gold tieback.

'Oh, hi.' The woman swivelled towards Sabrina. Her accent was soft, with a twang to it signalling she was a long way from home and she'd a bobble hat in one hand and was busy tugging off her mittens. 'It's bitter out there today. That wind cuts you in two,' she said shuddering for effect. 'I'll never get used to the winters here. It's lovely and warm in here though.' She cast about and saw the bar heater Sabrina turned on when it was particularly cold to give the shop's temperamental central heating a helping hand.

'Do you mind if I stand in front of that and warm up for a moment?'

'Not at all, that's what it's there for,' Sabrina said, positioning herself behind the counter and arranging the jar of pens she kept there as the woman moved over to the heater.

She stood with her back to it so she could look around the shop.

'I love that chandelier.' She shoved her mittens in her pocket and ruffled her blonde hair, flattened from her hat, as she gazed up at the sparkling pendants.

'Ta very much. I found it at a car boot sale, would you believe, and I fell in love with it the moment I saw it.' Sabrina had known it was perfect for the look she was trying to create for the shop. Her aunt had given her free rein to re-decorate, wanting her to put her mark on the place. It was Sabrina's business as much as it was hers, she'd said, and Sabrina had stepped up to the challenge of refurbishing with relish. She was proud of what she'd managed to put together.

'Do you sell ready-made dresses and made to order?' The woman asked waving her hand in the direction of the shelf full of pattern books and rolls of fabric a safe distance from the heater. 'Who knew there were so many shades of white?'

'We do, yes. And there's lots of variants on cream and white as well as all the different materials.' Sabrina's practised eye studied the woman for a moment. She'd a medium pale skin with warm undertones. With her appraisal done she strode over to a roll of shimmering material. 'This here is called oyster and it's perfect for your colouring.'

'That's gorgeous but with the time frame I'm working with I think I'll be opting for a ready-made dress only I haven't a clue where to start.'

'That's what I'm here for,' Sabrina said reassuringly. 'And I say start with what you like.'

The girl smiled. 'That sounds a good plan.' She was sufficiently thawed out to step away from the heater and she made her way over towards the ready-made gowns she'd been appraising when Sabrina had ventured out from the work-room.

'Have a look through and let me know which ones take your fancy. I'll hang them in the fitting room for you to try.'

'Thank you.' She began to sift through them. 'I'm getting married this month and when I rang my mum back home in Australia, she told me I had to come here to your bridal shop on Bold Street. She was adamant in fact.' She frowned, marring her pretty features momentarily, as though this was a puzzle to her. 'It was all a bit odd really. She said she'd been good friends with a girl who'd ties to the shop. She said it held a special place in her heart and that this girl whoever she was would explain everything to me when I called in. I've no idea what she was on about but the call was costing me a bomb so I didn't hang about to find out.'

'Is she from Liverpool then, your mam?'

'She is yes.'

'Ah, no mystery then. It will have been my Aunt Evie, Evelyn Flooks she'd have been talking about. She must have made her dress for her.' Sabrina twinkled. 'She's sewing out the back.' It wouldn't be the first time a bride-to-be had been sent here by their mother or gran who'd fond memories of her own special dress being made at Brides of Bold Street.

'No, she didn't. My mum was married in Adelaide, Australia, a few years after she emigrated and Evelyn wasn't the name mentioned. The line was bad. It was one of those awful echoing calls where you talk over one another all the time but I'm certain she wasn't talking about an Evie or Evelyn.'

'Oh, well I'm sure we'll get to the bottom of it. It's lovely to have a recommendation from the other side of the world, though. Do you mind me asking what brings you here to Liverpool?' Sabrina had been accused of not paying attention in a lot of her classes at school. She'd been too busy designing dresses in her mind's eye or doodling them in the back of her exercise books. She'd learned enough in geography though to know that Australia would be bathed in sunshine about now whereas the day outside the door was bleak. She couldn't imagine what would have lured the young woman from sunnier climes.

'Not at all. I'm on a working holiday or at least I was. It was only going to be for a year because I wanted to see where Mum and my Uncle Davey come from. There's only the two of them on her side.' She offered up by way of explanation. 'I stayed with my aunt Bernie and Uncle Don initially but then I got rooms above the pub where I found work. It's my Andy's dad's pub and meeting Andy wasn't part of my travel plans. I'm only twenty and I thought I'd be footloose and fancy-free for years to come but I fell for his cheeky grin straight off the bat and I knew he was the one. That was a year ago now.' She got a soft look on her face at the mention of her fiancé's name and Sabrina smiled, well used to lovestruck young women. 'My mum, dad and Uncle Davey along with Aunty Doris and my cousins, Lisa and Melody are travelling over from Australia for our wedding.'

She must have read the perplexed expression on Sabrina's face.

'I know a winter wedding seems a mad idea and I feel a little bad luring them all away from an Australian summer but we don't have a choice.' She paused and stared at a simple gown in a shade not dissimilar to the one Sabrina had said would flatter her skin tone. Her sigh was heavy.

'I love this but I can't very well have shoestring straps in winter.'

'Ah, but that's where I come in. I've a lovely faux fur lined cape that would work well with that dress and I can always put sleeves in the gown.'

'Could you?'

Sabrina nodded, smiling at the way the young woman was looking at her like she was some sort of magician.

'I like the leg-of-mutton sleeves but I don't want a Princess Diana style dress. Something more fitted. I don't have her height and I'd look like one of those toilet paper dolls in a dress that big.'

Sabrina laughed, knowing exactly what she was on about because Aunt Evie's friend Ida had a doll in a blue crochet dress sitting overtop of her spare loo roll! It gave her the creeps to be honest because it was unsettling to have an enormous pair of blue eyes watching you sat on the throne. She was glad too she was after something different. They'd been inundated with orders for gowns similar to the elaborate and fussy design the Princess of Wales had worn.

'Shall I hang this one up in the fitting room for you?'

'Yes, please. I thought this was going to be hopeless because I never saw myself as a winter bride. I always wanted a beach wedding. You know barefoot on the sand, my white sandals in my hand, a flower behind my ear.' She sighed. 'It's not to be though because Andy's mum's not well. She's not well at all which is why it's all a rush. She'd not make the trip out to Australia where we originally planned to have the wedding and well, we want her to be part of it all. It's going to be special.' Her lips set in a determined line.

'It's lovely you're so determined to make your fella's mam a part of it all. I'm sure it will be a wonderful wedding. It's great your family's able to travel over for your big day.'

She nodded. 'I'm Nicole by the way.'

'Sabrina, and it's lovely to meet you, Nicole.'

'Sabrina?'

'Yes.'

'How odd.'

Sabrina wasn't sure how she should take that. It wasn't the most common of names but she'd hardly call it odd.

'Sorry, I didn't mean that how it sounded. It's just I'm sure that's the name Mum mentioned. Yes, I'm certain. Obviously, you can't be the same one because that would have been in the early sixties. You don't happen to know if there was there someone else here back then by that name, do you? Or, could you ask your aunt for me? Only Mum will be on at me to find out how she is when I tell her I called in.'

Sabrina's heartbeats amped up a notch. She was uncertain how to answer so instead she asked a question. 'What's your mam's name?'

'Patty, she'd have been Patty Hamilton back then.'

The name, just as Sabrina had suspected, didn't mean anything to her but if Nicole's mother knew her it only meant one thing. She must have gone back in time again. She must have met Nicole's mam when she was a young woman like her daughter standing here now was. It was the only explanation.

She eyed Nicole hesitantly. The truth was fantastical and she wasn't sure what she'd think of her if she told her how it was she thought she'd come to meet her mam. There was nothing to be gained by not telling her though especially as her mam had asked her to explain everything. 'Erm, Nicole are you in a rush?'

'No, I don't start until six this evening. I was determined to go home with a dress today too.'

'Good. I can help you find just the thing but first, I've something to tell you and you might want to take a seat out the back while I do.'

Chapter Seven

Liverpool, 1952

Patty

Patty didn't know what she'd expected. Their mam had aged with the grim reality of their daily lives but while she'd withered their father had clearly thrived. He looked younger than he had when she'd last seen him. He was fuller in the face, his hair neatly trimmed and his jawline smooth. His suit was well cut and fitted him perfectly. He was their father but he was a different daddy to the grey-faced one she remembered.

He stared at her and Davey, drinking them in, and then held his arms out to them both. Patty let out a sob and ran into them, Davey taking his cue from her even though his own memories of this man were hazy.

'You poor, poor things,' he said holding them tightly. 'What you must have been through.'

Patty breathed in his scent. He smelled the same. A mix of cigarettes, starch, and the musky aftershave he'd always favoured. It was this familiarity that broke the dam and she allowed herself to cry then. Properly cry as she hadn't had the chance to do since their mam had died. She'd had to be brave for Davey and the relief she felt at an adult taking that burden from her shoulders was immense.

Everything was going to be alright.

THE WORLD SO FAR AS Patty was concerned was looking a lot brighter as they sat at the table in the kitchen with a plate of beans on toast in front of them. Sheelagh, as they'd learned their stepmother was called, had begrudgingly banged it down in front of them before shooting her husband an annoyed look.

'It's the shock,' their father said, waving away his wife's unwelcoming behaviour as she stalked from the kitchen, presumably to check on Amelia.

Patty didn't care how Sheelagh behaved toward them, not now their daddy was here. He'd look out for them.

Their dinner tasted as wonderful as anything she'd ever eaten because she was sitting at the kitchen table with him and her brother who'd virtually inhaled what was on his plate.

'I'll eat later, once I've got you both sorted.' Anthony Hamilton swirled the ice in the tumbler he was holding before taking a sip of his drink and eyeing them speculatively. 'I bet you're dead on your feet after the day you've had.'

Patty nodded, mopping up the sauce with her toast and spying her brother running his finger across his plate before popping an orange finger in his mouth. She frowned at him. If Mam had been here she'd have slapped him on the hand for that.

Sheelagh hadn't come back and Amelia occasionally made sure her presence in the house was known. Anthony smiled as she gave a particularly virulent shriek.

'She reminds me of you as a baby, Patty.'

The questions Patty wanted answering burned but before she could put them into words her father pushed his seat back.

'I've put your case in the room you'll be sleeping in tonight. How does a hot bath and then bed sound?'

It sounded blissful she thought, deciding there'd be time enough for questions later. She got up and gestured to Davey to do the same before carrying their plates over to the sink.

'Leave those, Patty,' Anthony said holding open the kitchen door. They followed his lead into the hall where a telephone table and chair were the only furnishings. The hall was carpeted as were the stairs. Patty thought of the cold boards of their room in Toxteth as her stockinged feet sank into its plush weave.

The walls, she noticed, as she followed her father up the stairs were painted a sage green which made the hall and stairs seem dark. When they reached the landing she saw a row of photographs all in pride of place where they couldn't be missed. There was one of baby Amelia wrapped in a lacy white blanket in her mother's arms and another of her sitting up against cushions in a frilly dress. There was her father looking very smart next to Sheelagh who was dressed in a white suit and hat clutching a small posy.

It was the photo of the three of them, her father, Sheelagh and Amelia all smiling at the camera that made her tummy hurt though, It was like standing outside in the cold looking in through the window at a warm and cosy scene she and Davey would never be a part of.

'Here we are,' Anthony Hamilton said, reaching the end of the landing and opening a door. 'You can sleep in here tonight.' He beamed at them both as though wanting their approval.

Patty dragged her eyes away from the pictures and hurried down to him. The room she saw, ducking under his arm, was spartan with a bed made up in the corner. The bold orange bedspread the only splash of colour in an otherwise beige room. It smelled musty as though it hadn't been aired in a while.

'Sheelagh's sister stays in here when she visits from London,' he offered up by way of explanation.

Patty thought, given the smell, she mustn't have stayed in a long while. She rallied up a smile though and told him she and Davey would be just fine.

'Mine and Sheelagh's room is at the other end of the hall next to Amelia's room. She sleeps through now so you won't have to worry about being woken by a crying baby.'

Patty and Davey were well used to the sounds of crying babies echoing through the walls of Osbourne Court.

'Davey, you can wait here while Patty has a bath.'

Davey was already opening his case to dig out his teddy.

'Gather up your clothes and I'll get Sheelagh to wash them for you,' Anthony said, a look of distaste on his face at the sight of the grimy bear.

'Not teddy,' Davey stated firmly, holding the toy to his chest.

Anthony sighed, 'Alright not teddy but I'll dig you out a pair of my pyjamas tonight. You can roll them over at the waist and Patty you can borrow one of Sheelagh's old nighties.'

Patty glanced back at her brother as she followed her father from the room. He looked very young sitting on that orange bedspread and she smiled watching him put his thumb in his mouth and cuddle teddy to his chest once he was certain his father wouldn't see him.

The bathroom was like nothing Patty had ever seen. It was pastel peach and the water was scalding. Her father fetched her a fresh towel and, as promised, a clean nighty and, as she sank into the foamy, rose-scented water she felt her shoulders, which had been in knots all day, relax. She lathered herself with the soap even washing her hair with it and then sank down in the bath to rinse herself clean.

She'd have soaked in there until the water was cool if it were only her but she didn't want Davey to have a cold bath so she dragged herself out of the tub before her skin could pucker like a prune.

She patted herself dry and helped herself to the talc on the vanity before slipping the nighty over her head. She found a comb in the drawer and tugged it through her tangled wet locks. She smelled of lux soap, talcum, and something else. It was Sheelagh's perfume she realised, wishing she'd her own nighty to wear. It didn't feel right wearing something that belonged to the woman who'd taken her mam's place. Besides, she liked sleeping in her clothes. It was warmer.

Maybe tomorrow their dad would take them shopping for new clothes. They could have butties and maybe even a cream cake at the tea shop she'd seen when they'd come in off the beach earlier. She smiled, being careful not to trip over the too-long gown, as she made her way back to their room to tell Davey it was his turn.

'Be sure to wipe around the sides of the bath when you pull the plug, Davey,' she ordered as he picked up the pyjamas their father had given him and took off in the direction of the bathroom.

Patty saw their clothes had gone from the suitcase and wondered briefly what she'd wear tomorrow but she was too tired to care. The steamy bathroom and soothing bath along with a comfortably full stomach had made her sleepy.

She pulled back the covers and clambered between the sheets to wait for Davey to come back, listening to the distant sounds of the home she hoped her and Davey would become part of.

Patty was about to get up to bang on the bathroom door to make sure Davey hadn't nodded off in the warm water when her brother appeared. She laughed, seeing him trying not to trip over himself in the oversized pyjamas.

'Did you wipe around the bath like I told you to?' She'd hate for a ring of dirt to be left behind, picturing the look on Sheelagh's face if there was.

He nodded before clambering in alongside her. He pulled his teddy out from under the pillow where he'd left him for safekeeping, not entirely trusting his dad not to take him and put him in the washing machine along with their clothes. There was a certain smell to teddy that made him feel safe.

She'd have to get up and put the light out, Patty thought reluctant to climb out of the warm bed, but before she could do so a knock on the door sounded.

'Come in,' she and Davey chorused.

It was their father and he smiled at the sight of them, hair still damp from the bath snuggled together under the covers. He came and perched down on the end of the bed.

'Was it a good bath?'

They both nodded, neither wanting to admit to what a luxury it had been and both suddenly shy once more. Patty could smell alcohol and cigarettes on his breath. She didn't remember him drinking before when he'd lived with them.

'I've missed you two,' he said, reaching over to pat the mound under the blankets that was Davey, his eyes misty. 'More than you can ever know.'

Patty was suddenly wide awake and she pulled herself up to sitting, her arms resting on top of the orange spread as the words tumbled out. 'Then why did you leave us, Daddy?' Tears sprang unbidden and a plump one trickled down her cheek.

Anthony looked sad as he reached forward and wiped it away. 'I didn't want to leave, Patty, but I wasn't well. Not physically, up here.' He tapped his head. 'I had a nervous breakdown. Believe me when I tell you I never intended to keep walking away from you all but it was as if my body had taken on a mind of its own that day. Something in me had snapped.'

'But where did you go?' These were the questions Patty had wondered over so many times in the ensuing years since that dreadful day when he'd not come home.

'I went home to the house where I grew up. My parents took me back in and got me the help I needed so I could get well again. Then, when I was better I took up the position in the family furniture factory that was supposed to have been mine all along and with their help bought this house when I married Sheelagh.'

'But why didn't you come back to us when you got better?' Her voice sounded childish and whiny but she didn't care and it rose in pitch as she added, 'Why wasn't it us living with you here? You already had a family. How could you marry someone else?'

Anthony Hamilton ran his hands through his hair and for a moment sank his head into them before looking at his children once more. 'I don't expect either of you to understand but the job, this house, they came with a condition that I forget my life with you and your mother. My parents wanted me to wipe the slate clean and start afresh.'

'But why? Why do they hate us so much?'

'They don't hate you, they hate Catholics. I told you I don't expect you to understand but it's deep-rooted and your mother's family, they were no better. They wiped their hands of her because of me.'

'They were wrong to do that, yours and mam's.'

He sighed and it sounded heavy as though he'd summoned it from the depths of his very soul. 'It's the way things are, Patty. Some things you can't fight against. Your mam and I were very young when we met. We thought we could rise above their pettiness but it was so much harder than we thought it would be. I never intended to stay away either. I thought I'd get back on my feet and go back to you but the days since I left had turned into weeks while I got myself well again and then for the first time in a long while I felt worth something working in the family business. By the time I'd settled into my job, months had passed. I didn't know how to go back and face your mother or you two. I was ashamed for leaving the way I had with no explanation. It was easier in the end to stay and then your mother found me.'

Davey pressed his back into Patty's side curling himself into a ball as he listened to what their father was saying.

'I'd met Sheelagh by then and there was no going back. I offered to pay for yours and Davey's keep but Geraldine was a proud woman, she wouldn't have it.'

It was like a knife twisting in Patty's stomach hearing this. How could their mam have been so selfish? How could she have turned down his help? That their lives needn't have been so hard was a bitter pill to swallow.

'Don't think badly of her, Patty, or me. As I said we were young when we met and thought our love would be enough to rise above all that prejudice. Life's not that simple though.'

Her father read her conflicting emotions correctly.

It was Davey who spoke up next, poking his head out from under the covers to ask, 'What's a bastard, Dad?'

'Where did you hear that?' His voice was sharp.

Davey unfurled himself and looked to his sister for reassurance that he hadn't said something wrong.

'I asked where you heard that?'

Patty gave a small nod.

'Sheelagh said we were bastards. She said she wouldn't have that woman's bastards under her roof.'

Anthony flinched hearing this and mumbled something she didn't catch under his breath before answering.

'You have to understand. It was a shock for Sheelagh you two turning up the way you did today.' He looked at Patty then Davey. 'She's a sweet-natured woman who's well-loved in the neighbourhood and a good mother to Amelia. It was the shock.' He echoed this as though trying to convince himself.

Patty swallowed down the retort that had risen up. She wanted to shout at him that it had been a shock to them to find out their father who was married to their mam had wed another woman in the ensuing years since he'd left. And, that his new wife was so kind she'd not so much as offered his children a drink or bite to eat, insisting they stand like statues until he arrived home from work. Instead, she asked, 'How could you marry Sheelagh if you were married to mam?' They'd come this far she needed to hear it all now.

His voice was quiet when he spoke and he wouldn't look at them. 'We weren't married, your mother and I.'

'But she had rings, I remember her engagement ring and she wore a wedding band. She was Mrs Hamilton.'

'We weren't married, Patty. We got engaged and all hell let loose with our families and by then Geraldine was pregnant with you. We were both turfed out and decided to set up home on Lowry Lane. I bought her a plain band to wear to stop people gossiping and although we planned to make it official we never got round to it. We felt like we were married. It was enough or at least it felt like it was enough.'

They hadn't been enough though, had they, Patty thought, her brain whirring. They'd not been enough because if they had he wouldn't have been able to walk away and forget about them as he had done.

She stared at her father and he read the accusation there in her eyes. He'd no idea what they'd endured while he'd been here with his new family living a life of luxury.

'So, now you know. I'm sorry.'

It sounded trite. It was pathetic and he knew it because he'd that same stoop in his shoulders Patty remembered him having the day they'd had to leave their house on Lowry Lane. Defeated, worn down.

'Get some sleep. Goodnight.' He didn't attempt to kiss either of them goodnight before getting up from the bed. He walked from the room turning the light out on his way.

Patty stared unseeingly into the blackness and at that moment she hated him.

Chapter Eight

Liverpool, 1981

Sabrina

'Aunt Evie, this is Nicole. She's on a working holiday here in Liverpool, all the way from Australia,' Sabrina said with a curious Nicole standing alongside her taking in the industrious workroom out the back of the bridal shop. 'Her mam suggested she call on us to see about a last-minute wedding dress. She lives in—' she turned to Nicole.

'Adelaide. She left Liverpool in the early sixties. It's why I came here. I wanted to see where Mum and my uncle grew up. I felt as though I knew the city before I even arrived because I've grown up with their stories of what it was like here and all their mad expressions. I think they sugar-coated a lot of their childhood for my benefit. Their mum died when they were young, my mum was only ten and they didn't have an easy time of it after that.'

Evelyn had stopped sewing and was inspecting the young woman who pronounced her words with a drawling twang. She was a few years older than Sabrina and had the sort of face that made you want to look twice. Her eyes were very blue, like glittering twin jewels and her hair was blonde. She looked Australian except she didn't have a tan. She always thought of Australians as being tanned people.

'A hard age for a girl to lose her mam alright,' Evelyn said sympathetically, thinking privately any age was a hard age as she recalled Sabrina as a lost three-year-old. She swung the conversation around to herself. 'Now then, Nicole, you don't happen to know my cousin Jimmy, do you? He emigrated out your way years ago and is terrible at the letter writing.' She asked this as she always did when she met someone from that part of the world. She did the same with Canadians having a long lost cousin, Marnie who'd crossed the water years ago.

'No, I can't say I do.' Nicole grinned, blinking at the brightness of the little woman with the owl-like glasses and shop coat.

'Aunt Evie, Australia's huge you know. The chances of Nicole knowing your cousin Jimmy are very slim,' Sabrina shook her head as though she herself were well-travelled and worldly and knew all about these things. She supposed, thinking about it that she was well-travelled just not in the conventional sense.

'There's no harm in asking, Sabrina. The world's a small place, you know.'

She couldn't argue with that. It was true enough, Sabrina thought, thinking of Adam and his dad. If she didn't keep things moving along though Aunt Evie would be asking Nicole if she'd had a pet koala or a kangaroo called Skippy as a child next!

She dragged the chair their brides-to-be usually sat on when waiting for any last-minute alterations to their dress over to the worktable, swallowing down the question that had risen unbidden as to whether Nicole had ever met Olivia Newton-John. She knew it was up there with Skippy the kangaroo but she'd have loved to have asked it anyway. Just in case.

'Here we are, Nicole.' She gestured to the seat. 'Would you like a cup of tea? It's getting on for that time.' There'd be time for a bite to eat later.

'I'm gasping,' Evelyn piped up, deciding the matter as to whether tea should be made.

'Sounds lovely,' Nicole said, wondering what on earth Sabrina was going to tell her that required her to step out the back of the shop, take a seat, and have a cup of tea. She sat down and watched as Evelyn finished the hem she'd been in the middle of sewing before snipping off the cotton.

'Sabrina before you disappear help me with the Megan.'

'We give the dresses the names of our brides-to-be,' Sabrina explained, helping Evelyn place the heavy dress on a padded clothes hanger. She held it aloft while Evelyn pulled the plastic covering over so it covered the dress like a rain poncho. 'Nicole's getting married this month, Aunt Evie, and her mam, uncle and the rest of their family are coming back to Liverpool for the wedding.'

'A Christmas bride,' Evelyn smiled.

'Yes, more or less. We've set the date for December the twentieth,' Nicole replied. 'I'm hoping if I'm to be married in winter that we at least get snow for the sake of the photographs.'

'Quite likely. Last year it was a white Christmas,' Sabrina said, picking up her own mishappen mug and her aunt's teacup and saucer, placing them on the tray to carry upstairs to their flat. 'I'll be back in a jiffy.'

She wasn't privy to the conversation going on as she put the tray down on the bottom step of the stairs leading to the flat but she was guessing Nicole would be quizzing Aunt Evie as to whether she remembered a Sabrina from the 1960s. She couldn't dwell on it because she'd her rituals and the light needed to be flicked on and off three times before she left it on. Satisfied all was as it should be, she bent down to pick up the tray once more carrying it carefully up the rickety stairs to their flat.

It was a process she repeated when she opened the door to the flat. Sabrina's insistence on doing this drove her aunt potty but despite her protestations that Sabrina wasn't manning a lighthouse and guiding the ships in, she understood their origins.

Sabrina's rituals made her feel safe. She could control the number of times she turned the lights on and off whereas there were aspects of her life she'd had no control over. Like finding herself all alone on a busy street at the age of three; her mother gone.

Everybody needed someone to look out for them in life and she was blessed Aunt Evie had happened along to take her in. This was why she carried down a bowl of porridge each morning for Fred. Off she'd go, carrying the steaming bowl carefully down the stairs and out the front door of the shop onto a street only just beginning to wake up for the day.

She'd trot past flamboyant Esmerelda's Emporium pausing briefly to admire whatever weird and wonderful outfit was on display in her shop window before moving on to where Fred slept rough; a bag of bones under a mound of coats and blankets in the doorway of an empty shop.

He'd not been there this morning and Sabrina had been glad he'd had the sense to find proper shelter overnight. The weather was far too cold for him to hunker down in the open. She was terrified she'd venture down one morning and find he'd died in his sleep of hyperthermia. She knew there was a hostel he'd reluctantly head to when the weather turned particularly vicious which gave her some reassurance.

Aunt Evie said she was far too soft for her own good. She'd known the uncertainty of an alcoholic father as a child and had no sympathy for those who loved the bottle more than their nearest and dearest. Fred had chosen to live the way he lived she'd tut but Sabrina knew that for all her protesting, beneath her sometimes hardened shell lurked a heart of gold. If Sabrina hadn't been there to take a bowl of hot oats down to the dear old vagabond each morning, she'd have done it herself.

A whiff of smoke from Aunt Evie's after dinner ciggie the night before tickled her nostrils as she opened the door and bent to retrieve the tray once more before stepping into their living room. She grimaced at the fishy smell left behind from her aunt's supper wafting from the small kitchen tucked away over in the corner of the room as she carried the tray over to the worktop and put the kettle on.

The furnishings in their living room were tired and could be described as antwacky but they made up the only home Sabrina could remember living in. She'd rather put up with the old sofa's spring that dug into her leg when she watched tele than some fancy new furniture she was frightened of sitting down on, any day!

The paperchains she was working on were draped over the back of the sofa. Sabrina had been making the honeycomb-patterned decorations each year at Christmas for as long as she could remember. Aunt Evie had made noises about how she was making them earlier every year and that next year she'd be at it in flamin' July. Sabrina had just carried on with her folding and stapling. She loved Christmas and her paper chains dangling from the ceiling gave their little flat a festive air.

It was chilly in here, she thought, shivering despite her sweater, and glancing over she saw Aunt Evie had forgotten to close the window. She'd opened it this morning before she joined Sabrina down in the shop to give the room an airing as was her custom but she'd forgotten to close it which wasn't like Aunt Evie. She was in her early seventies but her mind was as sharp as it had always been.

Sabrina moved over to close it then retrieved the packet of garibaldi biscuits before making the tea. As she waited for the kettle to boil she wondered what Nicole's response would be to the story she was going to tell her. The knowledge she must have travelled back in time once more had her feeling tingly.

If, as Nicole had said, her mam had met somebody called Sabrina who worked at Brides of Bold Street than it meant she must have arrived in the 1960s. Perhaps she'd even stepped back to 1963 the year she'd become separated from her mam and Aunt Evie had taken her in. The thought made her breath snag and her hand trembled as she poured the boiling water into the pot.

One thing was certain though, another adventure await-ed her and this time it might lead her back to her mother.

Chapter Nine

Liverpool, 1952

Patty

The red gates creaked behind Patty and Davey as their father closed them before picking up the two little cases that Sheelagh had bought for them. Patty's was brown and Davey's was blue and both had shiny brass clasps. Their battered old suitcase wouldn't have been in keeping with their father's smart coat, polished shoes and trilby hat, tilted just so on his head. As such, Sheelagh had insisted on buying new.

Where once Patty had thought their daddy handsome, now she thought him a peacock.

The suitcases weren't the only new purchases. They were filled with freshly bought clothes, all folded neatly and packed by Sheelagh so as not to crease. Patty had vowed not to wear any of them having decided they'd been bought by the Wicked Witch, as she had taken to calling her stepmother when she was out of earshot, to appease her father's guilt at offloading them into the care of others.

Much to the Wicked Witch's chagrin, she'd refused to wear the dress she'd selected for her this morning. She'd slapped Patty hard on the legs but she refused to give in. She wouldn't give her the satisfaction. She'd refused to brush her hair and wash her face too. She'd wanted to look every inch the abandoned child because that's what she was.

Until the dress she'd had on the day she'd arrived on their father's doorstep was retrieved from wherever it had been tossed and brought to her she'd refused to cooperate. She'd heard Sheelagh mutter to their father that at least the dress was clean and wouldn't be seen under Patty's new coat.

She'd had no choice about wearing the red coat with gold buttons. Her old one had gone out in the rubbish and there was no point in catching a chill. She'd not be able to look after Davey if she were sick. She'd not be like her mam and let stupid pride take the place of common sense except where her dress was concerned. She'd wanted something from her old life to take with her.

'Isn't it grand?' Anthony Hamilton said, gesturing to the Victorian mansion up ahead. There was a faux jolliness in his tone as if he'd convinced himself he was dropping them at a holiday camp and not a children's home. 'You'll have a lovely time here. Think of all the playmates you'll have.'

Davey had a tight hold of his sister's hand and they hung back for a moment staring at the largest house either of them had seen. It loomed imposingly through the mist of the morning at the end of the treelined driveway. The trees, given the time of year, were stripped of their leaves and looked ghostly. To Patty's mind, it was as if they wanted to lean in and snag their clothes with their spindly branches—to catch hold of them and never let them go.

'Is it a castle?' Davey whispered.

'No,' Patty said shortly. She'd seen the sign Strawberry Field Children's Home beside the gate. It was far from a castle.

'Look at all the chimneys.' Davey was awestruck. 'There's too many to count.'

Patty shivered inside her coat. The house was spooky, like something out of a storybook where nothing good happened to the children involved in the tale.

From the minute they'd lost their mam, she'd felt as if she'd stepped between the pages of a fairy tale with the evil stepmother and the father who wasn't strong enough to know his own mind. Hansel and Gretel, Cinderella, Snow White; they were all merging together. The only comfort she could glean was that these stories had happy ever after endings but right now Patty couldn't imagine one for her and Davey.

She tried to focus on the warmth of her brother's mitten-covered hand in hers and ignore the impending sense of dread creeping over her. She'd kept her promise to her mother. They were still together.

The house had too many windows to count and she felt as though hundreds of eyes were peering down at her through them. Were children clustered together staring at the new arrivals? Sizing them up and getting ready to put them in their place.

Her feet took root in the ground like the trees ahead of her and refused to budge. She was frightened and Davey, sensing it, gripped her hand even tighter.

'Hurry up, the matron's expecting us,' their father threw back over his shoulder. 'Patty, come on,' he urged. 'Davey looks frozen. Let's get inside to the warm.' He carried on, his loping gait seeing him reach the front entrance in no time.

He was right, it was cold, their breath was coming in dragon-like puffs and she forced her feet to move. Put one in front of the other, Patty, she told herself, mutinously dragging her heels toward the front door to the left of which a car was parked.

Their father waited for her and Davey to catch up before pressing the doorbell firmly. 'It's for the best. You'll see. It wouldn't work,' he said, half to himself and half to them as they waited for the door to open.

Patty refused to look at him. She wanted to shout and scream and pummel him with her fists for not having tried to make it work. A stronger man would have put his foot down and told his wife the way it was going to be, but not her father, oh no! He was leaving them for the second time.

Less than a week they'd stayed with him. How could he possibly know it wouldn't work? Sheelagh had decided there was no room for them the moment she'd laid eyes on them, never once warming in her frosty attitude toward them.

Patty cast her mind back to the first night in the house she'd hoped would become her and Davey's new home as they waited for the door to the children's home to open.

It had taken her forever to get to sleep as she lay next to her brother. She was unaccustomed to the softness of the mattress and the silence of the house had unnerved her. She was used to hearing thudding up the stairs, children crying, and doors banging, nevertheless, she'd eventually nodded off only to be woken by raised voices.

Patty didn't know how long she'd been asleep but her head felt woolly. Davey hadn't stirred but then he was always a heavy sleeper. She tried to drop back off but couldn't because curiosity as to what had Sheelagh and her father so heated was getting the better of her. In the end, she pushed the covers aside, careful not to disturb her brother.

She made her way across the floor of the dark room to the door and opened it, poking her head out to listen. The hallway was deserted and the doors to the rooms at the end, where Amelia's nursery was, along with her father and Sheelagh's bedroom were closed. The voices were coming from below.

Tiptoeing down the hall, she sat on the top stair tucking her nighty under her feet to ward off the chill. She was in time to hear Sheelagh shout that it was them or her and Amelia.

'I won't have them near our daughter, Tony. The girl's hair was alive. Goodness only knows what diseases they've brought into our house.'

Patty scratched at her head. It itched all the time, so much so she barely registered it.

Her father's voice was placatory. 'But, Sheelagh, they've nowhere to go.'

'That's not my problem but I'm telling you they are not staying here! Think of the scandal of it. I mean, your illegitimate children under our roof—I wouldn't be able to hold my head up at church and I won't be reminded of your fancy woman every time I look at them. You must see that.'

A silence stretched long and Patty shivered inside the nighty. She heard her father speak after a while but his voice was too low for her to catch what was being said. Sheelagh, however, came across loud and clear.

'Tony, to all intents and purposes they're orphans. You made your choice when you left them with their mother. There are places, places where they'd be well looked after.'

'What are you saying, Sheelagh? That I should send them to an orphanage?' There was horror in his voice.

'Don't be so melodramatic. It's not the Victorian era. We don't have workhouses anymore. My father has connections through his work with the Salvation Army. There's a perfectly lovely children's home in a grand old house over on Beaconsfield Road in Woolton. I'm sure if he put in a word for us, room could be found for them there. They'd be well looked after, better than they have been judging by the state of them. And, they could forget the papist nonsense their mother instilled in them. You'd be doing the right thing allowing them to be brought into the faith.'

'I can't put my own flesh and blood in a children's home, Sheelagh. How can you even ask that of me?'

'Tony, listen to me because I am serious when I tell you I won't have my reputation in the community ruined because you couldn't keep it in your trousers with that, that woman.'

Patty had heard the door bang downstairs and had scarpered back to bed to hold her brother close to her. She'd comforted herself off to sleep by replaying her father's part in the conversation. He wouldn't let them be put in a home.

Now, here they were about to be deposited at Strawberry Field Children's Home.

Chapter Ten

Liverpool, 1981

Sabrina

The shop was quiet and the hum of the Singer silent as, with their tea poured and a plate of the currant filled biscuits Sabrina was especially partial to within easy reach, Evelyn spoke up.

'Nicole here's been telling me how her mam was eager for her to come here to our shop for her wedding dress. She said she'd been good friends with a girl called Sabrina who was tied to the shop before she left for Australia.' Her expression was unreadable behind her glasses.

Nicole nodded her agreement and looked at Sabrina. 'Evelyn said you'd explain the connection. I don't know why Mum made such a big mystery out of it all. She's not usually the dramatic sort. I'm guessing she must have been your mum, am I right?' Nicole took a biscuit from the plate Evelyn slid toward her.

'Erm, no, you're not, and this will sound mad to you, Nicole, but hear me out will you?'

Nicole, biscuit halfway to her mouth nodded.

'There's a strange phenomenon here on Bold Street. A timeslip. I don't know what's behind it or why it affects some people and not others but it affects me and I'm certain it affected my mother. One minute you can be walking down the street minding your own business and the next you sense a change in the atmosphere, a sort of thickening of the air and a feeling that something's different and then, when you look about, you realise the cars have changed as have the shops. What was Hudson's Bookstore has become Cripps Dressmakers.'

'Are you talking about time travel?' Nicole raised an incredulous eyebrow.

'Yes, I suppose I am. It happened to me you see. I found myself back in the nineteen-twenties.' Sabrina squirmed putting voice to this. It did sound mad but it was the truth.

'I don't see the connection with my mum.' Nicole shook her head. This was not what she'd expected to hear and she was beginning to regret having agreed to come into the workroom with Sabrina. She was crackers.

Sabrina could see her struggling to comprehend what she'd just heard but she'd stayed in her seat which was something, she thought. Although, by the look on Nicole's face if she didn't convince her in the next few minutes she wouldn't stay seated for long. 'It's easier to understand if I start at the beginning.' She took a deep breath and dived in. 'I came to live here above Brides of Bold Street with Aunt Evie as a three-year-old in nineteen sixty-three. She found me wandering outside Hudson's Bookshop further down the road, only it was Cripps Dressmakers back then. I always assumed my mam had abandoned me but now I'm not so sure.'

Nicole interrupted then, directing her question to Evelyn, 'Didn't you go to Child Welfare or whatever it's called here?' Her tone had an accusatory ring to it which saw Evelyn put her teacup down bristling like an indignant budgie as she opened her mouth. Sabrina stepped in before she could say her piece.

'There was never anything in the papers about a missing child and the police never announced a child had disappeared, Nicole. It was as if it hadn't happened. Aunt Evie decided I'd be better off with her than in the care system because there were stories going about that children from orphanages were being sent abroad even though they weren't always orphans. She was worried this would happen to me and when my mam came looking for me, as she was sure she would, I'd be long gone.'

Evelyn nodded along with Sabrina's words.

'Aunt Evie thought perhaps my mother had been in an accident and somehow lost her memory. She was certain once she recovered she'd try and find me then but no one ever came to claim me. I think I had a lucky escape to be honest because my life could have turned out very different. Aunt Evie's been a mother to me,' Sabrina stated loyally.

Evelyn's ruffled feathers were smoothed and she tried not to let the emotion show on her face as she dipped her head to sip from her teacup.

A ringing sound from the shop pierced the momentary silence and with a sigh Sabrina excused herself getting up to answer the telephone. 'Please stay and hear me out, Nicole,' She said before she left Evelyn and Nicole alone.

When she returned Nicole was talking. 'Mum and my uncle were placed in a children's home after their mother died. That's all I know. They never talk about why they came to Australia. They're a closed book on the subject. I always found it odd. There're parts of them closed off to me. I think maybe that was another reason I wanted to come to Liverpool, to see if I could understand them a little better.'

'People have their reasons for not wanting to talk about the past, Nicole. Sometimes it's the only way they can move forward into the present,' Evelyn stated. She spoke from experience. She too was a closed book on parts of her past which not even Sabrina was privy to. Ray Taylor knew what had happened back before she'd found the strength to rise above it and open her bridal shop. Each time she saw him, she was torn between hating the reminder of what had happened yet, at the same time, she'd always be grateful for what he'd done. It was their secret.

'That was Stephanie about her dress,' Sabrina supplied, sitting back down at the table. 'She's going to pick it up tomorrow at four so that gives me plenty of time to get the rest of those sewed on.' She pointed to the tray of slowly depleting pearl beads.

Nicole eyed the dress at the opposite end of the table where they were sitting. 'It's very pretty. I love pearls even though they're supposed to mean tears if you wear them on your wedding day.'

'I don't think it counts if they're beads and not the real thing.' Sabrina grinned. 'When we've had our tea, I've a lovely dress to show you. The entire bodice is beaded.'

'You'll tell me the rest of your story first though, won't you?' Even though she was sceptical about what she'd been told so far, Nicole's curiosity was piqued enough to want to hear everything. She needed to find out where her mum fitted into the picture. It was a hard sell to imagine stepping back in time to another era though. A hard sell indeed.

'Where did I get to?'

'You were telling Nicole how you came to live here. These biscuits aren't doing my dentures any favours.' Evelyn pulled a face as she tried to dislodge a currant and Sabrina's mouth twitched.

'Well stop eating them then,' she said, helping herself.

'And let you polish off the lot? Fat chance. Nicole, you'd best have another one before she chomps down the lot.'

Nicole smiled. Quite mad the pair of them might be but she found herself liking them, nevertheless.

Sabrina picked up her story. 'My bezzie mate and I, Florence, I call her Flo, went to see Mystic Lou. She gives psychic readings from her upstairs premises a few doors down from here.'

Evelyn made her feelings about the psychic clear with a rude snorting sound.

'Ignore her, Nicole,' Sabrina said with a flap of her hand. 'We went because Flo wanted to know what the future held where our love lives were concerned; she's obsessed. Only Mystic Lou told me something completely unexpected.' Actually, she'd told Flo something completely unexpected too, Sabrina thought, recalling the lemony expression on her friend's face when instead of hearing her future lay with her dream fella, Tim Burns, she'd been told to watch out for a fella in tight trousers! They knew full well who she was referring to and while Tony—he of the tight trousers—had made his feelings toward Flo known, to date she was playing hard to get.

'What?' Nicole brought Sabrina back to the here and now, eager to hear what this Mystic Lou had said to her.

'Well, amongst other things she said there's a woman who looks like me from another time who's been searching for me.'

Nicole didn't have to roll her sleeves up to know the hairs on her arms were standing on end.

'I didn't know what to think when I heard this. I thought it was far-fetched poppycock but the publican at my local happened to mention there've been tales going round of people stepping back in time on Bold Street for years. He'd encountered a few poor bewildered souls himself wondering where they were and not understanding how they'd got there. And, when I relayed all this to my boyfriend, Adam, he told me a story his uncle used to tell anyone who'd listen about something so odd that had happened to him on Bold Street, he'd never forgotten it. He said he'd encountered a strangely dressed woman who'd been distraught. She was looking for her daughter. He thought she must be on drugs or something. Anyway, she asked him what year it was and he said nineteen sixty-three which was the year my aunt found me and this woman shook her head and said no, it couldn't be because it was nineteen eighty-three. She set off then and when he looked to see where she'd gone a second later, she'd vanished into thin air.'

Nicole's pretty blue eyes sat huge in her face. 'That is strange, and you think that woman was your mother?'

'I think so, yes.'

'I don't understand where my mum fits into this, though.'

'You said your mam told you she was close to someone called Sabrina who had ties to this shop back in the sixties. Well, I think it was me. I think I must have gone back in time again to search for my mother.'

'No, Sabrina.' Evelyn's voice had a warning tone as she realised this was the connection to Sabrina's visit in 1962. Nicole however had already begun to speak.

'But how did it happen that first time. You said you wound up in the nineteen-twenties?' Nicole couldn't believe she was giving any of what Sabrina had just said credence.

'Well, when Adam told me his uncle's story, I got it in my head to see for myself if there was any truth in it all. I went to Hudson's, you know the bookshop I told you used to be a dressmaker's, where Aunt Evie found me. It's a shop I'd walked past hundreds of times before but this time I paced back and forth in front of it. Nothing happened and I made to go home, feeling foolish, when I realised things around me had changed. The motor cars were like those you see at vintage car rallies and the men and women were all dressed oddly. I went straight back to the shop here but Aunt Evelyn was a young woman and she didn't know me. I panicked, not knowing what to do and wandered about for an age, and in the end, I went and sat in the church at the top of the road.'

Nicole frowned. 'You mean the bombed-out church?'

'St Luke's, yes, only it was untouched and a woman who was the cook for a big house on Allerton Road took pity on me and found me work there as a kitchen maid. I was gone for months, or at least I thought I was, and every chance I got, I came back to Bold Street to try and get back to the here and now but nothing happened. Then, one day,' she clicked her fingers, 'it happened. I'd only been gone a few days but I'd spent months in nineteen twenty-eight. Don't ask me to explain this because I don't understand any more than you but it's what happened,' Sabrina finished with a shrug.

Evelyn nodded confirmation of all this.

'Weren't you worried when Sabrina vanished?'

'No. You see I knew it would happen. As Sabrina said, she came to see me in nineteen twenty-eight when I'd not long opened the shop. She told me then what would happen. All of it. Me finding her outside Cripps, her disappearing in nineteen eighty-one to go back in time and, like you, I thought she was stark raving mad. When I found her as a small child, just as she'd said I would, it all came back to me.' She sighed and shook her head. 'I want her to leave well alone. It's a dangerous game traversing time and who's to say, if she goes back again, she'll find her way back to us next time?'

Evelyn's hands were clasped tightly under the table because she knew something she'd decided not to mention on account of Sabrina not needing encouragement. Who was to say she couldn't change the past by remaining silent? Sabrina did not need to know she had visited her here in the shop in 1962.

'Stop talking about me like I'm not sitting right here, Aunt Evie,' Sabrina said. 'And it's not that simple as you well know.' Sabrina turned her attention to Nicole. 'I know it's a lot to try and understand.' She shrugged again. 'Like I said I don't understand and Aunt Evie doesn't either but I do know I've got to keep trying to find my mam.' The familiar stab of pain at the thought of her looking for her lost daughter and never finding any answers shot through her. 'What you've told me today means I must travel back again. I have to have done so if I met your mam twenty years ago.' She eyed Nicole. 'It sounds crazy doesn't it?'

'Crazy enough to be true,' Nicole said.

'Yes,' Sabrina echoed. 'Crazy enough to be true.'

Evelyn's lips tightened.

Chapter Eleven

Liverpool, 1952

Patty

The door to Strawberry Field opened and a middle-aged woman in a crisp uniform with a headdress, from beneath which peeped a kindly face, smiled warmly, first at Anthony and then at each of the children. Patty felt her trepidation at what lay ahead lessen a little.

'Come in, come in,' she trilled, ushering them inside and they filed into the expansive entrance. The ornate tiled floor shone and no speck of dust could be seen clinging to the wood-panelled walls or sweep of bannister rail. She closed the door behind them. 'Now then, you must be Patricia and David.' Neither answered and so their father, having taken off his hat the moment they'd crossed the threshold, confirmed that yes, they were.

'Welcome to Strawberry Field, my dears, and don't look so frightened, you'll both be charging about the place with the other children in no time.' She gave them another warm smile before shooting a reassuring glace at their father.

She received no smiles in return from the trio.

In the distance, Patty could hear children's voices and she sniffed, certain she could smell cabbage which didn't bode well because she hated cabbage. She could smell polish too and wondered if the floors had been freshly shined.

'Now then,' Matron spoke up once more, her tone more businesslike than it had been a moment earlier. 'It's time to say goodbye to your father, children. I find it's best in these circumstances if we don't draw this out.' She shot Anthony a meaningful glance.

Patty studied her shiny new shoes; the leather hurt her heels. She was sure she was starting with blisters. She'd have rather had her old shoes back even if they did have cardboard inserts to stop the water seeping through the holes in the soles. The Wicked Witch had thrown them out in the rubbish, too though. Another part of her old life tossed in the bin to be taken away and dumped.

Davey followed her lead, only he scuffed his foot against the tiles in a manner that earned a cluck of disapproval from the matron. He stopped doing it but wouldn't raise his head either.

Their father laid a hand on each of their heads briefly and his voice cracked as he told them they'd settle in in no time and that it really was for the best. 'You'll see. You'll be well looked after here.'

'I can assure you they will be, Mr Hamilton.'

He hovered half a second longer and then, peering under her lashes, Patty watched as he put his hat on and took his leave. As the door shut behind him she felt trapped like an animal in a cage with no way out. There was no point running after him though. No point at all.

'Right then,' Matron said brusquely. 'That's that. Wait here a moment.' Off she clacked down the hallway.

'I'm scared, Patty. I want to go home,' Davey whispered, glancing around fearfully. 'I don't like it here.' There was a portrait of the king in all his finery hanging on the wall and Patty stared at it for a moment before his stern gaze made her turn her attention back to her brother.

'We don't have a home, Davey. This is it.' There was no point sugar-coating it or making promises she couldn't keep. 'We're going to have to make the best of it here, you and me.'

'Sing to me,' he pleaded, but at that moment a dark-haired youngster poked her head around a doorway. She stared at them both with her conker-shaped eyes and pasty face, sizing them up before calling out, 'Youse aren't wanted either.' She scarpered as footsteps sounded on the polished floor tiles once more.

The matron reappeared along with a short, stout woman with grey hair stretched tightly from a face that was pale, smooth and unlined. 'This is Miss Acton, children. Patricia, she's your housemother.'

'Hello there, Patricia, you can come with me and I'll get you settled in.' Her accent was lilting, reminding Patty of the voices that would carry around Osbourne Court. She immediately liked the woman and sensed she was kind-hearted.

'What about my brother?'

'He'll be taken care of. Don't fret,' Miss Acton said but Patty wasn't reassured.

'I don't want to leave him here. Can't he come with us?'

'Patricia dear, don't make a fuss. You're not helping matters.' Matron's tone was clipped. 'We've separate quarters for boys and girls. You can come with me, Davey.'

Davey had begun to cry and his grip on his sister's hand was fierce.

'It'll be alright, Davey. I'll see you soon,' Patty said, not sure if she believed what she was saying.

He refused to let go of her hand and Patty felt tears threaten but she refused to let them spill over. She didn't want her brother to see she was scared and that she didn't want to leave him either.

Miss Acton inclined her head and there was a look in her eyes that told Patty it would be better for her and Davey if she did as she was told.

'Davey, you go with Matron. I'll see you soon.'

He wiped his running nose on the sleeve of his coat and Patty was grateful Matron hadn't seen. She was already beginning to walk away, clearly used to children doing as they were told. Instinct told her she wouldn't put up with any nonsense. 'G'won now, Davey,' she urged not wanting to mark their cards as disobedient children. Only when she saw him pick up his case and hurry after Matron did she do the same and follow Miss Acton up the stairs.

She tried to put the thought of her brother's tear-stained face and his pleading voice from her mind as she concentrated on keeping up with her housemother. For a portly woman, she was setting quite a pace.

Patty followed her down the rabbit warren of corridors before coming to a halt outside a door that Miss Acton opened. 'Bath time, Patricia,' she said cheerily gesturing her in. 'Or do you prefer to be called Patty or Pat?'

'Patty, please.' She hated being called by her full name. The only time her mam had referred to her as Patricia had been when she was in bother for something or other.

It was an odd time to be having a bath, Patty thought, entering the room which had a wooden slat floor in the middle of which sat an enormous cast iron tub. 'Right then, young miss, we'll have you cleaned up in no time. Off with that dress while I get the bath run.'

Miss Acton rolled up her sleeves and turned on the taps while Patty stripped off. Before she knew it she'd a strong-smelling concoction being rubbed into her scalp. It made her eyes water. 'This will get rid of them nits,' Miss Acton declared with an extra vigorous rub before checking on the bath. 'I comb my girls' hair through each evening too.'

Patty blinked to stop the stinging.

'You have a wash and rinse that off in there,' Miss Acton pointed to the bathwater. 'Don't be messing around either, it's not for playing in. We've swings in the garden for that. When you're done empty the bath and give it a swish round with the cloth. I'll be back in a jiffy with some fresh clothes for you to put on.' She scuttled out of the bathroom, pausing before closing the door behind her, 'And watch your step getting out the bath on those duckboards.'

Patty clambered into the water which was only just warm and got washed quickly as she'd been instructed to do before rinsing her hair out in the water.

Miss Acton, true to her word, reappeared with a dress and cardigan for her to put on, telling her to be sure to get all that stuff out of her hair.

Patty dunked her head under a second time and then, having no wish to linger, she swished the sides of the bath clean as the water gurgled down the drain. Despite Miss Acton's warning to be careful on the slats she nearly slipped as she stepped over the side of the tub, only just managing to right herself in time.

The bathroom felt claustrophobic with only a high window to let in light and she was keen to get dried and dressed in the clothes that smelled freshly laundered so as she could ask Miss Acton if they could go and find Davey now. She'd only just buttoned her cardigan up when her housemother opened the door once more.

'Good girl. Alright, then I'll take you to your room and show you where you can put your things.'

Patty traipsed after Miss Acton once more as she led her up the stairs to the third floor and when she disappeared inside a door at the end of the corridor she paused, her eye caught by the sight of names etched into the timber panels just outside the entrance. 'Esther, Helen, Ann,' she read wondering who these girls were who'd been bold enough to scratch their names into the wall. She jumped as Miss Acton reappeared. 'Don't be getting any ideas about doing the same as them either or you'll be sorry like they were,' she clucked. 'Now come on with you, Patty, we haven't got all day.'

Patty entered the dormitory which was filled with rows of iron beds less than arm's distance from each other. She counted sixteen of them in total, all with the sort of blanket that would scratch your skin neatly folded at the bottom.

Miss Acton was fiddling with the door to a locker. 'Here we are. This is where you can keep your things and these are yours too.' She showed Patty a tin cup with a toothbrush in it already inside the locker. To her surprise, the mug had her name on it.

'But where will Davey sleep, Miss Acton?'

'He's in the boys' wing, of course.' The housemother looked at her as though she'd grown a second head.

It was no answer at all Patty thought, watching as she clip-clopped down the middle of the room coming to a halt in front of one of the beds. 'This is your bed, Patty, and one of the drawers there is yours too.'

Patty wondered if Davey's room would be the same and if he'd be teased by the other boys for sleeping with a teddy bear. He liked to hear her sing of an evening too, because like it had settled their mam it helped him get off to sleep too even if he'd pains in his tummy from not enough to eat.

She walked down to where Miss Acton was patting the bed and placed her case down on it.

'Why don't you get unpacked and settled in and I'll come and get you in time for dinner.'

'Thank you, Miss Acton,' Patty replied dully. The house-mother smelled of lavender which was a welcome relief from the pervasive scent of polish.

As her Irish housemother disappeared off to other parts of the home, Patty sat down on her bed. She'd never felt so alone in her whole life and a tear traced a path down her freshly washed face. How could he have left them like this? The injustice of it frothed like the foamy waves she'd seen on that long-ago outing to the beach in happier times. She longed for something familiar to cling to but staring around the echoey space she could find nothing.

'*We must make the best of things, Patty,*' The voice sounded sharply in her head. Her mother's voice. She was watching over her, Patty thought, as a warmth stole over her. She'd heard those words each time they'd moved and their circumstances had grown worse. 'We must make the best of things,' Patty whispered before wiping her tears away with the back of her hands and unlatching her suitcase. She put her hated new clobber away in the drawers and the locker she'd been shown. Then, taking a deep breath, she made her way from the dorm room and back down the stairs to see what lay ahead for her and Davey.

Chapter Twelve

Liverpool, 1981

Sabrina

'That could've been a disaster if I'd met you at the Swan,' Florence Teesdale chirped, tottering toward Sabrina's bedroom after her friend. She waited while Sabrina did her light-flicking ritual three times, and then her small but tidy room was bathed in light.

It was Friday, and apart from looking forward to an evening down at their local, the girls had other, different reasons for anticipating the night ahead.

On Florence's part, she was desperate for her weekly fix of bad boy, Tim Burns, and on Sabrina's, she wanted to talk to Flo away from her Aunt Evie's wagging ears about her encounter with the young Australian girl, Nicole. She couldn't wait to see Adam either, who'd be joining them along with his mate Tim and the rest of the lads later on.

Evelyn, in the process of putting her lipstick on, peered over the top of her powder compact and called after them, 'You two look like the flamin' Bobbsey Twins,' before snapping the mother-of-pearl embellished compact shut.

'Ignore her,' Sabrina said, flinging open her wardrobe and staring at its contents, hoping inspiration would jump out at her.

'She's not wrong, though,' Florence said, flopping down on Sabrina's bed to wait while her friend changed. Spying an open packet of Opal Fruits she helped herself.

Both girls were dressed in their Calvin Klein jeans and had their new sweaters on—identical white with a diagonal print—bought at the C&A sale. They'd agreed at the time matching tops wouldn't be a problem so long as they checked in as to who was wearing theirs any given night. Their plan hadn't worked.

'What do you think? The red satin blouse or the black vest with my white shirt underneath?' Sabrina held both out seeking approval.

'Definitely the red satin. You look gorgeous in that. The colour works a treat on you.'

Sabrina hung the vest back in her wardrobe and shut the door. Adam had already seen her in the red blouse, she thought, slipping her sweater over her head, a little disappointed about not giving her new top an airing but Flo couldn't very well change or borrow anything of hers, not with her bust, and there'd be plenty of other opportunities to wear it.

Her friend had stood up to peer at her hair in the dressing table mirror. She wrinkled her nose and gave her verdict, 'Look at the state of my fringe, girl. That fog's costing me a fortune in hair gel.' She fluffed at it. 'Winter and me hair don't get along. I need to move somewhere like Spain. I'd have good hair every day in Spain, I would.'

Sabrina laughed, buttoning her blouse before tucking it in. 'No, you wouldn't. You moan when it's too hot because it makes your hair frizz. You look gorgeous. Shall I leave mine down?'

'Yeah, but backcomb the sides for more volume,' Florence ordered, retrieving a tube from her bag. She squeezed its clear gel contents into the palm of her hand, spiking her fringe until she was satisfied she'd returned it to its former glory. 'Can I have a squirt of your Charlie, Sabs? Mines run out, thanks to the terrible twins.'

'Course you can.' Sabrina reached for her comb.

'Ta. I'm not sure which one of them thought it was clever to use the last few sprays I was saving for tonight as loo freshener. Neither of them is owning up to it. You know what they're like, more impenetrable than the Berlin flippin' Wall when they've been up to no good.'

Sabrina smiled. She loved Flo's family even if the lot of them were all mad.

Florence moved on to reapplying her lip gloss. 'When I cornered them about it, they said that it was Dad I should be shouting at because in a roundabout way it was him that made them do it.' She smacked her lips together.

Sabrina sniggered at their logic. Flo's eleven-year-old twin sisters, Shona and Tessa didn't miss a beat and they'd an answer for everything.

'It's not funny, Sabs, they're driving me potty, always helping themselves to me stuff. I want to put a lock on me door but Dad says, "There's to be no locks on doors, Florence Teesdale. Not in my house. What if there's a fire? What then eh?'" She did a good impersonation of Mr Teesdale when he blustered, which was often. 'I need me own space.'

Sabrina had heard this many times and she knew her pal was well aware that if she were to move out, she'd only be able to afford a damp, smelly, bedsit. There'd be no one to give her a shake of a morning and pour her a cup of tea to make sure she wasn't late for her job down at the shipping office by the docks. Nor would there be a hot meal waiting for her when she got home at the end of the day. Flo knew full well the terrible twins, as she called them, were a small price to pay for her home comforts. Still, that's what bezzie mates were for. To listen to one another's gripes and assure them all would be well with the world.

Sabrina watched as Florence, about to put the lid back on the bottle she'd sprayed enthusiastically behind her ears, hesitated. She pulled out the neck of her sweater and angled the bottle to give her ample cleavage a quick squirt.

'You never know your luck,' she grinned cheekily as Sabrina laughed, carrying on teasing the sides of her hair for all she was worth. 'Tonight, queen, could be the night if Tim Burns plays his cards right.'

Sabrina paused in her backcombing, tempted to say something, but then, thinking better of it, she put the comb down. It was pointless to tell her Tim Burns wasn't worth it. He wasn't the settling sort and even if he did look Florence's way he'd only break her heart. She'd be better setting her sights on Tony who, Adam had informed her was a nice guy. She'd relayed this to Florence who, unimpressed, had said, 'A nice guy who wears his trousers so tight he just about has to walk on tippy-toes.'

To which Sabrina had replied with a cheeky wink, 'But it's what's underneath the trousers that counts.' Now, she realised, Flo had moved on.

'Do you know what I caught Tessa at this morning?'

'What's she been up to now?' Sabrina nudged her mate aside so she could have a better look at herself, she enjoyed hearing about the twins' antics. They always made her giggle. She'd have liked a sibling, a partner in crime, growing up but then again she'd had Flo and she was as good as any sister. The Teesdales too treated her as a fourth daughter, albeit one who got special privileges like first dibs on the crunchy burnt bits of raisins left on the tray of scones Mrs Teesdale always seemed to have at the ready.

On close inspection, Sabrina decided a second coat of mascara was in order.

Florence put her gel back in her bag and zipped it up. 'She came down for breakfast and I knew something wasn't right straight away but I couldn't put my finger on it. Then I twigged. She'd a chest you could rest a mug of tea on. She'd only gone and stuffed my best Marks and Spencer's bra, you know the lacy one?'

Sabrina nodded.

'With loo roll. Mam went mad, not because she'd been nicking my stuff again but because she'd used all the toilet paper in the house. Four rolls worth. She gave her the money doesn't grow on trees lecture and made her roll it all back up again. She was still at it when I left for work.'

'Don't tell me stories like that when I'm putting make-up on. I nearly stabbed myself in the eye then,' Sabrina said, shaking with laughter as she replaced the wand and stood back to give herself the final once over. Florence did the same.

'What do you think?' Sabrina said.

'I think we look gorgeous, girl.'

They grinned at each other.

'C'mon then,' Sabrina said, linking arms through Florence's and venturing forth.

'Ignore her,' she said for the second time as Evelyn made a show of waving her hand and saying that no one would come within a one-mile radius of the pair of them for fear of being gassed.

Sabrina slid into her bomber jacket. 'Enjoy the bingo, Aunt Evie.' She flicked her hair out from under the collar and opened the door. She switched the lights in the stairwell on and off three times as was her custom. As before, Florence, well used to her friend's idiosyncrasies, didn't say a word as she called out, 'Ta-rah then, Aunt Evie.'

'And say hello to Ida for me,' Sabrina added, as she did every Friday before pulling the door to.

'Humph, I'm sure she's got that bingo hall rigged,' Evelyn muttered about her long-suffering friend. The two women had known each other most of their lives and were very competitive when it came to their bingo.

Sabrina, halfway down the stairs, finished her sentence for her. 'Three weeks in a row, she's won. I'm telling you there's something not right.'

Florence laughed as Evelyn pulled the door open and shouted down after them. 'I heard that Sabrina Flooks! And it's four weeks, not three.'

'She's ears in the back of her head that one. I'm sure of it,' Sabrina said, stepping out the back door onto Wood Street, half expecting her aunt to call out that she'd heard that too.

'It's eyes not ears,' Florence corrected adding, 'It's freezin' out here.' She huddled into Sabrina as they picked their way over the cobbles in the direction of the pub.

The yellow street lights pooled eerily on the slick bricks, and the warehouse-style buildings in polar opposite with the quirky frontages of Bold Street loomed large on their right. Up ahead, they could see the lights through the windows of the Swan and hear a faint beat signalling the jukebox was on but had yet to be cranked up.

'Me hair's flopping, Sabs,' Florence yelped as they were enveloped in the thick, damp evening air.

'You'll still look gorgeous, even with a flat fringe,' Sabrina reassured her, dragging her towards the pub. There was no collection of motorbikes outside as yet to signal Adam and the rest of the lads were there. But then, she hadn't expected there to be and besides which, she needed to talk to Flo. As they drew nearer, the door swung open and they heard a burst of laughter and someone shouting.

The girls, well-practised at the art of tottering along in heels on cobbles, reached the pub in no time and pushing open the door they walked through the smoky haze towards the bar. It was a route they could have traversed with their eyes closed.

The jukebox was playing The Police, Every Little Thing She Does is Magic and Mickey

behind the bar had begun pulling their pints as soon as he saw the two regulars heading towards him. He bestowed his gold-toothed smile on them and enquired as to how their day had been.

'Good, ta.' Florence dimpled, quickly fluffing her hair before pointing up to where the Steering Wheel Club was hidden away overhead. It was an exclusive club for the likes of Liverpool's VIPs to gather without being bothered by the minions below. 'Anyone rich, famous, and single up there I should know about then, Mickey?'

Mickey laughed. 'That'd be telling, queen.'

The two of them bantered back and forth while Sabrina went to nab a table. She sat down and watched a minute later as Flo made her way carefully over, carrying the pint glasses full to the brim. A lad sitting with his girlfriend was in danger of dislocating his neck watching her progress and Sabrina smiled watching his girlfriend put the boot in under the table.

'There we go. Not a drop spilt.' Florence placed the glasses down on the table and sat down opposite her friend.

Sabrina picked up the glass and raised it. 'Cheers.'

Florence clinked hers against Sabrina's and they both took a sip of their lager before looking around the familiar space. It was quiet but give it a couple of hours and the place would be heaving.

'Did you enjoy *Raiders of the Lost Ark*?' Florence asked.

Sabrina nodded, 'It was good. Definitely worth going to.' She'd gone to see the film with Adam mid-week.

'Only Carol from work broke up with her fella, you know the one who was Tim Burn's cousin?'

Sabrina nodded.

'And she asked me if I want to go and see it with her. She's got a thing for Harrison Ford.'

'That's understandable.' Sabrina grinned.

'Ooh, and I can't believe I forgot to tell you but I lost just over a pound this week, Sabs. I tell you this running is the biz. It's definitely working. I'd had a second helping of Mam's rice pudding on Monday—'

'Did you have a dollop of jam in it?' Sabrina butted in, her mouth watering at the thought of Mrs Teesdale's creamy, sweet rice pud.

'Of course. It wouldn't be proper not to. Anyway, I was dreading stepping on the scales of doom at this week's meeting. I thought Bossy Bev would strip me of my role as Bootle's Weight Watchers poster girl but, I'm pleased to inform you, my crown is intact! I, Florence Teesdale reign supreme over Bootle's well-padded women.'

Sabrina raised her glass. 'To the reigning queen!'

They clinked and had a hearty sip of their pints. The pints at the Swan didn't count where Flo's weight loss regime was concerned in her opinion because she always burnt the extra calories off on the dance floor.

Sabrina smiled to herself thinking running was a loose term for the slow-paced jog Florence had undertaken a couple of nights a week after work and then feeling the waistband of her Calvin's digging in thought she was in no place to snigger. She'd have to start getting out there with her.

'Bossy Bev made me stand up and tell them all what the secret to my success is,' Flo continued still on the Weight Watchers theme.

'What did you say?'

'I told them exercise was key and now she's on about me starting a jogging group.'

Sabrina snorted into her ale.

'It's not funny.'

'It is, Flo.'

'Ahright it is.' She grinned. 'But you know you'll have to come if she rallies up enough interest. I wonder if I'll get a whistle like Miss Hounsell had. I'd quite like a whistle.'

Sabrina conjured up an image of their no-nonsense physical education teacher at high school.

'More bounce, Florence, more bounce,' she trilled.

Florence shuddered. 'Don't! I hated that vault. I always got stuck halfway.' She envied her friend who'd been far more agile in gymnastics and who was also naturally slender. Sabrina, unfairly, was able to have her cake and eat it too although she was begging to differ these days saying her metabolism was catching up with her.

'Have you bumped into Tony on these jogs of yours?' Sabrina now asked slyly. She'd only been running once with Florence and they'd come across Adam's mate, Tony who was obviously enamoured with Florence.

'I might have. He sort of appears from behind a tree, like. Imagine being in Canada soaking in nature when all of a sudden a bear appears cos that's what it's like.'

Sabrina began laughing.

Florence grinned back at her. 'It sounds funny but he's hairy like a bear. It's not easy to talk to him either, Sabs, because those shorts are a terrible distraction. I don't know how he can breathe in them let alone run.'

Sabrina began to clutch her middle at the images spring-ing to mind at her friend's colourful description. 'He's not that hairy and his shorts aren't that bad either.'

'They flamin' well are and he is. It's like a great big grizzly bear in skimpy shorts. Anyway, how's your week been?' Florence was keen to move them off the subject of Tony and his soprano shorts as she thought of them.

Sabrina stopped giggling, her face suddenly serious as she put her glass down and leaned forward in her seat. 'Flo, I heard something today.' She filled her friend in on her conversation with the young Australian, Nicole. 'You know what it means, don't you?'

'That you must have gone back again.' Florence stared glumly into her pint.

Sabrina nodded.

'I know you want to find your mam, and I know you said you wanted to go back again to look for her, Sabs. I under-stand why you need to, too. I do. But it's not exciting any-more. It's scary. Anything could happen to you and how do you know if you'll be able to get back to us? You might get lost in time. It happened before when you and your mam were separated.' She rubbed her temples. 'The whole thing gives me a bleedin' headache.'

Sabrina reached across the table and rested her hand on her friend's forearm. 'But you see, Flo, I don't have a choice do I? Because it's already happened. I've already met Nicole's mam back in the sixties. I can't change the past. And this could be it. This could be when I find me mam.'

Florence pursed her lips. 'I wish we'd never heard about any of this. I wish we could go back to how things were before.'

'We can't though, Flo.'

They were distracted from any further debate by the arrival of a cluster of lads all wearing leather jackets and clutching motorbike helmets.

As Sabrina locked eyes with Adam, she knew she wouldn't change any of what had happened. Not a thing.

Chapter Thirteen

Liverpool, Two years later, 1954

Patty

The girls were restless, spread out on their beds in the dorm. Some were trying to read, some were chatting and helping one another tie their hair up and some were doing as Patty was doing, glueing her latest cutting into her scrapbook.

Today was the day of the Salvation Army's garden party and the staff and children of Strawberry Field had been in a state of excitement since breakfast. The minutes until it was time to head down to the grounds below were ticking by painfully slowly.

'Why is it that time goes so slowly when you're waiting for something nice and once it's happening it whizzes by as though someone's twirling the hands of the clock around?' Patty's best friend Bernie lamented, looking over at her from the next bed. She was lying on her tummy with her chin resting in her cupped hands. 'Remember when we got picked up by taxis?'

'And taken to Crosby Beach, yes.'

'And we got to have tea and cream cakes in those posh tearooms.'

Patty laughed. 'Miss Acton kept saying, 'remember you're little ladies representing the Salvation Army itself, eat your cakes accordingly.' She mimicked their housemother's Irish brogue but didn't look up from what she was doing.

Bernie giggled. 'You sounded just like her.' She kicked her legs back and forth. 'And we came home with a balloon each and a bag of sweets. You gave your balloon to Bridget Kehoe who cried like a baby when hers popped.' Her friend had a kind heart, Bernie thought before remembering what she'd been going to say. 'My point is, that outing was the same. I looked forward to tasting that cake all morning and then before I knew it, I was back here, trying to dab cream off my dress before Miss Acton noticed it!'

'Hmm, you're right, nice things do whizz by,' Patty said, recalling how they'd all wound up with cream down their fronts despite doing their dainty best not to scoff the delicious cake treats. She remembered too the excitement setting off on that unexpected outing. They'd formed an orderly crocodile line like the ones used for walking to church and school before Miss Acton at the front of the line had trilled, 'Check your socks are up, girls. You're representing the Salvation Army you know.' It had been her favourite phrase of the day.

They'd all dutifully pulled their socks up then watched as she raised her umbrella to signal they were off!

'Why's she got her umbrella? There's not a cloud in the sky,' Bernie had whispered to Patty, squeezing her hand in anticipation of an afternoon out as they trooped along to the bus stop.

'I think she's going to use it as a sunshade, you know like in the pictures we saw at school of the Japanese ladies in their kim... kim—'

'Kimonos and they were parasols not great big black umbrellas like Miss Acton's,' Bernie had finished for her. 'And she's a hat on.'

It had been strange seeing Miss Acton's round face peeking out from under a sun hat.

'Yes, but she does like to be different,' Patty had whispered back. It was true, Miss Acton veered toward being eccentric.

'I suppose so, and her skin's paler than the milk. She'd go bright red and peel like Margaret Traynor always does at any hint of sun on it. She can't be too careful.'

The girls giggled, ignoring Cynthia Wilson as she tapped them on the shoulder to ask what was so funny; she could be a tattletale could Cynthia. Their own skin was tanned a nutty brown with a smattering of freckles across their noses and cheeks in evidence of time spent running around in the expansive, secretive grounds of Strawberry Field during the summer months.

Patty blinked as she came back to the here and now, smoothing the newspaper cutting before carefully wiping the excess glue from the sides of the paper. 'You'll crease your dress lying on your bed like that, Bernie.' She sat up straight, satisfied with the job done. 'There! Isn't she pretty?' She angled the book to show Bernie. 'This is my favourite picture.'

The photograph was of their new queen in her beautiful gown of gold and silver, with the sweep of purple robe spanning the stairs on which she stood. Next to her were her six maids of honour. Of course, the newspaper clipping was in black and white but Patty had pored over enough articles to know the ins and outs of the colours of the ceremonial dresses and as such, when she viewed them, she viewed them in colour.

The children, especially the girls and staff of Strawberry Field were no exception to the royal fever sweeping the country and Patty and her friends had begun to keep scrapbooks of the coronation and the royal family. They'd swap and barter for cuttings from the newspapers they managed to get their hands on, thanks to various kindly staff members bringing them in for the eager girls to scour.

Bernie pulled herself up to sitting and swung her legs over the side of the bed in order to see the photograph better. 'I'd have loved to have been one of her maids of honour. She's my favourite.'

She pointed to a fair-haired young lady. Bernie was desperate to be blonde like Patty and the woman in the picture and had declared more than once that as soon as she walked out those red gates for the last time she was off to the hairdressers to ask for a Diana Dors! 'I wonder how heavy those tiaras are?'

She stood up then, smoothing her pretty frock down before picking up the Bible resting on the drawers that separated their beds.

'Jolly good job it's the New Testament,' she remarked, placing it on her head before practising her regal walk up and down the centre of the room.

'You're mad, Bernie Phillips.' Gwen who'd the end bed by the window laughed, watching her prance towards her, the book teetering ominously.

Bernie and Patty had bonded the first night Patty had spent in Strawberry Field over a shared dislike of their full names being used. Bernie had reached across in the darkened dormitory and offered the new girl her hand, sensing her fear and loneliness. She'd squeezed it and confided to Patty the only time she was called Bernadette was when she was in trouble. Her kind gesture had distracted Patty from her worries as to how Davey was coping and she'd listened as Bernie told her the circumstances that had brought her here to the home.

Her story, like Patty's and the other children who lived here, was a sad one. Her mam had run off with another fella and her dad hadn't been able to cope with her and her four brothers. So, they'd found themselves packed off to various homes around Liverpool.

It hurt that they'd been split up she'd told Patty and she hoped they'd find their way alright. She knew two of her brothers had been adopted which she felt was a blessing for them given her auld dad was fond of the drink and using his fists. They were better off beginning new lives in new families.

She was happier here at Strawberry Field than she had been at home too because here she got fed three times a day and no one came crashing in late at night singing and carrying on before getting maudlin and then eventually angry. She didn't lie in bed of a night on tenterhooks.

She couldn't blame her mam for wanting to make a better life for herself, Bernie had said, adding that it was just a shame she'd not seen fit to take her and her brothers with her. She'd an irrepressible spirit did Bernie and a kind heart. They'd been firm friends ever since that first night.

On the bed directly opposite Patty's, Mary, who sucked her thumb and had an overbite she could whistle through, was flapping her scrapbook willing the glue to hurry up and dry. Patty knew her favourite pictures of the royals were the family ones. They all yearned to be part of such a perfect family with a beautiful mother, a handsome father, and brothers and sisters all of whom loved each other.

Patty had been here at Strawberry Field for nearly two years now. She'd not long celebrated her twelfth birthday and a cake with pink icing had been delivered to the home which had caused great excitement amongst the girls in her dorm. It had been shared out after tea by Miss Acton and to Patty it had tasted like sawdust, the crumbs getting stuck in her throat. She'd forced it down though not wanting a reprimand for being ungrateful.

It was her father who'd arranged for the cake to be sent. He'd done so last year too and on Davey's birthdays, a cake with blue icing would appear. As if a cake would make up for abandoning them. She tried very hard not to think of her father and the baby sister she'd never get to know. Bernie had told her from the get-go that she should let her old life go because this was her life now and it didn't help always harking back to the past.

Patty took her friend's advice and adapted quickly to the daily routines at Strawberry Field Children's Home. This was made all the easier with Bernie having taken her under her wing.

She'd told her she'd be fine so long as she toed the line. Matron, she'd informed her knowingly, was all bark and no bite. As for their housemother, Miss Acton, she was as soft as butter despite her sharp tones and when she got excited you couldn't understand a word she said her accent got that thick! You had to watch her with the nit comb of an evening though, she was a holy terror with it she'd whispered into the darkness of the dormitory ignoring Cynthia telling her to shurrup. Bernie's own mane was curly and dark and had been on the receiving end of the comb just that evening.

She'd been right too and many an evening Patty had the dreaded comb tugged through her fine sheet of fair hair as she and the other girls sat fireside singing the Irish songs Miss Acton had taught them. It could have been worse. They could have had to learn pious hymns like what the younger girls in the dormitory down the other end of the corridor had to sing each evening under the hooky nosed Miss Garston's instruction.

It was Miss Acton who'd put Patty forward at church for the choir. Each night along with a turn with the nit comb they'd a turn singing a solo verse of one of the songs they'd been taught. That evening they were singing Banks of the Roses and Patty had been given her favourite verse all about getting married in the month of May. She thought it would be a lovely thing to have the sun shining on your wedding day.

As such she'd opened her mouth and the emotion of all that had happened to her and Davey had been poured into that one short verse and when she'd finished, to her surprise, the girls were staring at her open-mouthed, Miss Acton included.

'You sing like a nightingale, so you do. That's a gift God's given you there, Patty Hamilton,' she'd said, wiping a tear from her eye. 'And I'll not see it ignored.'

She'd been true to her word and each Sunday, Patty slipped her robe on and sang the songs of praise next to the older members of the choir with all her might. She loved to hear the way their crisp, pure voices harmonised to bounce off the church's old stone walls and to see the rapt expressions on the congregation's faces. Singing helped fill the hole the life she'd led up to this point had left in her soul.

She fancied Miss Acton was gentler with the comb when it was her turn on account of her singing too. Patty always felt sorry for the girls with the thick heads of curly hair like Bernie because it seemed to get in a terrible tangle with that comb which would end in an almighty tug-o-war. She was a determined woman was Miss Acton.

Still, Patty didn't miss the burning itch of her scalp and supposed the nit comb was a small price to pay for being rid of that awful discomfort. She enjoyed their fireside sing-a-longs too and the girls she shared her room with often asked her to sing them a song. It made them feel happy, they said.

Their days at the home were routine and there was a strict timetable to adhere to during the week when they were all up early for breakfast, school, and then home for chores and tea. All of the children learned the value of hard work and while some complained over their assigned chores written up on the roster, Patty didn't mind, although, she was always heavy-footed dragging her heels when it was her turn in the laundry. She quite enjoyed the floor polishing though. When no one was looking she'd sit on her cleaning rag and slide across the floor. She could get quite a bit of momentum going and Matron always commented on what a good job she'd done with the floors when she'd finished. Bernie said she'd wear a hole in her knickers one of these days!

Sundays were her favourite day because after church the afternoon was their own to get lost in play in the grounds of the home. The garden, with its trees and shrubbery, was enormous and gave them the freedom to run wild. They all relished their time in the magic garden as she and Bernie called it.

She checked in with Davey then too. At ten he was turning into a cheeky so and so, whose mouth had seen him on the receiving end of more than one clout round the earhole. She tried talking to him and telling him being cheeky wasn't clever but he paid no attention, too busy rallying up a group of children to play his favourite game of hide 'n' seek.

'The boys are down there,' Bernie informed the dormitory. She'd taken the book off her head and was peering out of the window to the grounds below. 'And I can see the band. I can see your Davey, Patty. He's very close to the sandwiches being set out on the table. I hope the boys don't scoff all the treats before we get down there. Where's Miss Acton!'

'I'm right here, Bernadette, now come away from that window.'

Bernie flushed pink at Miss Acton's timing.

'There'll be plenty for all to eat and not even your Davey boyo would dare touch those sandwiches before Grace has been given, Patty, so stop looking so alarmed. Mary Murphy, you know better than to have your shoes on the bed! You shouldn't be lying around like so, girls, you'll get your dresses creased. Chop, chop come along now, we've a party to be going to.' Miss Acton tsked but her eyes were dancing and Patty could tell she was just as excited as they were about the party.

She looked pretty in her sundress, Patty thought, and her hair wasn't pulled back as tightly as she usually wore it with curls escaping around a face shaded by her sun hat.

There was a flurry of movement as the girls organised themselves before filing out of the dormitory and down the stairs.

'I'm going to win the sack race!' one of them called out.

Patty was guessing it was Agnes, a sly girl with eyes too close together. She'd been practising with her pillowcase after lights out, thudding up and down the row between the beds in their dormitory, looking like a demented kangaroo with Mary and her quiet friend, Sarah doing a few laps behind her. They had their sights set on winning the wheelbarrow race with Mary proving to be a very good wheelbarrow.

It was hard to imagine Miss Acton sleeping through all that thudding but, if she'd known they were wide awake when they should be asleep, she'd let it slide just as she did now. Leading the charge as ever, she informed them they were to behave like little ladies this afternoon because they were representing the Salvation Army itself!

Patty and Bernie grinned at each other. The day stretched out before them, gloriously sunny and full of possibilities.

Chapter Fourteen

Liverpool, 1981

Sabrina

Friday night had been full of loud music and dancing. Florence had desperately tried to make eye contact with Tim but to her dismay, he'd set his sights on a Farrah Fawcett wannabe. She'd spent the evening chasing around after him on the dance floor while trying to avoid Tony who'd been breaking out Travolta moves in his tight trousers.

Sabrina, who loved to dance, had elbowed her friend more than once, telling her not to be rude as she circuited the dance floor all but trying to get in between Tim and Farrah whilst keeping her distance from Tony. She and Adam had wound up grooving alongside him not wanting him to look like a Nigel no mates. When Sabrina had cornered her pal in the Ladies about it, she'd said, 'I don't want to encourage him, Sabs.'

To be fair, Sabrina had thought, Tony didn't need any encouraging. He was making his interest in Florence very clear. If only she could see that he'd be a much better bet than the fickle Tim! She couldn't help herself saying tongue in cheek, 'Ah but, Flo, it's written in the stars you and him. Stop fighting your destiny.'

Florence had muttered something unrepeatable to that.

The night had ended with Flo stomping down the cobbles, her breath erupting in annoyed, misty bursts because Tim had disappeared from the pub with the blonde with the flicky hair. Adam had a tight hold of Sabrina's hand as he walked the two girls home.

Sabrina had almost forgotten Florence was there as she lost herself in the goodnight kiss Adam leaned in for when they reached the back door. Florence, however, had made her presence known, announcing she was fed up with standing about in the cold. It had dampened their ardour and Sabrina and Adam had broken apart. He'd kissed her on the tip of her nose and told her he'd see her tomorrow night. She'd gripped the doorframe, smiling at him as he lingered reluctant to part, but Florence had said a firm goodnight to him nearly jamming Sabrina's fingers in the door as she shut it.

Sabrina woke when her alarm shrilled nowhere near enough hours later feeling bleary-eyed. Florence was snoring next to her. She banged the alarm off and left Florence, who hadn't even stirred, sound asleep. It was alright for her, she thought, her head thumping as she ventured into the darkened kitchen, she didn't have to work on a Saturday morning.

By the time she'd sat at the table and drunk her tea, she was beginning to feel a little more ready to face the day. She grinned as she stirred the porridge in the pot a few minutes later, hearing Florence give an undignified snore. She was adamant she didn't snore. One day she'd get her on tape!

Aunt Evie had appeared by the time she was pouring the bubbling, creamy oats into bowls leaving some warming in the pot for herself and Flo to have when she deigned to get up. Evelyn had sat down at the table pouring herself a cup of tea from the pot. 'Good grief, that girl sounds like the number ten express pulling into the station.'

Sabrina laughed but her aunt turned her attention on her. 'Late night was it?' she asked with a raised eyebrow as Sabrina put her breakfast down in front of her. She was well aware it was, having heard her and Florence giggling their heads off at some ungodly hour. 'And there's some of that emollient cream in the bathroom. Put it on your chin before you go down to the shop, Sabrina, or else all our customers will know exactly what it was you were up to last night.'

Sabrina's hand flew to her chin and she blushed, realising her skin was tender from all that late-night snogging. 'Eat your porridge, Aunt Evie,' she muttered, taking the other bowl and heading out the door and down the stairs once she'd flicked the lights, to see if Fred was there.

She didn't miss a trick did Aunt Evie, even with glasses as thick as milk bottle bottoms, and she wasn't worth talking to until she'd had her breakfast and her morning visit or constitutional as she called it.

There was no sign of Fred and she was about to make her way back to the shop when Esmerelda's door flew open. Her head, covered in a hot pink turban, darted out like a chameleon's tongue catching a fly. 'Morning, Sabrina. No Fred?'

'Morning, Esmerelda. No, I think he must be taking himself off to a shelter of a night which is a blessing.'

A plume of smoke curled up in front of Esmerelda. She was never without her sleek black cigarette holder with a

Topaz ciggie dangling from it. 'He won't be needing that porridge then?'

Sabrina took the hint. 'No, would you like it, Esmerelda? It's only going in the bin.'

'Does it have sugar on it?'

'A dessertspoonful.'

'Well, it would be a shame to waste it.' Esmerelda reached out and her nails, Sabrina saw, were the same pink as her turban.' She took the bowl from Sabrina then, telling her she should call into the emporium when she had a minute because she'd a pair of black and gold culottes that would look fabulous on her.

'I will,' Sabrina said, carrying on her way. She enjoyed admiring the wilder fashions that vied for attention alongside all the other weird and wonderful things for sale in Esmerelda's Emporium but admiring them was as far as she got. She wasn't bold enough to wear any.

'Aunt Evie,' she said, entering the flat a few minutes later. 'I've just had proof that Esmerelda eats from time to time.'

Evelyn was convinced her neighbour existed on a diet of gin and cigarettes.

FLORENCE HAD TAKEN herself home shortly after Evelyn and Sabrina opened for business, having arranged to spend the afternoon beautifying herself with Sabrina at her house.

The morning passed by quickly with Nicole calling back into Brides of Bold Street for two reasons. The first being she was having second thoughts about the dress she'd originally thought was the one for her and the second was to tell Sabrina how excited her mum was that she'd connected with Sabrina.

'She told me what you said might sound farfetched but it's all true.' Nicole shook her head. 'I still can't wrap my head around it, to be honest. But you must go back in time again at some point to meet Mum.' She shrugged. 'Otherwise, it makes even less sense.'

Sabrina knew how she felt and she agreed with her, not wanting Aunt Evie to overhear that, yes she must travel back in time again because it was the only explanation as to how Nicole's mum, Patty knew her.

'I can't stop thinking about the lacy dress you showed me either, Sabrina.'

'Do you want to try it on one more time?'

'Yes please.'

Nicole finally made her mind up when another young woman and a crowd of her mates piled in and made a huge fuss of her saying how gorgeous she looked.

She left the shop with a tissue-wrapped, long-sleeved dress with a lace overlay along with a faux fur-lined cape and a promise she'd be back when her mum and the rest of her family arrived.

Sabrina barely had time to catch her breath before it was closing time and she found herself upstairs eating a hastily made cheese buttie while Aunt Evelyn twirled her red and white scarf around her neck. She was off to the match and called a cheery ta-rah before heading off to catch the number 17 to Anfield Stadium as she did every Saturday afternoon.

Sabrina cleared up the lunch things and threw some clothes in a bag to wear later before heading for Florence's.

She pushed open the Teesdales' front door a short while later calling out a hello.

'We're in the kitchen, Sabs.'

Sabrina poked her head around the door to where Tessa and Shona were kneeling at the coffee table in the front room cutting out dresses for their paper dolls. 'Ahright, you two? Are you behaving yourselves?'

Two identical angelic faces grinned up at her with a touch of the devil dancing in their eyes. 'Flo's making something for you two to put on your faces. She says it will make your skin soft,' Shona said, pausing in her snipping.

'She won't let us use any of it,' Tessa lamented.

'I'll see if there's any left over for you. But you've got to promise if there is you don't move from the bathroom while you've got it on,' Sabrina said and they brightened, going back to their cutting out as she made her way to the kitchen.

She kissed Mrs Teesdale on the cheek and seeing the paraphernalia spread out on the worktop asked, 'Are you making what I hope you're making?'

'Steak 'n' kidney pudding.'

Sabrina beamed. She loved Mrs Teesdale's suet pastry; nobody made a pie crust as light and airy as hers.

Florence was whipping together a concoction of lemon and honey and satisfied it was the right consistency, she put the whisk in the sink and she and Sabrina made their way up to her room.

Ten minutes later they'd a Blondie record blaring, their hair twisted back in towels, and were busy daubing the sticky mess over their faces.

'I bet Tim would fancy me if I looked like Debbie Harry,' Florence said, shooting the album cover a mournful glance. 'Or one of the Bucks Fizz girls.'

'I'm sure if you were to whip your skirt off like they did on Eurovision you'd probably grab his attention,' Sabrina sighed, 'But, Flo, you know he's not worth it.'

Florence ignored her. 'I'm going blonde.'

Sabrina shook her head. 'Oh, Flo, no.'

Florence got up then and fossicked around in her handbag to produce a box of hair dye. 'California blonde, to be exact.'

Sabrina tried for the next ten minutes or so to talk Florence out of dying her hair but she'd dug her heels in. So it was, she found herself mixing the colour tube into the peroxide while Florence went and washed the face-pack off. She'd opted to leave hers on a while longer, hoping it would clear the red rash on her chin. She hoped Florence didn't live to regret her proclamation that blondes have more fun!

Florence settled herself on the stool by the dressing table with a towel draped around her shoulders and while Sabrina brushed the thick colourant onto her hair, she filled Flo in on Nicole's latest visit.'

'You're going to try to go back again, aren't you?'

Florence's eyes were watering and Sabrina thought she might be about to cry but then realised it was the fumes from the dye. She nodded. 'I'll tell Adam when I see him tomorrow. He's taking me on a mystery ride.' He was at the Saturday afternoon match with Tim, Tony, and the rest of the lads and she'd see him later at the Swan but there'd be no time for a proper conversation there. She'd tell him about the connection between Aunt Evelyn and his dad tomorrow too.

'Oh, Sabs, I don't want you to.'

'I have to. We've talked about this, Flo.'

'I know but I still don't want you to go.'

Sabrina squeezed her friend's shoulder. 'Don't worry.' She gave her a reassuring grin to mask her own fear and said, 'Now stop going on because I've got to concentrate.' She worked the colour through the ends. 'There, all done,' she said as she rubbed the last few drops she'd squeezed from the bottle into her roots. 'Phew, it reeks in here.' She flapped her hand in front of her nose before heading over to the window to fling it open.

The door burst open. 'Sabrina said we can have what's left of your face-pack,' Tessa said before shrieking. 'Eew! It stinks in here.' She took in her sister perched on the stool. 'Does Mam know you're dying your hair purple?'

'Mind your own business, and it's not purple its blonde.'

Shona peered around her sister to see what was going on and Florence shrieked at them both to clear off. They scarpered with the remains of the face-pack and Sabrina hoped they'd stay in the bathroom while they slathered it on their faces. She didn't want to be responsible for them getting the sticky condiments everywhere.

An hour later, all hell let loose. Mrs Teesdale burnt the steak 'n' kidney pud as she dealt with the howling twins whose faces were covered in itchy red hives thanks to an allergic reaction to the face-pack while Sabrina tried to console Flo who was sobbing. 'I look like a flamin' leprechaun.'

'It's not that bad, Flo,' she offered up weakly as her pal held up one of her greenish blonde locks. So, much for California blonde, Sabrina thought, wondering if she'd be able to find a hairdresser's who'd take an emergency booking at half past four on a Saturday afternoon.

Chapter Fifteen

Liverpool, 1954

Patty

The Salvation Army band, decked out in their finery, played Marching as to War with gusto as, overhead, fluffy clouds scudded across a blue sky and the sun beat down on the excited group gathered for this, the garden party at Strawberry Field.

Families from the neighbourhood mingled with one another, drawn by the music, a sneak peek behind the red gates of the home and the promise of fun. Women in their smart army uniforms with their odd little bonnets tied under their chins, busied themselves overseeing the food being brought out and the housemothers kept an eye on the games being played.

'Look at the size of those strawberries, Bernie.' Patty's mouth watered at the thought of a bowl of the plump red berries along with a dollop of cream.

A gentle breeze sneaked in through the shrubbery causing the trees to rustle and the sheets commissioned as tablecloths to flutter under their loads. Lazy plumes of cigarette smoke floated past on the sweet summer air, along with laughter and the general hum of joviality. The atmosphere was festive and boisterous on this most glorious of days when not a single child present at the garden party would be told to quieten down or form an orderly line.

Patty had come second in the egg and spoon race. Agnes, true to her word, had come first although Patty was indignant that she'd been the victim of foul play because Agnes had stuck her foot out as she'd gone to overtake her and sent her and her egg flying. It was most unfair!

Agnes had got her comeuppance however in the wheelbarrow race when she'd wound up with prickles in her hand and Miss Acton had had to put down her cup of tea and pick them all out for her.

To Bernie's competitive delight she'd won the sack race and had a small bag of sweets in her pocket as a result. 'I'll share them with you later, Patty. We'll have a midnight feast.' She grinned at her friend who was appeased by the thought of clandestine sweets.

They'd agreed to stash treats that wouldn't go stale or soggy in the pockets of their dresses for their planned feast. The blancmange wobbling away over there would be no good! The trick, they'd decided, would be in waiting until all eyes were on the band playing and not the trestle tables. Oh yes, they were in for a fine old time later on.

They'd Enid Blyton and the girls from *Malory Towers* to thank for the idea. They were their favourite books at the moment. Both girls could relate to being left in a new world where it was sink or swim like their favourite character, Darrell Rivers had been. Although there was a world of difference between Strawberry Field and the Cornish clifftop boarding school where so much fun was to be had. Today, however, gazing at the delicious treats that lay in store for them, there was no place either child would rather be.

There'd be no call to fill a party plate for another ten minutes or so and, puffed from the games, Patty and Bernie flopped down on the grass to pluck at the daisies forming a white carpet.

'I'll make you a crown, Princess Patty.' Bernie grinned, beginning the task of threading delicate daisy stem through stem.

Patty lay down on her back, breathing in the scent of the grass, as she stared up at the blue sky. There was a big world outside their small one, she thought. She rolled onto her side, her elbow propping her up as Bernie carried on with her task.

'What are we going to do, Bernie?'

'What do you mean?'

'When we leave Strawberry Field?'

'You're going to be a famous singer of course.' Bernie stated this as though it were a given.

Lonnie Donegan's new record was storming the charts and there was a sense of excitement about the changing music scene according to Tina with the modern, pixie hairdo and pedal pushers that had the other staff frowning. She helped in the kitchen and liked to have the radio tuned in to the hit parade. Tina kept the girls abreast of what was what when it came to popular records.

Upon hearing Patty singing as she was apt to do in the kitchen, given the acoustics and the fact it distracted her from the mundane chore of peeling potatoes Tina had said,

'You've a voice that's a cross between, Alma Cogan and Doris Day, girl. You're as pretty as either of them too.'

She'd hefted a bag of carrots onto the worktop and added, 'Listen, queen. What you want to do when you leave here is get yourself a decent haircut, proper clobber not like that antwacky clobber they make you wear in here, and a manager. You've got to have a certain look about you and all the big recording stars have managers. It's not just about your voice these days. It's about image too and if you get that right with your looks and voice you could be as big as them lot on there.' She pointed to the radio. Given Doris Day's song Whatever Will be, Will Be (Que Será, Será) was currently at number one, Patty had thought this high praise indeed.

'We must stay together though, Bernie. You, me and Davey. No matter what.'

'And we will. Me and Davey will be your managers. You'll be so famous you'll need two of us running around after you.' Bernie had no idea what a manager did but she was certain she could learn and Davey was turning into a lad who could talk his way into and out of anything. Well, almost anything. She threaded the last flower through and told Patty to sit up. She did so and Bernie ceremoniously placed it on her head. 'There, I crown you Princess Patty.'

'Patty!'

Davey's shout saw Patty turn her head and scan the milling crowd for her brother but she couldn't spot him.

Bernie nudged her. 'Up there.' She pointed to a tree with low hanging branches and Patty glimpsed her brother halfway up the trunk, balancing on a sturdy bough, almost hidden by the foliage as he swung himself up to the next not so sturdy branch like a monkey swinging its way around the jungle.

She shaded her eyes with her hands, wincing as she saw him snag his good shirt on a twig and, from the way in which he pulled away to free himself, she knew he'd have ripped it. She gritted her teeth, half at the sight of him climbing higher and higher and half in the hope he wouldn't be in bother for tearing his party shirt later.

A lad she didn't recognise was laughing as he stood in the shade squinting up at him. It was egging Davey on Patty thought, knowing how much her brother loved an audience. The lad looked more her and Bernie's age than Davey's. There was something familiar about him too but she didn't think he was from the home.

'Who's that over by the tree?' she asked Bernie, holding her breath as it looked for a second as though her cocky brother might fall right out of it. She breathed out in a gush as he regained his balance. He'd break an arm or a leg, or worse if he wasn't careful.

'He's one of the boys who climbs in over the fence from Menlove Ave,' Bernie stated. 'John, I think he's called. Matron goes mad about it. She's told Mr Norris to report to her if he sees any of them in the grounds. She went around and talked to their parents but they still do it.'

The children from the home didn't mind the neighbourhood interlopers. It was a case of the more the merrier when it came to hide 'n' seek and the likes. Lumbering old Mr Norris, whose garden clippers might as well have been an extension of his arm wouldn't care either so long as they didn't give him any lip. He was fighting a losing battle with the grounds he never seemed to tame in his weekly visits, which suited the children just fine because the wilderness they claimed as their own was all the more exciting for being overgrown.

She'd seen the boys shimmying down the brick wall that separated their grounds from the outside world and thought them quite daring because the wrath of Matron was a frightening thing to be on the receiving end of when she was in full force.

'I'd better go and tell him to come down before he falls out of the tree,' Patty huffed, annoyed at him taking her away from her thoughts.

She made her way over to the shaded, woodland area, her daisy crown still in place, while the band began to play a rousing rendition of All Things Bright and Beautiful. It was one of her favourite hymns.

She ignored the lad at the bottom of the tree who was tapping his feet along to the beat of the music as she hollered up at her brother to get down.

'Don't be a spoilsport, Patty.' He grinned down at her impishly and Patty couldn't help the twitch at the corners of her mouth. He was a monkey alright, her brother, and without a father in his life, he was prone to running wild but there was an infectious sense of adventure about him which Patty didn't want to quash.

'And who're you then?' she demanded, hands on hips as she turned her attention away from Davey to properly look at the lad she was standing next to. He looked familiar alright.

He met her gaze. 'I'm John and why've you got that on your head?'

Patty had forgotten her daisy crown and she hastily removed it. 'You're not one of us.' Her hands went back to rest on her hips.

'No. I'm from over the wall. I live with my aunt and uncle but I come here all the time. It's my place too.' He stared her down and she liked him all the better for it.

'Leave him alone, Patty. He's my pal and he's as good as one of us, even if he is always falling over his feet,' Davey shouted down. 'Aren't you, John? Needs glasses he does.'

'I am and I don't.' He peered up in the general direction of Davey's voice.

'Patty's my sister. She's a singer,' Davey called down. 'She's really good. Go on give him a tune, Pats.'

Patty felt her face heat up. 'I sing at church in the choir.'

'I know. I'm a choir boy. I've seen you at St Peter's.'

'And John's in the boy scouts,' Davey said, a note of awe in his voice. He was desperate to join the scouts.

They both ignored him.

'I'm going to be a musician. I'm learning to play the banjo. Me mam's teaching me.'

'See, I told you he's as good as one of us. He doesn't live with his mam just like we don't live with our dad.'

John frowned.

'Don't listen to him, he's only ten.'

'He told me he was fourteen like me. I thought he was small for his age, like.'

Patty laughed, 'Well, he's a fibber. I'm twelve nearly thirteen, he's two years younger than me and he's gorra a gob as big as he is.'

The lad grinned and Patty liked his eyes. They were gentle eyes, a soft brown. 'Sing us a song then,' he said.

'What?'

'Worrever.' He shrugged.

She eyed him for a moment, weighing up whether or not she'd rise to his challenge.

'Go on, Patty.' Bernie had moseyed over to see what was going on. 'Sing that Julie London one, that's me favourite.'

Patty took a deep breath and did what she always did when she sang—lost herself in the words. The people around her faded into the background as she heard the imaginary music and gave her rendition of the husky song.

'You can sing, ahright, I'll give you that,' John said when she'd finished and Bernie and Davey had stopped clapping. 'But that wasn't the right song for your voice.'

Patty was put out; who was he telling her what suited her voice? 'And who made you the expert, then?'

He shrugged, 'I can feel the music.'

'Ignore him, Pats, he doesn't know what he's talking about,' Bernie said loyally. 'I get goosebumps when you sing that.'

'Davey Hamilton get down from that tree before you break your neck! This minute do you hear me.' Miss Acton had appeared and was staring up at her brother from under the brim of her hat. 'Off you go you three, or you'll miss out on the strawberries and cream.'

They didn't need to be told twice.

Patty sat later, enjoying her sweet. She'd been miffed at what that lad, John had said but she wondered if there was truth in it. She'd have liked to have asked him whether he thought she'd do better with poppier numbers, but she didn't see him again for a very long time.

Chapter Sixteen

Liverpool, 1981

Sabrina

SABRINA THREW HER JACKET on, called out ta-rah to her Aunt Evie who was still sulking over Liverpool's loss the day before and flicked the lights three times before haring down the stairs. She'd decided to wait for Adam downstairs. This was to avoid Aunt Evie giving him the Spanish Inquisition because she didn't want her connecting the dots where Ray Taylor was concerned before she'd had a chance to tell her herself. The guilty thought that she'd had ample time to come clean with her aunt reared its head and she quashed it like she was stomping on grapes for wine. Nothing would spoil her day.

Sitting down in the workroom, on the chair normally reserved for clients, she glanced at her watch. He'd said he'd pick her up at ten and it was three minutes to the hour now. There wasn't much point in picking up Stephanie's dress to stitch the additional pearl beads around the hem she'd decided she now wanted. Think Shufflebottom, Sabrina, she told herself scowling over at the dress.

She twiddled her thumbs listening out for the rumble of his bike, thinking back on the events of the previous afternoon.

Poor Flo had been beside herself with the state of her hair but Mrs Teesdale, having dabbed calamine lotion all over the twins' faces had come to the rescue. Her friend, Mavis, had a daughter in hairdressing and she'd called around, introducing herself as Clare and demanding money up front before she undid the damage the home dye job had done.

With the twins sitting cross-legged on the bed, the pink lotion on their faces beginning to crack, Mrs Teesdale wringing her hands in the doorway, and Sabrina kneeling beside her friend holding her hand, Clare applied a special silver toner to Florence's hair. They'd all held their breath as it was rinsed off in the bathroom, exhaling when they saw it had had the desired effect of neutralising the green. Florence who'd hoped for sun-kissed locks was now white-blonde. Still, it was better than green.

The jury was out as to whether it suited her or not and Sabrina tactfully said she just needed to get used to it, that was all.

'If God had meant for you to be a blonde you'd have been born that way, Florence,' Mrs Teesdale declared before adding, 'Your dad's going to have a fit when he sees you.'

The twins would have sniggered but given the state of the pair of them they kept schtum.

Sabrina, given it had been her who'd applied the dye, felt immense relief her friend was not stuck with green hair. She'd have felt awful, even though Clare said it wasn't anything she'd done. By the time their emergency hair worker had left and Florence had bought the deep conditioning treatment, silver lights shampoo to stop her hair going brassy, paid for the emergency call-out and the toner Clare had applied, she was broke. She couldn't afford to head down to the Swan with Sabrina.

Sabrina loyal to the hilt opted to keep her company. She'd be seeing Adam in the morning she'd reassured Florence before moseying down to the corner shop for an emergency Saturday night in supply of chocolate.

SHE CAME BACK TO THE here and now, hearing the low rumble of an approaching bike, and getting up she flung open the back door eager to see Adam and to make sure he'd gotten her message. She'd rung Mick at the Swan and asked him to pass on she couldn't make it and that she'd see him in the morning. She hadn't wanted him thinking she'd stood him up.

She watched as he slowed and came to a stop outside the back entrance of the shop, the black fuel tank gleaming. He stilled the engine and balanced the bike with his feet resting on the cobbles as he tugged his helmet off and removed his sunglasses. He ran his fingers through his shock of black, brown hair and Sabrina's stomach did peculiar things as his mouth stretched into a lazy grin.

'Ahright there, gorgeous?'

She smiled, suddenly ridiculously shy as she looked coyly up at him from under her lashes the way Princess Diana did in all the photos. She could smell the exhaust fumes from the bike and a jolt of excitement at the thought of spending a whole day together, just the two of them, ricocheted through her.

'Do I get a kiss then?'

Sabrina moved toward him and leaning down sank into a long slow greeting. When they came up for air she knew her carefully applied lippy would be long gone but she didn't care so long as there was more where that had come from.

'Did you get my message?' she asked, tucking her hair behind her ear.

'From Mick you mean?'

She nodded.

'Yeah, is everything ahright, like?'

'It is now, Florence had a hair disaster.'

He raised a dark brow.

'She's only gone blonde!'

'Like Farrah Fawcett,' he winked.

'Erm, not exactly, more Debbie Harry.'

'Tony loves Debbie Harry.'

Sabrina grinned. With the two of them playing matchmaker, Flo didn't stand a chance.

'Are you hopping on then?' He unhooked the helmet and passed it over to her.

Sabrina was well versed at doing it up and she snapped it into place before retrieving her sunglasses from her jacket pocket. She'd been caught out before with the wind stinging her eyes and she'd no wish to do a repeat performance of her Gene Simmons' impersonation. She swung her jeans-clad leg over the back and snuggled in to Adam. She loved the smell of his jacket and she leaned her face into it for a moment feeling the smooth coolness of the material. 'Where are we going then?'

'Not telling. It's a surprise. Ready?' he asked, revving the engine.

'Ready.' She was desperate to find out where he was taking her and wrapping her arms around his middle she leaned into him as they puttered off down Wood Street with him only notching the speed up when they'd turned onto Ranelagh Street.

Sabrina watched the buildings speed by before they disappeared under the Birkenhead Tunnel and emerged over the water in Birkenhead. They cut through the Wirral peninsula and Bebington before veering inland toward Chester. It was only when she spied a castle, perched on a rocky crag overseeing its surrounds, that she had an inkling where they were headed.

She was right she thought, as he slowed the bike and pulled into the parking area below the imposing castle. She hopped off the bike as he kicked the stand down and did the same. They removed their helmets and she gazed up at the ruin.

'It's five hundred feet up that. Beeston Castle. I love it here,' Adam said, pocketing his sunglasses and holding out his hand for her to take. 'Mam brought me here when I was a kid in the holidays. I used to imagine I was king of all of England running about the ruins overseeing my lands below.'

Sabrina soaked up this insight into the little boy he'd been as he led her to the ticketing office where a family were just setting off through the stone walls encasing the grounds.

They followed behind them a minute later. Sabrina paused at the bottom of the hill, shading her eyes at the glare despite the moody sky. Apart from the chatter of the children ahead, it was peaceful. There was no traffic noise and she could hear birdsong from the surrounding woodland.

She let Adam lead her up the sharply inclined path towards the footbridge that would take them across the ditch and in through the imposing castle gates.

'It's thirteenth century,' Adam said as they crossed the bridge. 'Not the bridge, that's newish.' He grinned. 'The castle I mean.'

'I didn't know you were a history buff,' Sabrina puffed.

He shrugged. 'It was the only subject I paid much attention to in school.'

Sabrina passed under the gates with a feeling of reverence as she tried to imagine all those that had gone before. The interior, she saw, was mostly ruined and it was encased by thick stone walls shaped to fit the rocky outcrop on which the castle sat. They wandered about in silence, both lost in the overwhelming sense of the past.

Adam led her through a passage cut into the thick walls and she wondered how it was that she wasn't transported back to another time here. It seemed so much more fitting than a busy urban city street. It was what it was though and she'd already resolved to see if whatever mysterious forces were at work on that particular stretch of Bold Street would take her back in time tonight.

They investigated the well next and Sabrina got vertigo looking down into its black depths.

'Richard II's treasure is supposed to buried somewhere on the grounds. It's never been found,' Adam informed her before they strolled over to where they could look out at what lay beyond. His arm snaked around her waist, pulling Sabrina in next to him, as they stared out over the plain below.

'That hazy line along the horizon there is Wales,' Adam said. Their eyes met and she wondered if he was remembering the white lie she'd told him when she'd returned from her 1920s sabbatical about having been in Wales. She'd come clean not long after and told him the truth about her adventure, including the fact she'd never been to Wales.

'We'll go there one day soon,' he stated now, turning to gaze back at the vista spread out below them. 'There was no chance of their enemies taking them by surprise up here.'

It was true, you could see for miles in all directions Sabrina thought, her attention settling on the medieval outline of another castle spread out over a hill in the distance. 'What castle's that?' she asked, pointing to it.

'Peckforton Castle but it's not really a castle, it's a Victorian country house. They use it for films and the like. I like the rawness of Beeston better,' he added.

Sabrina liked this new side she was seeing of Adam. There were depths to him she'd not seen before. She wondered what his mam had been like. 'You must miss your mam,' she ventured. It was the first time she'd broached the subject with him.

He nodded. 'Yeah, I do. I can still hear her laugh sometimes. It's like she's still with me. She had a great laugh; it came all the way from here.' He pointed to his belly. 'Me dad always said she guffawed.'

Sabrina smiled, unsure whether he'd carry on.

He gazed straight ahead as he said, 'She was too young to die. Her heart, it just stopped one day. I was fifteen at the time and me dad did his best with me but,' he shrugged, 'we're not close me and him even though we work together.'

He never mentioned his work other than to say he'd had a good day, Sabrina realised. Whereas she could waffle happily about her dresses and customers for hours.

'I never thought I'd follow him into the business. It just sort-a happened, like. I'm good at it too. I've the gift of the gab, like him. You need that in our game. You've got to be able to talk the talk or you'd never get any deals across the line.' He gave a wry laugh. 'He can talk ahright me dad but not about stuff that matters. I always felt he kept a part of himself back from me and Mam.'

Sabrina wondered if that part had anything to do with her Aunt Evie. 'Adam, I haven't had a chance to mention it before but my Aunt Evie and your dad know one another. In fact, they go way back. I only made the connection between Ray Taylor, I mean your dad, and you being his son the other day.' It was another white lie and her body stiffened waiting for his response. She angled her head to look up at him.

He returned her gaze with a frown, 'Really?'

Sabrina nodded. 'It's a small world.'

'It's that alright. Me dad knows half of Liverpool though. He's had plenty of dealings on Bold Street.' He moved them off the subject and told her about a fella his mate, Tim knew who'd done a road trip across America on a Harley Davidson. 'Imagine that?' A dreamy look settled on his handsome face.

'Imagine,' Sabrina murmured. 'Erm, talking about travelling.' She filled him in on Nicole's visit to the shop and when she'd finished she said, 'It's time I tried to go back. This could be it, Adam. This could be when I find me mam.'

Adam dropped his arm from her waist and leaned the side of his body against the wall as he faced her. 'I don't want you to go, Sabrina.' He was echoing Florence's sentiment.

'I know. Neither does Flo or Aunt Evie but you know I have to. How can I not?'

'No, you don't have to.' He shook his head. 'I've had time to think about it and it's like playing Russian roulette. The odds aren't in your favour. Time catches up to when you and your mam were separated in two years. You'll be reunited then. Nineteen eighty-three's around the corner. Your mam's been waiting this long to find you, what's another two years?'

Sabrina's heart began to beat a little faster and her face heated up despite the wintery air. 'Adam, I thought you understood?'

'I do. I get it. But that doesn't mean I have to like it. I want you to promise me you won't try and do whatever it is you do to make it happen.'

'I can't promise that and I don't do anything, it just happens.' She took his hands in hers. 'If you had the chance to see your mam again, you'd take it wouldn't you?'

He wrenched his hands free and his face shuttered closed. 'That's not fair, Sabrina. There's no chance. She's dead. Nothing can change that.' His voice was flat and he shoved his hands in his jacket pockets. 'C'mon, I'll take you back. It looks like rain.' He began to walk toward the gates.

'Adam!' Sabrina called after him but he kept walking.

Chapter Seventeen

Liverpool, Two years later, 1956

Patty

Patty was in no mood for singing because her throat was getting more painful by the minute and her voice felt thick as she embarked on the mound of carrots waiting to be peeled that afternoon. She'd been feeling strange since she'd woken up and had felt progressively worse as the day dragged on. Both Bernie and Tina remarked on this and Bernie, concerned at how peaky her friend was looking given the scarlet fever scare at school, told her to go and lie down before the bell went for tea. 'I'll finish your lot,' she said.

Patty didn't argue, she felt too poorly for that and telling the pair of them it was just a head cold she had coming on, she dragged herself up to their dorm. When Bernie came back upstairs she found Patty lying on her bed not caring that her shoes were still on. For Patty's part, she was aware Bernie had returned from the afternoon chores but couldn't rouse herself to sit up and chat. She'd a thumping headache, her throat was on fire now, and she felt shivery.

She desperately wanted to close her eyes too because the light was beginning to hurt them but Cynthia Wilson had appeared at the foot of the bed and was wearing the supercilious expression she recognised as meaning she knew something Patty didn't. She didn't have to wait long to find out what it was.

'Your Davey and his gang are down with Matron again, Patty.'

'Had your ear to the door have you, Cynthia?' Bernie piped up pulling her nose out from the book she'd just settled down to read in the ten minutes before they were summoned to the dining hall. There was no love lost between the pair. Not since Cynthia had told Miss Acton, Bernie, who'd a terrible sweet, tooth, had helped herself to a slice of cake out of the tin in the kitchen's larder.

'Oh, shurrup, you.' Cynthia scowled at her nemesis before focusing on Patty again, her lips pursing in a sanctimonious manner as she said. 'He was caught shoplifting this time. Him and his pals went into town after school. I don't know what it was they stole but they'll be for it now.'

Patty's brain was in a fuddle but Cynthia's news penetrated the fog. She'd swing for Davey when she saw him. How could he be so stupid? His misdemeanours were adding up and he was very close to being shipped off to a home for juvenile delinquents, or so Miss Acton had said the last time he'd been hauled up for breaking a window. Shoplifting was another matter altogether though. It was a step up from throwing a stone at a window.

Her father's face flickered to mind and she hazily recalled having seen him walking up the drive to the main entrance the other day. She'd gazed down from the window in their dormitory calling Bernie over in a tone that had her friend come running.

'Look, that's my dad, I'm sure of it,' she'd said, willing the figure to look up so she could confirm it was him but he was intent on his destination.

'How can you be sure, Patty? You can't see his face and it's been four years since you last saw him,' Bernie had questioned.

'It's the tilt of his hat and the way he's striding.' She'd recognise his long-legged stride anywhere; she didn't need to see his face. She was assailed with the urge to bang on the window. She wanted him to acknowledge her, his daughter, and she raised her fist to do so but it faltered as the little voice in her head reminded her he'd abandoned her and Davey. As he climbed the steps and disappeared from view her hand fell back down to her side. The moment had been and gone.

Bernie was sceptical but Patty had fretted. What had brought him to Strawberry Field after all this time? She doubted he had any intention of them coming to live with him and so it had worried at her he'd been sent for because of Davey's antics. It was clear her brother was lacking a strong male role model in his life. Surely he wouldn't go and live with their father and the Wicked Witch, while she stayed here?

She'd been desperate to know what had brought him to the home but hadn't dared asked Matron, and Miss Acton when she'd asked that evening said she knew nothing about his visit and that she should forget all about it.

She'd made a promise to her mam that she and Davey wouldn't be separated but the way he was going, there'd be nothing she could do to keep them together. She needed to make him see sense.

All these thoughts jumbled in on top of one another and she let out a moan as she tried and failed to get up.

'Oh, go away, Cynthia, can't you see Patty's not well?' Bernie flapped her book at her.

Cynthia stepped back quickly on hearing this. Just a week ago one of the girls at their school had caught scarlet fever. She'd been taken from school in an ambulance to the hospital and news had spread quickly that she was unwell with the dreaded fever. There'd been great debate as to whether the school should close in order to contain the spread of the disease but in the end, just the poor girl's classmates had been told to stay home and so far there'd been no other reported cases.

Cynthia minced off to annoy someone else and Bernie, book forgotten about, decided she didn't like Patty's pallor. This was more than just a cold coming on. 'I'm going to fetch Miss Acton,' she muttered tossing her book aside and getting up. 'I'll be back as quick as I can, Pats.'

'I'm alright, don't fuss,' Patty rasped even though she felt anything but; her throat was agony and she felt sick. 'I need to go and find out what's happened to Davey. My dad can't take him. I promised Mam, Bernie!' She raised herself on to her elbows but Bernie had already gone. The room spun and with no warning she vomited.

By eight o'clock that evening Patty was on her way by ambulance to the City Hospital.

PATTY'S EYES FLUTTERED open and she turned her head gently from left to right, trying to figure out where she was. The movement made her dizzy and she shut her eyes again briefly against the sterile whiteness of the space. This, along with the hushed atmosphere and smell of antiseptic, told her she must be in hospital. She'd no idea how she'd wound up here though.

She opened her eyes and took in her surroundings once more. There was a smattering of other girls filling up beds in the large ward which was half full. Their ages varied she noticed, one or two were quite young and some were talking quietly while others were resting.

Patty swallowed. Her throat was horribly dry. She tried to piece together what had led to her winding up here. Her last coherent memory was of feeling poorly in the morning as she went about her usual routine. She'd felt like she was sickening for a cold but had told herself to get on with things. She supposed she must have gone to school but it was all a blank after she'd gone downstairs for breakfast.

She didn't want to sit up just yet for fear of her head spinning. Her tummy felt tender and empty and she lay prone on her bed, staring up at the ceiling, becoming familiar with every crack in its time-worn, plaster finish.

She'd no clue how many minutes passed before she heard a woman's voice near the foot of the bed say, 'Well, well, well, look who's awake. Good morning, Patricia'

The authoritative tone startled her out of her semi-trance and she raised her head slightly to see who the owner of the voice was.

She received a smile from a nurse who reminded Patty a little of Miss Acton. That was comforting at least. Bossy was fine so long as it was tempered with kindness.

'I'm Nurse Flinders, Patricia. Now then, let's sit you up, dear.' Her manner was no-nonsense as she bustled around the bed and, reaching down, hefted Patty up with a pair of strong arms. 'There you go. That's better. Can't eat your dinner, flat on your back now, can you?'

Patty's head took a moment to catch up with the sudden movement and her stomach churned at the thought of food. She licked her cracked lips and concentrated on steadying her breathing until the nausea abated.

The nurse eyed the pillow behind her back for a moment and Patty found her voice to croak out. 'What's wrong with me? Why am I here?'

'You've had scarlet fever, dear, as have the other girls in here. It's the fever ward at the City Hospital you're on. You've been with us for three days and I don't expect you'll remember much of that but you're going to be as good as new by the time we pack you off home.' She smiled at Patty and patted her thigh under the sheet, 'You're in good hands here, dear. Now then, I'm going to straighten that pillow for you. Sit forward for me. One, two, three—that's it.'

Patty's fuddled brain tried to make sense of what she'd been told. Scarlet fever! She'd thought she was starting with a cold. She hoped no one else from the home had caught it. None of the faces in here looked familiar, she decided, stealing another glance at the other girls from under her lashes as she waited for the nurse to stop fluffing with her pillow. That was something; she'd have hated to have passed it on.

It was unsettling to know she'd lost three whole days she thought, doing her best to try and swallow. There was also something tickling her memory but she couldn't grasp hold of it. She'd a sense it was important whatever it was.

'There we are,' Nurse Flinders said, straightening, satisfied with her patient's position. 'I suspect you've a thirst on you.' She glanced at her fob watch. 'Lunch will be doing the rounds any minute. You'll get a nice glass of juice with that.'

Patty relaxed back into the pillow. Whatever it was she couldn't remember would come to her eventually. She was too worn out to worry about it now.

The nurse gave her one last appraising look. 'Try and eat something, dear, even if you don't feel much like it. We need to build your strength back up and it's better if you've food in your stomach for the antibiotics. The sooner you've put a little meat on your bones the sooner you can go home.'

She didn't wait for Patty to reply as she made her way past the empty bed beside hers. There wasn't so much as a wrinkle in the sheets, Patty thought, taking in the stiff cotton and thinking Miss Acton would be proud of whoever had made that bed. She watched as the nurse began fussing around a girl with carroty coloured hair who looked a few years younger than Patty. She was sitting with a book open in front of her.

Patty didn't hear what Nurse Flinders was saying to the girl though because she was distracted by the rattle of a trolley and a whiff of something that promised to be tasty and which, under normal circumstances, would have her mouth watering. These, however, were far from normal circumstances.

There was a shift in the air as the meals were placed in front of the girls one by one, all of whom were, like Patty, sitting propped up by a pillow, thanks to Nurse Flinders. It was obviously a relief to the monotony of being bedridden, Patty surmised, wondering if visitors were even allowed in the ward. There was no sign of flowers or get well soon cards. It was all very austere.

She did her best with what turned out to be cottage pie, all the while dreaming of jam butties, but she couldn't stomach the yellow mush she suspected was broccoli. The rice pudding and jelly for afters slipped down a treat though.

Nurse Flinders reappeared at Patty's side a short while later with a cup of water in one hand and a smaller container in the other. 'You've done well, dear,' she said inspecting her dishes. 'But are you sure you couldn't manage a mouthful of the veg?'

Patty shook her head emphatically and fancied she saw the nurse bite back a smile.

'Well, be sure to eat your vegetables tomorrow. Full of vitamins they are. I think you can manage the tablets now instead of the liquid.' She held out the container in which two pills sat.

Patty's eyes were like saucers as she stared at the size of them. She looked pleadingly up at the nurse but detected no sympathy to her plight.

'You're a lucky girl, you know,' she said in a clipped tone. 'I recall a time when we didn't have antibiotics to treat the fever with and there were a lot of children who didn't get better like you have thanks to these. So come on now, there's to be no fussing.'

Patty didn't feel lucky. Not in the slightest. She eyed the tablets for a beat longer and then tipped them from the container into the palm of her hand, bravely swallowing them one after the other with a big gulp of water. Her eyes watered and she tried not to gag as she put the empty cup and container on the tray with her other dishes.

'There, that wasn't so bad, was it?' Nurse Flinders smiled but didn't wait for Patty to reply which was just as well because she'd have said it was truly awful. Instead, she turned her attention to a younger girl of around five or six who was standing on tippy-toes trying to see out of the window.

'Back to bed, Eliza. You know you've to stay in bed if you're to get better. Plenty of rest is what the doctor said.'

'I want to know if me mam's coming to see me, maybe she'll be allowed to tuck me in today,' her plaintive voice whined.

'Now, now. There's no visitors on the fever ward, you know that, but you'll see her at the window.' The nurse moved swiftly towards the little girl who'd begun to cry and herded her back to her bed.

Patty didn't get a chance to dwell on there being a no visitors policy because the girl with the carroty coloured hair spoke up just then.

'I'm Edith.'

Patty's head swivelled toward her.

'Hello, Edith, I'm Patty.' Her voice, although still reedy, was stronger than it had been earlier thanks to the juice she'd had with her lunch.

They smiled at one another.

'I should be going home soon.' Edith plucked at her sheets. 'I can't wait. I feel like I've been here forever and I'm bored, bored, bored. We're not allowed to do anything and I've read the books I was given.'

'How long have you been here then?' Patty asked.

'Three whole weeks.'

Patty stared at her. She couldn't stay here for three weeks and it came to her then. The memory that had been niggling at the edges of her mind.

It was Davey, he'd been in trouble for stealing. She needed to get back to Strawberry Field. Then another piece in the puzzling gaps in her memory slotted into place. The sight of her father striding up the drive to the front entrance. Why had he come to the home after all that time? Davey had been causing so much bother, had Matron told their father he'd have to take him back? And now he'd been thieving, too. Their mam would be ashamed of him. She only hoped she got the chance to tell him that because it might make him see sense.

Her heart began to pump fast at the thought of her brother not being there when she got back to the children's home. She'd promised her mam they'd stay together. She gripped her sheets.

Edith, oblivious to her racing thoughts, said breezily, 'Oh, don't worry I'm sure you won't be in here as long as me. Most of the girls are here a fortnight and then they go home. I was allergic to the antibiotics that's why I've been cooped up here for ages and ages. I miss me mam, dad and sister and me schoolfriends. I miss me younger brother too, even though he can be very annoying.'

Patty needed to ask the nurse whether an exception could be made for her. She needed to get word to Strawberry Field and felt certain Miss Acton would come and see her if she asked. She'd be able to tell her what had happened with Davey. Perhaps she could say it would help with her recovery to have her mind put at rest. Before she could call out to Nurse Flinders though, Edith had begun to chatter once more.

'We're not allowed any visitors. Our parents can wave to us from the window down there.' She pointed to the large pane looking out onto the corridor. 'Some of the little ones find it upsetting seeing their mams and dads and not being able to have a cuddle.'

Patty, distracted, wondered whether she should tell her she was from a children's home and that there'd be no mam or dad standing at the window desperate to see how she was. A pang of something she'd not allowed herself to feel for a long time passed through her and in that moment she felt very sorry for herself.

If she'd a father who'd been strong enough to look after her and Davey she wouldn't be lying here now worried sick about her brother. Oh, she knew right enough she was no different to lots of children in the home and it did no good to dwell on such things, but at that moment she wanted to wallow.

The little girl whom Patty would imagine would forever be getting told off for talking in class carried on. 'I miss playing hopscotch too. I'm very good at it or at least I was. I doubt my legs will work properly after all this time in bed.

I tried to practise the other day but they were all floppy and bendy and Nurse Flinders went berserk when she caught me.'

Her glum face prodded Patty to respond. 'I'm sure you'll still be good at it once you're all better.'

Edith brightened at that. 'There are some nice things about being in hospital, Patty. Like the rice pudding and jelly. I see you ate all yours.' She craned her neck to inspect her ward-mate's empty lunch dishes. 'And I don't blame you leaving the broccoli. The vegetables are awful and, be warned, the nurses will try their best to make you eat them. Especially the ward sister, Sister Sourpuss I call her.'

Patty smiled. She was well versed with sourpusses; her domestic science teacher was awful as was her maths teacher. She'd been told she'd no aptitude for domestic science or maths, something she put down to her teachers. It was hard to be enthusiastic about a chocolate sponge when you had a teacher with a tongue sharper than a knife. Or about multiplication when a ruler was being slammed down on your desk each time your eyes glazed over, which was often in Patty's case.

She'd been told she should aim for a secretarial career as she'd good organisational skills and comprehension of the English language but Patty didn't want to be a secretary. She wanted to be a singer. Another thought raced in on top of the others. Would she still be able to sing? She vaguely recalled a horrendous pain in her throat.

'I doubt I'll get a bag of sweets each Sunday once I'm home either.'

Patty tried to keep up, finding herself distracted by the incessant chatter.

'Not that I get to eat all of them anyway. I'm sure the nurses help themselves to some of our treats from home. Sister Sourpuss says We don't want rotting teeth on top of an infectious disease.' She was careful to check Nurse Flinders was a safe distance away and to lower her voice as she said this and then she unfurled her hand and showed it to Patty. The skin was peeling. 'This means I'm on the mend,' she said knowledgeably before reaching beneath her pillow and retrieving a paper bag.

'You can't be too careful,' she said, again checking she wasn't in Nurse Flinders' line of sight. 'Nurse Mangan is a soft touch. She brought these in for me before the sourpuss could get her hands on them. I've a few left. Would you like a sweet?'

The thought of a sweet was heavenly. 'Yes please, if you've one to spare.'

Edith rummaged about before handing over a pink flying saucer and Patty tried not to flinch at the sight of the peeling skin. 'I'm not allowed chewing gum. I got it in my sister's hair accidentally on purpose when she was being very annoying. It had to be cut out in the end and she made a dreadful fuss.'

'Thank you.' Patty slipped the sweet in her mouth and sucked hard, relishing the burst of sweetness.

'Be extra nice to Olive. Her mam works in the Cadbury factory.'

The mention of the chocolate factory where her mam had worked made Patty's eyes tear up.

'Edith, Patty needs to rest not listen to your chitter-chatter,' Nurse Flinders said in a mock stern voice. 'And I hope you've not been passing out sweets. You know Sister doesn't like you having them except for on Saturdays.'

Patty forgot her tears and quickly swallowed her sweet feeling the lump work its way down her neck. She didn't want to get Edith into trouble.

Nurse Flinders looked from one to the other, certain she'd missed something. She had a nose for when things were afoot and these two looked like butter wouldn't melt in their mouths. A sure sign they'd been up to something. She stood there a moment longer and then, with a gentle shake of her head, told them both that it was quiet time now and Patty fancied she could hear the starch in her uniform crack as she left the ward.

Chapter Eighteen

Liverpool, 1981

Sabrina

'I'm going for a walk, Aunt Evie,' Sabrina called, zipping her jacket up and pulling a woolly hat down low over her ears.

'It's dark out,' Evelyn shouted over the sound of the television. It was only just gone five but the light had gone from the day.

'I need some fresh air.'

She was out the door before her aunt could push for answers as to why she'd been holed up in her bedroom all afternoon, emerging with puffy eyes and a red nose.

'Do you want me to warm you up some of the soup left over from lunch?'

Sabrina had already gone.

Evelyn turned back to the television. She'd had a lover's tiff with that fella of hers, she deduced. Time on her own to clear her head wouldn't do her any harm. She settled back in her seat to watch the wrestling. Another of her guilty vices, she thought, reaching for her Woodbines.

Sabrina strode toward Hudson's, her mind made up. The traffic was light and there weren't many people out and about. Those that were, were intent on getting wherever it was they were going. Bold Street took on a different feel once it was dark this time of year, she thought, glancing up at the twinkling Christmas lights strewn across the street. It looked magical, a proper winter wonderland. She couldn't summon enthusiasm at how pretty it looked though. She felt sick and had done since Adam had dropped her home.

She'd gotten off the bike, handing him the helmet, and had been about to speak to him. She didn't want to leave things on a bad note. They needed to talk and sort out what had happened up at Beeston Castle. He was already revving the bike's engine and, taking the hint, she'd unlocked the door and gone inside. Two could play that game.

She hadn't rung Florence because she knew her friend would take his side over her tempting another trip back to the past and so, saying a quick hello to Aunt Evie who was engrossed in a Dick Francis book, she'd taken herself off to her bedroom. She'd buried her face in her pillow and cried until her tummy hurt and then she'd rolled over onto her back until finally feeling as though the four walls were closing in on her she'd decided she would go and see if whatever it was that had happened outside Hudson's last time would happen again.

She reached the bookshop and began to pace.

Chapter Nineteen

Liverpool, 1956

Patty

Patty had grown stronger with each passing day spent on the fever ward. Being from a children's home she quickly accepted the routines of the hospital. She'd borrowed a book from Edith which was no *Malory Towers* but it had kept her mind occupied.

There was always great excitement on the ward when the visitors appeared in what the girls had dubbed the waving window. Treats, books, and comics would slowly filter through to them when the visitors had gone home but nobody came to see Patty. Not a single soul in the two weeks she was there.

She'd asked Nurse Flinders about getting word to Miss Acton at Strawberry Field. She'd stressed it was important but this had been met with a raised eyebrow and followed up with a curt, 'And do you not think we've enough to do, young lady? I'm a nurse, not a personal messenger.'

Having been put firmly in her place, she'd resolved to try not to dwell on Davey. There was nothing she could do except get well so she could go back to the home and see him for herself.

Edith and her continual chatter, sweet supply, and books, was a tonic for keeping her mind off her brother.

The fact no one had joined the cluster at the window to see Patty had been picked up on by one girl of around eleven or so who spoke with what Edith said was a plum in her mouth.

'She'll be from Crosby,' she said before mouthing 'posh' at Patty and making her smile.

'Where're you from then, Victoria?' she'd gone on to ask shooting a twinkly-eyed glance at Patty.

'Endbutt Lane in Crosby,' Victoria sniffed back, not understanding why Patty giggled.

Victoria had taken against Patty on the spot and whispered loud enough for her to overhear when no hospital staff were in sight that the reason no one came to let her know they missed her was because nobody *did* miss her. She was from a children's home where bad children go, she'd said cupping her hands either side of her mouth as she whispered to the girl in the bed next to her. 'She's either an orphan or illegitimate.' Illegitimate was a word she used with the same distaste the rest of them saved for describing the mushy vegetables they were served each dinnertime.

Victoria must have overheard her confiding in Edith, Patty thought and still fragile from her illness, had been unable to stop the tear escaping. Was that how people saw her and the other children at Strawberry Field? As bad children who were either orphaned or illegitimate? She was old enough to know Victoria was only parroting her mother and didn't know better but still her words stung. So too did the way the little girl she'd mock-whispered to had stared over at Patty as though she'd just landed from outer space.

Edith, who reminded Patty of a red-headed version of Bernie only younger and quite possibly fiercer, was having none of it. She'd tossed her sheet aside and leapt out of bed, flying across the room with surprising speed for someone who'd recently been unwell. Her fists were clenched and she'd been about to land Victoria one when Nurse Flinders' bellow brought her up short.

'It's a good job you're going home in the morning, Edith,' she'd said, shaking her head before ordering her back to bed in a tone that brooked no argument.

Edith had done as she was told and under the nurse's glowering gaze relayed what had been said.

Nurse Flinders shot Patty a sympathetic glance and her cheeks stained red both at hearing those ugly words again and because a twelve-year-old had felt she had to stand up for her.

The nurse had a quiet word with Victoria who went into a sulk, obviously unused to being told off.

Olive, whose mam worked in the Cadbury factory waited until the coast was clear before sneaking over to Patty. She gave her a shy smile and a row of chocolate before doing the same for Edith. She ignored Victoria who looked almost comical with her arms folded over her chest and her bottom lip out.

The sweetness of the act and the chocolate itself was almost enough to take away the bitterness of the words reverberating in Patty's head. *Orphan, illegitimate, bad children.* They were labels she wanted to shake off with all her might.

One day, she vowed silently, she'd have a family of her own and she would never, ever leave them as her father had her and Davey. She'd love them with all her heart and keep them close.

Patty was sad to lose her little friend the next day but pleased for her that she was finally going home. It was strange to see her dressed with shoes and socks on. she thought, as Edith hugged her.

'You're not to take any lip from her over there,' she said before glaring at Victoria. Letting go of Patty she made a fist with her right hand and pummelled it into the palm of her left hand. The smacking sound made Patty grin, she really was a feisty red-head, and Victoria's eyes bugged as she slunk down under her sheet.

'I'll miss you, Edith, time will drag without you to keep me company.'

'You'll get some rest though, without her constant monologue, there's always a silver lining,' Nurse Flinders said, not unkindly, before ordering her back to bed. 'Edith, your mother's waiting downstairs. No dawdling now, come on. I thought you'd be glad to see the back of this place.'

Edith looked back over her shoulder and gave Patty a final wave. Patty had bitten her lip to stop herself getting upset and rallied herself to wave back. Her life felt at that moment as if it had been full of goodbyes.

THE DAYS ROLLED OVER, all the same as each other, and a week or so later it was Patty's turn to be going home. She wasn't sorry to be leaving. Edith's company had made her stay bearable and sweet little Olive had left a few days earlier too. She'd had more than enough of looking at Victoria's spoiled face and listening to her whine.

There was trepidation at going back to Strawberry Field though. She'd talked herself into believing everything would be alright where Davey was concerned but she was terrified she might soon find out otherwise.

As she stepped outside the hospital entrance, she took a moment to gulp greedily at the fresh air. Looking about her, the colours seemed crisper and altogether clearer after the sanitised white of the ward. She saw Miss Acton waving out from where she was standing beside her teal Morris Minor. The bonny housemother beamed and it warmed Patty to see how pleased she was to see her. She knew she'd been fortunate in being placed under Miss Acton's care.

The woman, as round as she was little, tutted as Patty drew near. 'You look frail on it but we'll soon have that put right. The girls have missed you terribly, especially Bernadette. They're all excited you're coming home.'

She gestured for Patty to go around to the passenger side which she did, settling herself into her seat while Miss Acton squeezed in behind the wheel with an unladylike grunt.

Patty leaned her head back. The last time she'd ridden in a car had been with their father the day he brought them to Strawberry Field. She looked at the knobs on the dashboard, wondering which did what, and her fingers itched to touch them but she kept her hands clasped on her lap. After a few false starts, a loud belch from the exhaust, and much muttering on Miss Acton's part, they were off.

'I have to say you gave us all a terrible fright, Patty.' The housemother's voice verged on accusatory.

'I'm sorry, Miss Acton.'

'Yes, well, you didn't do it on purpose. It was me who called the ambulance and of course, the home was quarantined as soon as scarlet fever was diagnosed. Poor Bernadette was beside herself with worry until we'd had word you were out of the woods.'

Patty half listened as, like a babbling brook, she went on about how it was all a mystery her picking up the fever in the first place. She tuned in when she said it was nothing short of a miracle none of the other children had contracted the dreadful illness. It was a relief to hear this and she breathed easier knowing she'd not passed it on.

'I wonder if the fever has affected your vocal cords?' Miss Acton said, turning her head to look at her charge. Patty clenched her hands as she turned back in the nick of time to slam her foot down on the brake, narrowly avoiding the car in front of her. Unfazed she suggested, 'Why don't you run through the scales for me?'

Patty didn't want to give her any excuse for taking her eyes off the road a second time and so she launched into a round of middle C. Do-Re-Mi-Fah-Sol-La-Ti-Do.

'Hmm, a little rusty but once you begin practising with the choir again you'll be in fine fettle. The Lord is good, Patty. Oh, yes, He is good.'

'Yes, Miss Acton,' Patty answered automatically. She chewed her lip for a moment summoning up the courage to interrupt as she began nattering once more about school and how Patty would need to catch up with her work. She was desperate to ask after her brother and inquire once more as to the purpose of her father's visit to Strawberry Field but her tummy rolled over at the thought of what she might be told and she raised her hand to her mouth, chewing on her fingernail.

'Stop that right now.' Miss Acton tutted, muttering it was a disgusting habit.

Patty did as she was told, dropping her hand and clasping her hands in her lap to be sure she didn't do it again. Get on with it, she told herself before cutting her housemother off mid-sentence being sure to remember her manners, 'Excuse me, Miss Acton?'

'Yes, child?' She crunched the gears and Patty lurched forward in her seat.

As the car regained its equilibrium and juddered along, Patty brought up the topic of her father first. 'Do you remember when I told you I saw my father shortly before I got poorly?'

Patty wasn't sure if she imagined it or not but her housemother's grip got tighter on the steering wheel. 'Vaguely,' she said, an airiness to her tone that was at odds with her white knuckles. 'But it's not of any importance now.'

'But I've been so worried, you see, that he might have been told to take our kid back because I know he's been a handful.'

Miss Acton snorted at this but her lips remained sealed. Patty didn't mention having heard Davey had been caught stealing. To do so would only set Miss Acton off on a tangent about the breaking of the ten commandments. She could be very pious when she got started.

'I promised my mam before she died, you see, that I'd make sure we stayed together and a promise is a promise, Miss Acton. You've told us that yourself.'

The housemother shifted in her seat and gazed steadfastly ahead. 'I was going to wait until we'd got you settled back in, Patricia, because rather a lot's happened since you've been away.'

Patty didn't like the way she said 'away' as though she'd been on holiday and not sick in hospital. She didn't like the way her fingers were now drumming the steering wheel in an agitated fashion or the use of her full name either. Whatever it was Miss Acton was about to tell her, Patty knew she wasn't going to like it.

'Now then, I want you to think about your brother. What's best for him, do you understand? Not about yourself, Patricia, because this isn't the time for selfish thoughts.'

She glanced over at Patty who nodded stiffly.

'Good girl. Well, as you know, Davey wasn't on a good path and hasn't been for some time. He was well on his way to becoming a juvenile delinquent.'

Patty wanted to protest that he was just a lost little boy who needed a father but she dared not say a word until she'd heard the rest of what Miss Acton had to say.

'An opportunity presented itself shortly before you became ill. A rather wonderful opportunity for Davey to have a fresh start away from some of the bad influences he's been mixing with. This was why Matron summoned your father to see her. They had a long chat and between them, it was agreed it was the best thing for your brother because things simply couldn't continue the way they were.'

Patty wanted to scream at her to just spit it out.

She cleared her throat. 'Your brother's on his way to Australia, Patricia.'

Patty turned to stare at her housemother, not quite comprehending what she'd been told. Miss Acton took her hand off the steering wheel and gave Patty's leg a brief pat. 'I realise this will have come as a shock but you must remember what I said, dear. Think about what's best for Davey, not yourself.' The car swerved as she oversteered.

'But I promised me mam,' Patty whispered being thrown side to side.

'Yes, you said, but sometimes in special circumstances like this, a promise can't be kept. I think she'd understand, don't you? Because she'd want what was best for Davey too. In fact, I think she'd be very happy to know he was going to a country where he can eat oranges every day and the sun's always shining. Think of what a lovely life he'll have, Patricia.'

Patty was too stunned to cry. 'But how?' tumbled from her lips as a thousand and one questions vied for attention. Where would he live? Who would take care of him? When would she see him again? Would he be allowed to write to her? How would she find him? And so it went on. She barely heard Miss Acton's reply.

'By ship, of course. I'm told the boys were beside themselves with excitement at the thought of being on a big ship at sea for six weeks. Oh yes, they were thrilled by the grand adventure ahead of them all. That's what you must hold on to, dear.'

Patty's ragged fingernails were digging into her palms and her breath was shallow.

She wanted to hit Miss Acton, shock the look of excitement off her face. She couldn't believe Davey had wanted to go. And how could he have been sent away without her having the chance to hug him and tell him he'd be alright?

Her blood thundered in her ears as she thought about her father and how he'd consented to his son being sent away to the other side of the world and she hated him for it.

She turned to Miss Acton. 'I'll find him you know. You can't keep us apart.'

'Really, Patricia, dear, you've had a shock and you've not been well,' she spluttered. 'It was for the best.' There wasn't quite the same conviction in her voice as she took in Patty's white face.

Patty didn't respond. She'd meant every word she'd said. If she died looking, she'd find her brother.

Part Two

Chapter Twenty

Liverpool, 1962

Patty's fingers flew over the keys of the Imperial typewriter at which she was sat. There were seven other girls in the room with her, all clacking away in silence. She could smell the heady mix of cigarettes and the overtly sexy smelling Tabu perfume coming off Fiona in waves, the combination of which and the lack of ventilation in the close office space was giving her a headache. Still, better that than the whiff of fish she thought she'd caught off herself earlier. It was the bane of her life living above a fishmonger's!

Fiona had earned herself a disapproving sniff from Mrs Frederickson, their supervisor, that morning due, to the length of her skirt which was above her knees and the redness of her lipstick. She'd already been spoken to about the wearing of heavy perfume to work. 'It isn't fair on those around you, Miss Hughes, coming in smelling like you're off to a dance hall and not the office.'

'You don't mind do you, girls?' Fiona had stopped chewing her gum long enough to ask.

There'd been a quiet tittering among the cluster of typists already seated at their typewriters ready to begin their working day. Nobody else would dare stand up to Mrs Frederickson the way Fiona did. It was a great source of entertainment watching them butt heads.

'This is a factory typing pool, Fiona,' the supervisor retorted, 'Not Lime Street after dark.'

Fiona hadn't been fazed in the least as she winked at the others, false eyelashes firmly glued in place, before shrugging out of her coat. The other day, Patty had been on her hands and knees in the lavatory helping her find her lashes which had a tendency to spring off at inopportune moments. Knowing her, Patty thought, looking up from where she was already seated and flexing her fingers in readiness to begin the day's work, tomorrow's skirt would be even shorter.

Fiona sailed close to the wind and the only reason she got away with her tardiness and tartiness was because she was a favourite of Mr Cox's, one of the managers at the car manufacturing firm where they were employed. Something, Mrs Fitzpatrick reminded them of on a daily basis they should be grateful for given the current climate.

Out of the eight girls in the pool, five were copy typists and only three shorthand typists. This had Fiona, the owlish Sandra, and Patty in hot demand with the managerial staff at the company. To summon them for dictation made the men in suits upstairs puff with importance as it was only the company secretary and managing director who had personal secretaries.

The girls would have to sign out before taking to the stairs, reporting back to Mrs Fitzpatrick as to how many words they'd taken before settling down to the task of transcribing their notes.

Mr Cox's soft spot for Fiona, however, wasn't because of her exceptional shorthand and typing skills. He'd a roving eye did Mr Cox and while Mrs Fitzpatrick frowned upon Fiona's skirt length, Mr Cox was appreciative and praised her work often so the supervisor had no choice but to lump it.

Patty would have liked to have been more like Fiona with her carefree naughtiness but she kept her head down and got on with her work. She didn't rock the boat, partly because years in a children's home had taught her it was best to keep a low profile and partly because she couldn't afford to. She needed this job. It was her ticket to Davey.

Each week when she picked up her brown pay packet, she'd arrive home to the smelly flat you could barely swing a cat in that she shared with Bernie and divvy it up. There was money set aside for the rent and feeding the meter. Then there was food, which, if it had come down to it she'd have gone without if she had to choose between eating and entry to the various music clubs around Liverpool. She went as often as she could but her and Bernie's joint savings took precedence. They had to.

She'd never once wavered in her plan to find her brother. She was determined they'd all be together again and that Bernie's words all those years ago as to her and Davey managing her singing career would no longer be mere words bandied about in the kitchen of Strawberry Field. They'd become reality.

Fame and fortune awaited her, and Bernie and Davey would be along for the ride. She just knew it.

She'd had a letter from her brother in the early days after he'd been sent away. She'd been so excited when Miss Acton had handed it to her with a broad smile as though this made everything alright and that here was the proof the decisions made over her head were the right ones. Patty had felt certain Miss Acton had read the contents of the envelope before passing it on though she didn't dare accuse her of this.

Their relationship had shifted and never gotten back on the same footing after what Patty had seen as deceit on Miss Acton's part. Her housemother had known why her father had been sent for and yet she'd told Patty she hadn't a clue. If Miss Acton had been honest as to why he'd come to the home all those years ago when she'd asked then she might have had a chance to stop the wheels for Davey going to Australia being set in motion.

She'd no longer sung their evening songs with the same enthusiasm she once had. It was the only way she could think of to punish her housemother for the part she'd played in her losing her brother. She'd been angry for such a long time. She still was.

The letter had not made everything right. If anything, it had made things worse.

The words were brief and stilted as though Davey had been made to sit down and pen it. It hadn't told her much, other than to say he was in another home only this one was just for boys outside a city called Adelaide. The address on that letter was the most precious clue she had as to his new life and she'd committed it to memory.

Davey had gone on to say he'd made plenty of new friends and was learning the building trade along with all the other boys. He could mix cement and lay bricks, he'd said. He'd commented on how hot it was and that there were a lot of flies in Australia and then he'd signed it, your loving brother, Davey.

There was no mention of oranges.

Patty had cried as she passed it to Bernie to read. She could sense between the lines all the things he hadn't said. He was scared lonely and unhappy and there was nothing she could do to make things better for him. She'd written back straight away but no letter of reply had ever come.

Things hadn't gone to plan so far for her, Bernie and Davey. Life had seen to that. Life and the powers that be who dictated the path they'd had to take. A hostel, practical skills, and eventually work for Patty. Being a famous singer had never once come into the mix.

Patty hadn't minded insomuch as she'd been eager to begin her working life so she could start to save for her passage to Australia and when she'd left Strawberry Field she'd not looked back. She felt as though her work here in the factory office was a stop-gap until she could reassemble with Bernie on one side, Davey on the other once more and then her real life could begin in earnest.

It was this goal of reuniting with her brother that saw her through those grim early days when she and Bernie had been separated. The news that Bernie was to begin work as a machinist apprenticing on the job with accommodation near to where she was to work in the city had been a wrench. Aside from her hospital interlude, she'd not been far from Bernie's side since she'd arrived as a frightened child at the children's home.

Patty meanwhile had been placed in a lacklustre hostel while she attended Anfield Commercial College. It had been decided by those responsible for her care until she turned eighteen that she was suited to secretarial work and she'd proved them right.

She might have had an aptitude for it but her heart didn't lie in typing monotonous documents, day in day out, or taking notes while self-important, overfed men dictated the ins and outs of the car manufacturing process though.

Oh no, just like she'd not wavered in wanting to find Davey, she'd not given up on her dreams of one day becoming a singer. Now she and Bernie were together again she could sense this was within her reach. They just had to figure out how to grasp hold of it because it had also dawned on Patty there was money to be made and money would bring her closer to Davey.

A wintery light streamed in through the room's one window and despite its uninspiring view of the asphalted rear of the factory where she'd worked since she'd left college, Patty would've loved to have abandoned her post to peek out of it. This was because the workers on the assembly line would be having their break now. They'd be clustered down there in their overalls, stamping their feet to ward off the wintery bite as they smoked their ciggies.

She knew this because she'd risked a glance at the clock above the desk where Mrs Frederickson presided over them, her mean little mouth set in a permanent pucker of distaste as her watchful eyes missed nothing behind those horn-rimmed, glasses of hers.

It was three thirty.

He'd be down there.

Lee Carter was his name and he made Patty's heart flutter each time she saw him. Hers and all the other girls in the pool. He was a blue-eyed, blond Adonis who didn't have the pasty, spotty complexion of so many of the other lads Patty encountered in her daily life, which to be fair, weren't many. Nevertheless, he was always a bright spot on a winter's day. He seemed to shine.

He also sang in a band, Lee and the Sundials. She'd heard they'd performed at the Cavern but hadn't seen the band for herself yet.

Little Linda who sat on her left said they were great, a little bit Lee Dorsey meets Cliff Richard and The Shadows and they'd had the crowd screaming out for more. She'd done a little swoon mentioning Cliff Richard's name and had begun humming Lee Dorsey's hit Ya Ya then. Patty had had it stuck in her head all day. It was this that elevated Lee Carter from factory worker to swoon-worthy dreamboat in the eyes of the girls in the typing pool.

He'd a cockiness about him that made him all the more appealing as he milled about with the other lads, waiting for the factory doors to open. He gave off an air of being destined for bigger and better things which made him all the more attractive in Patty's eyes. He'd smiled at her this morning as she hurried past trying to ignore the wolf whistles.

All the girls got wolf whistles from the lads who worked the assembly line, even Sandra, and again she'd wished she was bold like Fiona who revelled in the attention. Patty would watch enviously as her workmate sucked in her tummy so her bosom jutted forth like twin bullets as she minced into the building of a morning, her skirts getting tighter and shorter by the day!

Fiona always had a cheeky comeback at the ready to put them in their places too. Whereas Patty had a tendency to turn beetroot and nearly trip over herself. Bernie said she'd have to get over her self-consciousness if she was going to get up on stage. She'd have to learn to enjoy being in the limelight.

Patty knew she was right but she couldn't help her face flaming every single time the lads turned their attention on her. It wasn't that she was sweet sixteen and never been kissed anymore but at twenty years old she was hardly a woman of the world either.

As a result of this morning's carry-on, she'd been hot and bothered by the time she walked into the office. Lee's smile had turned her insides to jelly.

Mrs Fitzpatrick had eyed her suspiciously as if she might be sickening for something but said nothing. She'd saved her breath for Fiona.

Now, Patty's sigh was heartfelt. Fiona was much more Lee Carter's type than she'd ever be. Dream on girl, she told herself as another voice whispered, if she could get talking to him, tell him she sang, he might talk his bandmates into letting her have a turn with the mike. The very thought of standing up on stage next to him made her fizz and pop.

She tried to focus on the long-winded document she was in the midst of banging out but her mind drifted off and instead, she saw herself on that tiny, cramped stage down the back of the Cavern, singing her heart out to the screaming crowd. Lee had picked up a guitar and was strumming it for all it was worth as he gazed adoringly at her.

She could almost feel the heat and hear the din. She could taste the excitement in the air. The same champagne-bubbles feeling she got when she was in the thick of it all, dancing shoulder to shoulder with the rest of the crowd, welled up and she was filled with the urge to down tools and march out of the office while belting out the hit song by Helen Shapiro, Walking Back to Happiness.

Oh, to see the look on Mrs Fitzpatrick's face!

One day she'd do it.

'Miss Hamilton.' Mrs Fitzpatrick's sharp tone brought her up short and she realised she'd stopped typing.

'Sorry, Mrs Fitzpatrick,' she murmured, dipping her head once more and carrying on clacking.

It was this moment's lapse that saw Patty mistype more than one line in the contract. As such, when the work was gathered up by Mrs Fitzpatrick and sent up to the company secretary for her final perusal, Patty's came back with an angry red line slashing through each page of the contract.

Mrs Fitzpatrick waved it at her and made a snippy remark about daydreaming on the job and Patty swallowed back a frustrated retort. She knew better than to answer back.

Little Linda flashed her a sympathetic glance as she put the cover over her typewriter. She'd planned on catching the bus with Patty who'd arranged to meet Bernie at the Cavern straight from work.

Bernie only worked a block away from the club and would bag a spot in the queue for them. She was able to go to the lunchtime sessions too which made Patty pea green. Although, she had to be careful to get back to work on time because she, along with all the other girls at the factory where she worked, had been told they'd be out of a job if they were late back from their lunch. Businesses all over Liverpool were fed up with their employees disappearing to go and see whatever band was playing in the cave-like club only to return to their workplace late, hot, and bothered not to mention over-excited.

Patty shed her secretarial skin and felt like the person she was supposed to be the minute she walked down into that hot, dark space, feeling the city's new beats wash over her. Davey was always there at the back of her mind but for a brief time while the music played she could be carefree and kick her heels up.

Now, she was going to be stuck here for at least another forty minutes retyping the stupid contract and the queue to get into the club would be down the street and around the corner! She'd miss the first band.

'I'll wait for you downstairs, queen,' Little Linda said. 'Don't worry you'll whizz through that in no time.'

Patty flashed her a grateful smile before threading a fresh sheet of paper through and setting to work. The sooner she had it finished the sooner she could go.

The other girls all tidied their stations and called out a ta-rah while Patty carried on grimly hitting the keys. She finished it forty minutes later and fidgeted in her seat as she waited for Mrs Fitzpatrick to check in with the company secretary as to whether this was up to scratch.

They'd no life either of them, that was their problem, she thought mutinously, as the ticking of the clock seemed to taunt her. They took pleasure in making sure she and the other girls who made up the typing pool didn't either whenever they got the chance.

To her relief, Mrs Fitzpatrick returned and in her clipped manner told her she could go home. She suggested an early night might be in order if she was to keep her mind on the job and Patty forced herself to bid her a courteous goodnight. She'd didn't want an additional lecture as to her attitude! With her coat only half buttoned she skipped down the stairs and burst through the doors onto the forecourt. Her eyes scanned the entrance, searching for Linda who normally would have waited at the gates for her. There was no sign of her though, and thinking she must have gone on without her she hurried off, eager to clamber on board the bus to take her to Victoria Street station.

She didn't blame her friend for not waiting, she thought, shoving her hands in her coat pockets for warmth, her step faltering as she heard a voice call out.

'Oi, luv, what's your hurry?'

She turned around and, through the gloom of early evening, blinked because there was Lee Carter leaning nonchalantly against the brick wall of the factory building. She clenched her hands in her pockets, feeling her nails dig into them as she assured herself she hadn't just conjured him up. She watched him grind out his cigarette with the sole of a gleaming black shoe before pushing off from the wall to swagger towards her.

Chapter Twenty-one

P atty tried to regroup in the few seconds it took Lee to reach her. She didn't want to give away how flustered she was by his being there. He must have been waiting for her to come out since half past five when everyone else had clocked out. It was well past six now and the last person she'd expected to be making his way towards her was him.

She'd not seen him in his civvies before and the sight of him with his hands thrust in the pockets of dark trousers he'd teamed with a white shirt and skinny black necktie, worn under a black jacket, made her knees go weak. He'd the collar turned up against the cold and his hair had curled slightly at the ends.

She knew what Fiona would say if it was her seeing him in his going out clobber instead of the usual blue overall he wore to work. She'd snap her gum and pat her fashionable new beehive hairdo before calling back, 'State of you and the price of fish!'

The words got stuck in Patty's throat though and she didn't have a beehive, her fine hair was better suited to the short swinging bob she wore it in these days. She was suddenly very glad she'd worn her pale blue two-piece to work. She knew the colour suited her but then she remembered she could have had her nighty on under her coat, which she'd now buttoned up to her chin, for all Lee knew.

'It's proper Baltic out here,' he said, his breath coming in a puff of white as he stood in front of her.

She looked up at him shyly, willing some sparkling banter to spill forth but to no avail. Her silence didn't seem to faze him though as he explained his presence.

'Your friend Linda told me you were going to the Cavern with her but that them lot upstairs had you working back late. She was going to wait for you but I told her I was going there meself and I was too much of a gentleman to see a lady standing about freezin." He winked at her. 'You don't mind do you, girl?'

'No.'

She received a grin by way of reply and he offered her his arm. Patty took it, glad one of them was self-assured as she caught a musky whiff of Old Spice aftershave.

'You're a mysterious woman, you are,' he said as they picked their way over the cobbles toward the bus stop at the end of the street. 'Mysterious Margaux with an 'x".'

'Me?' Patty was surprised. She wore her heart on her sleeve or so Bernie said. There was nothing mysterious about her.

'Yeah, you.'

That grin he kept flashing her was making her belly do strange things.

'I'm not mysterious and my name's Patty not Margaux with an 'x".'

'I know that, girl, but you look like a Margaux to me. You're not like the other girls here so I gave you a mysterious sounding name. I've been asking around after you but no one knows anything other than you share a flat with a pal over Kensington way.'

Patty kept the fact she'd grown up at Strawberry Field to herself. She didn't want to be pre-judged over something she'd had no control over. The snobbish Victoria's reaction to where she resided all those years ago when she was in hospital had cut deep and left her wary.

'There's not much to tell.'

'See, what did I say? A mysterious woman. Well, I'm going to make it me job to find out all about you, Patty Hamilton.'

'Oh, so I'm Patty now?' His banter was making her bold and she batted her false lashes at him praying they wouldn't decide to come unstuck then and there.

He grinned down at her but before he could reply the lights of the bus sluiced over them and it rattled past sliding into the stop up ahead.

'C'mon!' Lee grabbed her hand, pulling her along in a run which wasn't easy in kitten heels on cobbles but they reached the red open-top double-decker just as it began to pull away once more. He swung himself up onto the platform hauling her up behind him. The clippie shook his head and punched their tickets while Patty tried to catch her breath. Lee, still holding her hand, led her upstairs.

Normally on such a cold evening, she'd have opted to sit downstairs not up in the dancers where smoking was permitted. Tonight though, she didn't care where she sat so long as she was next to Lee and, catching sight of her windblown hair and flushed, excited expression in the window as he pulled her up the stairs after him she made a note to herself to try and discreetly sort her hair out once they'd sat down.

Lee slid into a seat near the front and she sat down alongside him.

A group of lads were right down the back laughing and ribbing one another but they were the only other hardy souls sitting up the top.

'Ciggy?' Lee retrieved a packet from his jacket pocket and held it out towards her.

She dropped the hand she'd been attempting to smooth her hair down with. 'No thanks.' She'd tried to master the art of smoking with Bernie. Both of them wanted to look so-phisticated like Audrey Hepburn as they sat about in cafés with a cigarette dangling from an elegant black holder. Nei-ther of them had taken to it though despite giving it a good nudge. Besides, given they worked from eight thirty in the morning until five thirty in the evening, five days a week there wasn't all that much time for sitting about in cafés. The spare time they did have was to be enjoyed dancing at the various clubs springing up about the city.

She watched as he struck a match and the glow lit his face for a moment and again she sought reassurance that this was happening. She really was here with Lee Carter.

'So, what do you do with yerself when you're not work-ing or dancing at the clubs then, Mysterious Margaux?'

The title he'd given her was growing on her. 'There's not much time for anything else.' Then she remembered herself and it was as if Bernie was whispering in her ear telling her to stop being a shrinking violet. 'You've been handed this op-portunity, girl, grab it!' she imagined her friend saying as she took a deep breath and spoke up. 'But I'm a singer or at least I'm going to be.'

He eyed her thoughtfully and drew slowly on his cigarette. 'I'm in a band,' he said before exhaling lazily.

'I know you are. I heard you're very good too. Lee and the Sundials.'

'That's us.'

'I thought you'd be playing tonight.'

'Nah,' he shrugged, 'We're booked to play the Cavern tomorrow. We've a manager, Alan Marsden, who sees to all that. You haven't seen us play yourself then?'

'No.'

'You don't know what you're missing, sweetheart.' He winked at her and she liked his conviction. It was no good thinking you were average in such a competitive business as music. She needed to take a leaf out of his book if she wanted to get a name for herself on the scene.

'You haven't heard me sing.'

'No.'

'You don't know what you're missing either.'

He threw his head back and laughed and Patty smiled too. She couldn't believe she'd come out with that but she was pleased she had.

'We could kill two birds with one stone tomorrow, girl. I'll call you up from the audience to take a turn with the mike.'

It was what Patty had hoped for. A chance to prove herself.

'Some of the other bands have been doing it. The crowd luvs it. The rest of the band will go for it.' Excitement flickered in his eyes as he appraised Patty.

'Tomorrow night then,' she said, nodding to reaffirm this really was going to happen.

'We'd better seal the deal.'

For a moment Patty thought he might insist on sealing it with a kiss but that was wishful thinking she realised as he held his hand out. Hers was dwarfed in his as he gave it a firm shake.

The clippie called out, 'Victoria Street station.'

'This is us,' Lee said and Patty got up making her way down the stairs. They jumped off as the bus slowed but it hadn't quite come to a stop and Patty nearly stumbled but Lee's arm snaked out and caught her in the nick of time. He kept it there and even though she liked the feel of his hand resting on her waist, Patty knew enough not to let on she was too keen. She swatted it away with her newfound confidence, 'Oi, cheeky.'

'God luvs a trier.'

He grinned and she took a mental photograph of the dimple in his cheek, knowing she'd be playing the events of this evening over and over in her head in bed later that night. It was a good job it was Friday night because she doubted she'd get a wink of sleep and at least tomorrow morning she could have a lie-in.

As they wound their way on to Matthew Street she could see a handful of people jostling one another to get in the door of the club but the burly man on the door was keeping them in line.

Lee breezed past the huddle of eager club-goers and said something to the doorman who stood aside to let him and Patty pass. A few shouts about queue jumping and pushing in rang out but he didn't seem to hear them as he sailed down the stairs with Patty hot on his heels. She felt like royalty.

They checked in their coats with the red-headed cloakroom girl and Patty caught Lee giving her an admiring once over in her blue box jacket and pencil skirt.

The infectious beat of the rock 'n' roll being played hard out by a group of lads all in matching leather gear washed over them and Patty's body began to spontaneously move to the rhythm.

She shouted up at Lee, 'I need to find my friends.'

'I'll catch up with yer, Alan me manager's over there.' He gestured over to a dapper man in a suit with short back and sides, not the longer hair of his compatriots. He was smoking and holding himself slightly aloof from the crowd as he watched the band on stage.

Patty was reluctant to leave Lee's side but she was also eager to lose herself in the music with Bernie and Linda so she ducked and dived around the room until she spied Bernie's blonde head bobbing about near the stage.

There was a third girl between them and as Patty homed in on them she noticed she was dressed strangely and dancing a little awkwardly as though unused to the music.

She was wearing jeans but not like any jeans Patty had seen before and she'd a sweater on which wasn't anything like the fashions Patty liked to keep abreast of when she window-shopped. She forgot about the girl's strange outfit as she felt her bum get pinched and, swinging round was met by three likely lads all grinning. She gave them a withering look before moving out of reach alongside Bernie.

'Patty!' Her friend didn't pause in her bopping. 'You've got some explaining to do, queen,' she shouted over the raucous music. 'Linda told me you had a personal escort here.'

Patty grinned and hollered back, 'I'll tell you all about it when they take a break.' Bernie nodded and Linda ducked her head around the girl in the middle and shouted out a hello.

The girl eyed Patty curiously.

'Who's your new pal?' Patty shouted in Bernie's ear.

'Her name's Sabrina.'

The rest of what Bernie bellowed was lost in the screaming and music. She'd have to wait until later to find out, Patty thought, beginning to do the twist.

Chapter Twenty-two

The leather-clad lads' set came to a raucous end and as they packed up their gear to clear the stage for the next group, Bernie and Linda announced they were busting and ducked off to join the queue for the lav. That left Patty and the girl she'd yet to be introduced to milling about on their own. Patty spoke up, eyeing her up and down once more, 'I'm Patty. Patty Hamilton, Bernie's bezzie mate.'

Patty Hamilton! Sabrina's mind raced. This was Nicole's, the young Australian with whom her conversation had triggered this trip back in time, mother. She looked just like her daughter.

She stared hard at her already knowing they were going to become friends.

'Sabrina Flooks,' the girl replied. She was pretty despite her odd get-up but she'd a frightened look about her. It was the sort of look Patty had seen before whenever new kids had arrived at the home. A lost look of not belonging anywhere.

'Do you work with Bernie then?'

Sabrina shook her head, mulling over how to word the story of how she came to meet the girl with the teased-back, blonde hair and kind brown eyes. She'd been an angel in Sabrina's book, sent to look after her when things had been at their bleakest. A sign that she'd be alright.

195

Patty was looking at her expectantly and as she'd done with Bernie she left out the part of her tale that would have people thinking she was doolally.

The part where she'd walked determinedly up and down the pavement outside Hudson's Bookshop without breathing a word of her plan to anyone. She'd walked back and forth to the point of blisters forming on her heels and, despondent, had been about to give up and go home. It was getting late and someone might call the police thinking she was casing the bookstore.

She'd been here before though and she hadn't given up. 'Give it one last go, girl,' she'd told herself, 'for your mam. G'won.'

That was when she'd felt the air thicken. It wasn't anything tangible like when a peasouper fog descended. It was more a sensation akin to wading through water. It had been followed by a feeling of rushing as though wind was whistling past her, only there was no wind.

For a moment Sabrina had felt unsteady on her feet as though the ground beneath her was out of kilter and she leaned against the shop frontage of Hudson's. It took a few blinks of her eyes to register that she was still on Bold Street only it was different to the one she'd been standing on only seconds earlier. For one thing, the street she'd been standing on had been dark, illuminated by street lights and the twinkling Christmas lights overhead.

Now, it was daylight.

She latched on to the Christmas lights strewn over the road in readiness for darkness and saw the cars passing under them were different. A blue Mini puttered past followed by a gleaming Austin Morris which she only recognised because Flo's dad had driven one when they were children.

Her eyes swept the scene either side of her. The street felt posher somehow. There was no sign of peeling paint on the shop frontages which gleamed with glossy black and smart gold detailing. Women in pillbox hats and cropped coats swished past her and the men were dressed sharply in suits.

She was garnering the odd curious stare and she realised how out of place she looked in her jeans, sweater and bomber jacket with her hair loose around her shoulders. She wished she could melt into the wall. For a girl who didn't like standing out this was the second time she'd been in this predicament.

Sabrina's attention turned to the bookshop she was standing in front of and she felt a frisson of excitement tinged with fear. If she'd needed confirmation that she'd stepped back to another time it was staring back at her.

Hudson's had been replaced by Cripps, Son & Co Outfitters just as it had been before.

A well-heeled woman pushed the doors open and stepped outside, pausing to eye Sabrina warily.

In a gush, Sabrina asked the stranger, 'What year is this?'

The woman's eyes were fringed with unnaturally long lashes and Sabrina was mesmerised as she watched them flutter as she replied, 'Nineteen sixty-two of course.' She took a step to distance herself from the bizarrely dressed young woman but then the good Samaritan she'd been raised to be took hold as she asked. 'Are you feeling alright, dear? You're very pale. There's a café up the road. Would you like a cup of tea?' She was already reaching into her handbag.

'No, thank you. I'm ahright, ta,' Sabrina replied as a crushing disappointment surged. To be so close to the year she'd gone missing and yet it might as well have been ten years. She hurried away. There was no time for tea and sympathy. She needed to get on with what she'd come here to do which was look for her mam. The sooner she could establish whether or not she was here on a fool's errand the sooner she could step back to her own time and make things up with Adam.

With no idea where to begin looking, Sabrina simply walked trying rather futilely to blend into the shop frontages. Nineteen sixty-two was only a year prior to when she'd gone missing. There was a chance she might recognise her mother going blithely about her business here on Bold Street, unaware of what would happen to her baby daughter the next year. She felt sure she'd know her as soon as she clapped eyes on her. She ignored the voice whispering that to simply bump into her was a tiny chance indeed. Nor did she give any thought as to how an explanation as to who she was would be received. She didn't know how any of this worked because she was two-years-old in 1962. What would she do if she saw herself as a baby? It was too strange to even contemplate.

If such an encounter were to happen, her mother would think her bonkers, of course, just as Aunt Evie had when she'd reached out to her when she'd tripped back to 1928. At least she could plant the seed that things had turned out alright for her. That she'd been found, and given a loving home. Perhaps when the inevitable happened and she vanished in a year from now her mam could take comfort in the words of the strange young woman she'd met who'd pro-claimed to be her daughter from the future. It was all she could hope for.

The alternative she mused hopefully, as she scanned the faces of every woman steering a pushchair down the busy street, was that she would stumble across her mother looking for her lost daughter as she traversed time herself trying to find her.

Sabrina had never once entertained the idea that her mam was anything other than desperate to find her.

Without being aware of it she'd reached Brides of Bold Street. The exterior was no different but the gown in the window denoted the era with its knee-length swing skirt. The lacework on the sleeves was superb, Sabrina thought ad-miringly. And then guilt wormed its way through her. Poor Aunt Evie. She'd told her she needed fresh air. What would she think when she didn't come home? Would she surmise she'd slipped back in time or would she worry something sin-ister had happened to her?

'You've been selfish, Sabrina, selfish,' she whispered. The urge to push open the door and run to the workroom where she was sure Aunt Evie would be giving the treadle of the old Singer what for, was overwhelming. She'd only been gone a short while but she was suddenly desperate to smell the fa-miliar mix of tea and biscuits underwritten faintly by Aunt Evie's ciggies of choice, Woodbines.

She moved towards the door and then hesitated.

She'd been here once before. Oh not *here*, literally. It had been 1928 and her aunt's business a fledgeling one, but the outcome would be the same. Aunt Evie wouldn't know her.

There'd be no misshapen mug produced from which to drink a cup of tea along with a garibaldi biscuit to nibble on. She'd be sent on her way.

In the end, she couldn't help herself. She pushed open the door, hearing the bell jangle as she stepped inside the shop. Her home.

'I'll be with you in just a tick, luv,' a voice that made Sabrina smile sang out from the workroom.

She wouldn't stay long, just a moment but long enough to stroke the fabric of the full Princess Margaretesque gown the lone mannequin on the shop floor was swathed in. As she did so, the familiarity of the shop, which although different thanks to her modernising touches, smacked of Aunt Evie, love washed over her. It rejuvenated her and she exited the shop before her aunt could come out and question who she was and what she wanted.

Sabrina carried on her way, traversing the length and breadth of Bold Street. Hours had passed and her feet were aching and sore. The blister that had threatened had now erupted.

Tears prickled as the futility of what she was doing sank in and she hobbled back to Cripps. She'd been foolish. She shouldn't have tempted fate. She should have telephoned Adam and apologised for upsetting him. His mam was a tender spot which she'd bruised further and he'd only not wanted her to do what she'd gone and done because he cared. She badly wanted to feel his arms around her, his lips on hers.

She continued to walk back and forth in front of the shop but it was to no avail and as the evening began to set in so did fear. She couldn't stay out here much longer. She was sore, chilled to the bone, and exhausted. She needed to rest and try and again later.

Sabrina looked around her and there it was at the top of the street, her sanctuary.

This time there would be no pews to sit on as only the shell of St Luke's remained but the flagstones out of the way of the passing foot traffic would have to do. She sat down on the Berry Street side and closed her eyes briefly. She'd have dozed off if she wasn't so cold and, opening her eyes once more she wrapped her arms around herself in an attempt to ward the cutting wind off. Her gaze was fixed on the denim of her jeans and she tried to think about nice things like the salty taste of Adam's lips after he'd been eating chips.

'Are you ahright there, queen?' a voice asked, and Sabrina looked up to see a girl with brown eyes that reminded her a little of Flo. Her blonde hair had telltale dark roots just beginning to show and her expression was open and concerned. The girl stepped off the pavement up onto the staggered flagstones on top of which Sabrina perched, huddled into herself.

This might be the only person who offered her kindness today, Sabrina thought, staring up at the kind face. Everybody else was rushing past eager to get home or to wherever it was they were going. Realising an opportunity had presented itself or rather herself, Sabrina decided not to mess about. She needed to grab it or she could very well wind up with hypothermia.

'Not really, no. I don't have anywhere to go tonight and I'm freezin.'

'You poor thing. I'm Bernie. Here put my coat on for a bit and warm yourself up.'

'I'm Sabrina and that's very kind but you'll be cold then.'

'I don't feel the cold me.' She grinned, already shrugging out of the forest green wool coat.

Sabrina gratefully draped it overtop of her own jacket. It was the sitting that had made her so cold but she'd run out of steam and had needed to rest. 'Ta very much. I'll just borrow it for a minute or two.'

'Where are you from, like? You sound like a Liverbird.' She sounded local, Bernie thought wondering what had brought her here to St Luke's with nowhere to go.

'I am but I'm erm, not from around here.' Sabrina was tight-lipped. She'd spoken the truth just in a round-about way.

If she didn't want to elaborate that was up to her Bernie thought seeing a need as she made her an offer. 'Listen, girl, you can sit out here in the freezin' cold or you can come with me. I'm on me way to a club. I've arranged to meet my bezzie mate there. You won't be cold in there! Then, you can have our sofa for the night. We've a flat over in Kensington.'

Sabrina couldn't believe her luck and could've kissed her. It wasn't the offer of the sofa that saw a tear escape and work its way down to her chin where it plopped off onto the coat though but rather the fact she wasn't alone anymore.

'C'mon now. None of that, we've dancing to be getting on with.'

'I don't think I'm going to be up to much dancing, I've a blister that's killing me.'

Bernie produced a plaster from her handbag, proclaiming to having every medical emergency necessity known to mankind inside it. 'You just never know when someone will need it, sweetheart,' she said passing it to Sabrina.

She wondered as she took the sticking plaster whether Bernie was an angel in disguise who'd been sent to help her. She saw to her heel and then, getting to her feet, insisted Bernie take her coat back. 'I'm toasty now.'

They set off back down Bold Street once more but this time Sabrina felt buoyant. She'd spend the night with Bernie and think about tomorrow when it came.

Sabrina realised it was the Cavern they were going to as they ducked off Victoria Street, emerging from the laneway on to Matthew Street. It wasn't the Cavern she knew though. The Cavern of her era was boarded up with talk of excavating and regenerating the underground club the Beatles had made famous.

The last time she'd made a trek here had been with Flo and half of Liverpool on a pilgrimage to mourn John Lennon. The news he'd been shot had been devastating for their city and they'd been in a daze for days afterwards.

This Cavern had bold black lettering visible as you drew nearer to let you know it was there and bills advertising who was playing were plastered above the nondescript arched entrance with its CAVERN sign. A burly, suit-clad bouncer on the door was keeping the lengthening queue of eager club-goers in order.

Sabrina recounted none of this to Patty, instead, she simply said, 'I'm from here originally but I don't live here now. I came back to find someone but had no luck and Bernie came across me freezin' my arse off outside the bombed-out church. I'm in a pickle and she offered me your sofa for the night which was very kind of her. I hope you don't mind? It'll only be for the one night. I'll get myself sorted in the morning and be out of your hair. I promise.'

There was still a piece of Patty that had never left the Toxteth Courts. It was the part that had instilled compassion in her. Because it was there, she'd been taught that you might not have much yourself but you always did what you could to help those who had even less. As such she replied, 'It's not a bother, Sabrina, so long as you don't mind our antwacky sofa.' She smiled to reassure the anxious-looking girl.

Bernie was a right one for taking wounded birds under her wing she thought as Sabrina smiled back at her gratefully. It was another reason she loved her pal with all her heart. Look at the way she'd gravitated towards helping her when she'd first arrived at Strawberry Field. They both knew what it was like not to have anywhere else to go and if Bernie thought Sabrina was alright then she was alright in her book too. But that didn't mean she wasn't curious about who, exactly, Sabrina Flooks was.

'Who are you looking for? Liverpool's a big city but everybody seems to know someone who knows someone.'

Sabrina had already decided she liked this girl and so she confided. 'I'm looking for my mam.'

'Your mam?'

She nodded. 'We were separated years ago and I heard she used to visit Bold Street often. It was the only place I could think of to start looking. It's like a needle in a haystack though. I was stupid to come back.'

'What about work then? Are you on a holiday, like?'

'No. I mean yes. I work in a bridal shop and I'm erm on a short sabbatical I suppose you'd call it. My purse was stolen today so I'm brassic, like.' The fib was a necessity, Sabrina told herself.

Patty thought a sabbatical was something only teachers took but she didn't voice this. 'That's terrible, girl. Did you report it?'

'I couldn't see the point. There were that many people around at the time it could have been anyone and besides, they'd have been long gone by the time I got to the station or managed to find a police officer.'

Patty nodded. That made sense. She scanned the sea of heads hoping for a glimpse of Lee as she replied absently. 'A bridal shop must be a luvly place to work. I'm a typist for a car manufacturing company. It's dead boring but it pays me way.'

Sabrina's face grew animated. This was a topic she was happy to chat about. 'It is. There's nothing else I'd rather do. I feel like I'm making our clients' dreams come true. It's as if I'm a fairy godmother of sorts when I see their faces when they try their gowns on for the first time.'

This was something Patty could relate to, not the wedding dresses but the passion behind Sabrina's words. She turned her attention back to Sabrina whispering almost conspiratorially. 'I'm a singer or at least I'm going to be and that's how I feel about singing. There's nothing else I want to do.' Patty was suddenly desperate to share the news of what had happened after she'd left work this evening and couldn't wait a second longer for Bernie to come back.

Instead, she bent Sabrina's ear, telling her how Lee Carter the lead singer in an up and coming local band who also happened to work at the same factory she did had waited for her after work. She'd reached the part about the invitation he'd challenged her with to get on stage and sing a number with his band the following night, adding, 'It's what I've dreamed of. A chance like this to prove what I can do but now it's going to happen I feel sick with nerves just thinking about it.'

'What's all this, then, girl?' Bernie reappeared with Linda behind her catching the tail end of the conversation.

Patty repeated what she'd just told Sabrina and Bernie nearly deafened her with an excited scream. Several heads spun around to see what had her excited before turning back to their own conversations. Sabrina, despite the day she'd had, couldn't help but smile as she found herself caught up in the girls' excitement.

'It's happening, Pats. It's finally happening,' Bernie stated. 'I can feel it in me water.'

Patty grinned back at her. Maybe this was the start of all the plans they'd had becoming a reality. One thing was certain, she'd have to put her best foot forward tomorrow night and sing like she'd never sung before.

'Oh my God, girl, he's coming over,' Linda said. It took all Patty's will not to spin around to see for herself but she was determined to play it cool.

'How's our star singer, then?' Lee appeared alongside her. 'Evening, ladies. You're all looking gorgeous tonight.' He draped his arm casually around Patty's shoulder and Bernie looked fit to burst.

Patty shrugged his arm off. 'I'm not your girlfriend, Lee Carter,' she said.

Bernie's eyes widened at this self-assured, unrecognisable version of her friend.

'The Dynamos are boss,' Linda said, her attention having been swayed from Lee to the lads setting up on the stage.

'They're ahright like but they're not a patch on Lee and the Sundials.'

'Says you!' Patty said.

Lee grinned. 'Places to be, ladies. I'll see you here tomorrow night then, Mysterious Margaux.'

He disappeared into the crowd and Patty watched him until she could no longer see him.

'He doesn't half fancy himself,' Linda muttered. 'And who's this Mysterious Margaux?'

'Not half as much as I fancy him,' Patty giggled not bothering to explain the name

The three girls laughed with her. The band was doing a soundcheck and Patty felt a tap on her shoulder. She spun around hoping it was Lee come back again. A girl she didn't know, with black hair, teased so high she'd struggle to walk under a bridge, and a hard set to her mouth leaned in and said, 'I'd watch out for Lee Carter if I were you, luv. He's an eye for the ladies that one. He'll break your heart.'

She moved off back to a crowd of girls who were preening and primping waiting for the music to start.

'She's only jealous, like,' Bernie said, having overheard the one-sided exchange. 'Ignore her.'

Patty flashed her a grateful smile but the girl's comments had made her feel a little ill.

The singer introduced the band and Linda said she was in danger of fainting he was so gorgeous. Patty resolved not to dwell on the warning she'd received as she concentrated on the band who'd taken to the stage.

It was then Sabrina's eyes settled on a fella across the room. She knew his face instantly. She'd have known it anywhere. Her voice had a wavering inflexion as she turned to the three girls, 'That man over there talking to the lad with the dark hair, in the far corner. Is that John Lennon?'

'Oh him, yeah he's in the Beatles, they're boss.' Linda stood up on tippy-toes to see who she was on about before turning toward the stage once more.

'They're going places, they are,' Bernie said.

Patty stared over too. 'You know, I think I met him once at Strawberry Field at one of the summer parties but I'm not sure. He was only a lad then. He said he was going to be a musician though.'

For the second time that day, a tear trickled down Sabrina's cheek. She wanted desperately to push her way over and say—*say what, Sabrina?* She couldn't change what had already happened. The band launched into a fast number and the crowd erupted.

Sabrina was jostled about as Merseybeat fever took over the room and she looked to the stage. When she looked back the Beatle had gone.

Chapter Twenty-three

'I didn't warn you it stinks of fish, sorry!' Bernie laughed as she, Patty and Sabrina ducked around the back of the darkened fishmonger's and made their way up the stairs to the flat above it.

It did smell fishy, Sabrina thought, but she didn't care; she was grateful to have a roof over her head for the night. She piled in the door behind the other two, standing next to Patty in the dark as Bernie shuffled into the room, hands out in front of her. There was the sound of jangling and she reappeared with coins to feed the meter.

A moment later the small space was bathed in light. Sabrina had to ball her hand into a fist to stop herself reaching for the light switch beside the door. It needed to be flicked on and off three times or... she didn't know what but it always gave her a sense of dread when her rituals weren't completed.

This wasn't her flat though and she was grateful to Patty who was pointing out the sofa. It was the distraction she needed and she moved over to the faded brown two-seater. The fabric on the arms was worn thin and the cushions on the seats lumpy but to Sabrina, who was ready to collapse, it looked heavenly.

'You can get your head down there tonight. It came with the flat and it's seen better days but its clean and we'll put a sheet down and find you some blankets.' Patty's smile was apologetic as she added, 'You won't be cold at any rate.' She moved over to the heater and it made a ticking sound as the bars slowly glowed orange.

'Thank you,' Sabrina murmured and she was grateful from the bottom of her heart to these two girls. 'I'll sleep like a baby.' She stared around the space that she was to spend the night in.

Patty followed her gaze about the room. 'There's a toilet, sink and bath in there but never much in the way of hot water, I'm sorry. Bernie and I usually top it up with the kettle and get in quick smart after each other. Our room's through there.'

Sabrina looked to the open door leading to a room that wasn't much more than an alcove. She could see clothes strewn across the bed and dirty laundry on the floor.

'That's down to Bernie, she's not one for picking up after herself.'

'I heard that, Patty,' Bernie said from the corner of the room designated for the kitchen. 'I'm rebelling against all those years of never being able to have a thing out of place,' she tossed over her shoulder to Sabrina.

Sabrina looked at Patty questioningly and Patty shrugged. 'Me and Bernie spent a good part of our lives in a children's home. Neither of us were orphans though. We were taken there or abandoned more like. Me brother, Davey was sent out to Australia for a so-called better life five years ago.'

'And I don't see any of my brothers. I've four of them but we're all scattered like,' Bernie stated.

'I know what it's like to be left,' Sabrina said. She'd been so lucky though. She could easily have been picked up and taken to the police station and put in a home. Or, like Davey, shipped to Australia. The thought of how different her life could have been if her Aunt Evie hadn't taken her in made her shudder.

Patty waited to see if Sabrina would say more but when she didn't she breezed on. 'The flat's only meant to be let to one but we don't give the landlord any grief and he doesn't give us any.' She sat down in front of the heater rubbing her hands together. Neither she nor Bernie had taken their coats off yet and Sabrina had no intention of removing her jacket either until the heater began to kick in.

Sabrina moved over to where Bernie was filling the teapot with boiling water. The kitchen consisted of a tiny worktop space, a sink, an old fridge that juddered as Sabrina looked at it as though to prove it were still in good working order and an even more ancient oven.

'Me mam didn't teach me much,' Bernie said to Sabrina 'But she did teach me to always warm the pot first. You could give that a swill out while I make us all some toast.'

Sabrina did as Bernie asked, her tummy rumbling at the thought of toast. She dropped a couple of bags in the pot and refilled it as Bernie sawed doorstops off a loaf before setting them to toast under the grill.

'Could you run those under the tap for us? While the tea brews.' Bernie pointed to the sink which had two breakfast plates with toast crumbs littering them along with a butter-smeared knife and two teacups.' Sabrina obliged as Bernie apologised that they only had the two cups, two of every-thing in fact and would she mind drinking her tea from an old jam jar. 'We're always in a rush of a morning to get off to work. We never seem to have time to tidy the breakfast things away.'

Bernie had filled Sabrina in on her work as a machinist on their walk to the Cavern earlier.

It wasn't long before the girls, in their stockinged feet, or socks where Sabrina was concerned and now divested of their coats and jacket were sat around the heater drinking tea and eating jam smeared toast.

Sabrina, whose stomach had been empty, didn't think she'd ever tasted anything so delicious and she thanked the girls again for their kindness in taking her in.

'We know what it's like to have nowhere to go, don't we, Pats?' Bernie said and Patty nodded.

Sabrina felt a bond form with these two girls. Their sto-ries were all different, hers most of all but they each under-stood what it was to be left behind.

Patty and Bernie reminisced about their time at Straw-berry Field. There'd been laughter and occasional mischief but also sadness and loneliness. They'd not been mistreated but they had missed out on what so many children took for granted; a family of their own to love and support them. And, then there was what had happened to Davey.

Sabrina could hear the desolation in Patty's voice as she spoke about losing her brother.

'But we had each other. We were each other's family weren't we, Bernie?' Patty said, injecting brightness into her voice.

Bernie nodded wholeheartedly.

Again, Sabrina counted her blessings that Aunt Evie had stopped when her three-year-old self had tugged at her skirt and asked where her mam was.

Patty was talking once more, telling Sabrina about the promise she'd made her mother as she lay dying to keep her and her brother together come what may. 'Me and Bernie we're going to go to Australia to find him and bring him home, aren't we, Bernie?'

Sabrina wanted to tell her that she would find her brother but then she'd have to tell her how she knew this. The toast stuck in her throat and she coughed to clear it. It was too soon. They needed to know her better and to trust her before she told them the truth about where she'd come from otherwise they would wonder if there was something wrong with her and whether they'd done the right thing in letting her stay.

'If I can knock them out tomorrow night when I sing at the club then maybe I'll get some gigs. The extra money will help our savings no end.' She beamed at Bernie over the rim of her cup. 'We'll be out there in no time, Bernie.' Her mind drifted imagining what her brother would look like now he was nearly a man.

Sabrina noticed Bernie looked uncomfortable at the mention of Australia and a moment later, as she told her about the fella she'd been seeing, she understood why. Bernie didn't want to go to Australia. She didn't want to leave her boyfriend but she'd not found the courage to tell Patty this.

'My Don's a baker. He works nights with Saturdays off. He sees us right with a loaf or two every day doesn't he, Patty?'

Patty nodded. It was her who looked unhappy this time round and Sabrina guessed she was worried Don might come between her and her friend's long-held plans where her brother was concerned.

Bernie drained her cup then and carried it and her plate back to the kitchenette. She muttered something about a surprise and disappeared into her and Patty's bedroom.

The other two girls watched curiously as she got down on her hands and knees and lifted the skirt of the bed.

'I wouldn't be doing that if I were you, Bernie. God only knows what's under there.' Patty was only half joking.

Bernie ignored her, sliding a package out. She placed it on the bed while she dusted her knees off and then carried it over to Patty. 'G'won then, open it.'

Patty looked up at her questioningly and then, unable to recall the last time she'd had a mystery present to open, she tore the brown paper off.

She gasped, staring down at the folded fabric within. Her fingers stroked it briefly and then she lifted it out and held it up to the light. 'Oh my God, girl, it's amazin'!'

A sleeveless, shift dress hung from her fingers. The colours shimmered in the light. Red, white and black squares on the front, blue, white and yellow on the back. 'Where did you find it?' She frowned then and Bernie read her mind.

'Don't worry I didn't dip into the savings. I made it at work from offcuts.'

Patty was mesmerised. 'I luv it, Bernie.'

'What sort of manager would I be if I didn't make sure my star client was dressed properly for her big break. I've had it under the bed for ages hoping it wouldn't get mildewy but I knew it'd happen, Pats. I knew I'd see you on the stage.'

Patty clambered to her feet and placing the dress reverently on what was to be Sabrina's bed for the night she threw her arms around her pal. 'Thank you.'

Bernie hugged her back and then pushed her away. 'Aren't you going to give us a twirl in it?'

Patty didn't need to be asked twice and she took off for the bedroom, stepping over Bernie's discarded underwear before closing the door.

When she emerged a minute later a transformation had occurred and this time it was Sabrina and Bernie who gasped.

Bernie recovered and clenching her hand she pretended it was a microphone as she donned a deep voice and said, 'Tonight, ladies and gentlemen, here at the Fishmonger's Palace we've a proper treat for you. Tonight,' she looked at Sabrina and whispered, 'drum roll,'

Sabrina obliged by slapping her thighs in the anticipatory beat.

'All the way from Kensington is Liverpool's finest Patricia Hamilton!'

'No, no, no, Bernie, I can't stand being called Patricia you know that.' It came to Patty then in a flash. If a girl wanted to stand out from the crowd she needed to be able to sing, yes, and look the part but she also needed a name that people would remember. 'My name's going to be Margaux with an 'x'. Just Margaux because that sounds much more mysterious than Margaux Hamilton.'

'Margaux.' Bernie tried it on for size. 'I luv it, girl.'

Sabrina nodded her agreement.

Bernie took a deep breath and said, 'Put your hands together and give Margaux a warm welcome.'

Sabrina didn't need a cue this time and she whistled and clapped. A banging sounded on the wall and they all looked at one another wide-eyed before bursting into giggles.

Bernie poked her tongue out at the wall. 'He's a grumpy old sod, ignore him.'

Patty, or rather Margaux, sashayed the few short steps into the centre of the room and struck a pose before launching into Connie Francis's hit Where the Boys Are.

Her voice soared, pure as birdsong, and Sabrina's mouth fell open. The penny had just dropped with a resounding clunk. She'd heard of Margaux. In fact, she was certain Flo's mam and dad had one of her records. She could remember her and Flo peeking around the door of their front room watching Flo's parents dance in a fit of nostalgia to an old record. She closed her eyes, conjuring the cover which had been peeking out behind another on the ground beside the stand the record player sat on. A pretty blonde woman with bobbed hair and enormous blue eyes ringed with lashes too long to be real was just visible. When she opened them again she knew she was looking at the same woman.

Both she and Bernie watched in silence, even him next door ceased to hammer on the wall as, at that moment, in the smelly flat above a fishmonger's in Kensington, a star was born.

Chapter Twenty-four

'How did you sleep?' Bernie shuffled in after ten the next morning yawning. Her hair was mussed and she'd smudges under her eyes from the previous day's make-up.

Sabrina couldn't believe she'd slept so late but then she hadn't a clue what time it was when they'd finally gone to sleep. She pulled herself upright and stretched. 'Well, ta.'

'I'll put the kettle on, Patty's having a wash.'

She rustled about the tiny kitchen and as the kettle began to whistle, Sabrina got up and folded the blankets and sheet away. The room was chilly once more and Bernie appeared with a few coins with which to feed the meter again.

'We keep the meter money in the jar on top of the fridge,' she said, instructing Sabrina to put the heater on.

She did so and went to join Bernie in the kitchen, the nighty she'd borrowed from her trailing on the threadbare carpet behind her.

The tea was made and Patty emerged looking fresh-faced and perky. She said good morning to Sabrina who was mid-yawn and then opened the cupboards over the worktop. She peered inside them as though expecting something to magically jump out for their breakfast and pulling out a box of cereal gave it a shake. It was nearly empty. They'd polished off the bread the night before and the dregs of milk left in the bottle were going in the tea.

She closed the cupboards with a sigh and then her face lit up. 'I say we have a splurge!'

Bernie spun round, milk in hand, to stare at her friend. Splurge was a foreign word to Patty. She raised an eyebrow and waited for her to explain herself.

'I'm going to be earning extra soon if it all goes well tonight. Let's go to Bill's around the corner and have a proper fry-up. C'mon, we deserve a treat.'

Bernie grinned. 'Well, I don't need convincing.'

Sabrina however shifted uncomfortably. She'd already imposed on these two's good natures. She'd not a penny to her name and she didn't want either girl feeling they had to treat her. Especially not when she knew how important money was to Patty and her plans to find her brother.

Reading her mind, Patty laid a hand on her arm. 'You too, of course.'

Sabrina shook her head. 'No, ta, I couldn't.'

'Yes, you can, can't she, Bernie? It's our treat.'

Bernie was emphatic. 'If you won't come then we won't go and we'll all miss out.'

Sabrina raised a smile.

'G'won,' Patty said. 'Get a wash and Bernie will dig out some gear for you.' Both girls had been too polite to question her strange clobber. 'So as you've something fresh to put on like,' she added hastily.

Sabrina, who'd had enough of being on the receiving end of stares the day before didn't care that Bernie's pedal-pusher trousers were a tad too long; she rolled the cuffs up. They looked a little odd with her boots but once she'd borrowed a sweater and the coat Bernie dug out she felt like she fitted right in.

'Let me sort your hair out, girl,' Bernie said, advancing on her with a comb and a can of hairspray.

Patty was tapping her feet impatiently while Bernie backcombed and teased Sabrina's hair within an inch of its life. Sabrina who'd given her free rein stared at herself in the mirror. She was beginning to look like she'd be right at home jiving to Twist and Shout. Flo and Aunt Evie would barely recognise her.

'It suits you,' Bernie declared, eyeing the homemade bee-hive. 'I should have gone into hairdressing, me. I've a flair for it.'

'She thinks because she dies her hair blonde she's missed her calling,' Patty whispered conspiratorially.

Sabrina felt a pang for Florence. 'Ta, Bernie,' she said as Patty urged them out the door.

'I'm starvin'!' Patty called, skipping down the stairs and announcing, 'it stinks of mackerel out here today.'

Sabrina was bringing up the rear and was the not so lucky last tasked with closing the door behind them as the next-door neighbour's door flew open. She'd one foot on the top of the stairs and she paused as a whiskered, rheumy-eyed old man with a missing tooth wagged a finger at her and shouted at her to stop making such a racket of a night before slamming the door closed.

'Don't worry about Mr Timbs, he says that every morning,' Patty laughed a moment later when Sabrina recounted what had happened. 'He luvs us really.'

The café with the uninspiring name of Bill's Café was a short walk down the street past the shops over which their flat perched and around the corner to where a long row of shiny Vespa scooters lined the length of kerb outside a café with red paint trim and a window looking out to the street.

'The mods are out in force then,' Bernie said, pushing the door open. 'It's a bit of a greasy spoon Sabrina but the coffee bars are no good when you want a good old full English breakfast.'

Stepping inside, they were instantly hit by the smell of cigarettes and frying bacon. A bluish haze hovered over the busy café where all but one of the tables was taken and a steady hum of conversation droned like bees.

Bernie shot over to nab the empty table, sitting down triumphantly before calling out to Patty, 'I want the works, Pats.'

After checking Sabrina could get a plate of sausage, bacon, black pudding, beans, eggs and toast down her, Patty instructed Sabrina to join Bernie. She did so, earning a whistle from a group of lads spread out over the tables by the back wall. They were all decked out in khaki army parkers with fur-lined hoods. There were cups and saucers in front of them and an overflowing ashtray was the table's centrepiece.

Sabrina's face flamed and she hastily sat down with her back to them at the table alongside Bernie.

Patty joined them a moment later also on the receiving end of a whistle. She muttered something about bloody mods thinking they owned the place and then she and Bernie fell about laughing reminiscing over a Teddy boy Bernie had dated not long after she'd left Strawberry Field.

'Do you remember the time he got a cob on polishing his shoes because he got nugget on his shirt and that was that, he wouldn't go out?' Patty spluttered. 'He was a proper peacock.'

Bernie grinned and explained to Sabrina. 'He was forever shining his shoes, winklepickers they were, and you could see your face in them by the time he'd finished. He was my first proper boyfriend like and a dead loss he turned out to be. He was always skint because he'd spent his wages on another of his fancy suits.'

A lad with spots on his cheeks and dark stubble decorating his chin elbowed his pal next to him and called out, 'Oi, luv! Yeah, you in the pink sweater, whar are your other two wishes because here I am, sweetheart.'

There was raucous laughter.

The cheesy chat-up line was aimed at Sabrina but Bernie stepped in with a lightning-quick comeback. 'Dream on, mate. She doesn't go out with lads who ride scooters. She prefers a man with a car.'

There was some catcalling and the café's barrel-like namesake, Bill, an apron tied around his beachball girth and a red face from the storm he'd been frying up in the kitchen waddled over. He was balancing three plates with the ease of someone who'd done it before, and pausing, he told the lads to settle down or they could sling their hooks before asking them if they were going to order something to eat because he wasn't running a doss house. Cigarettes were ground out and with much scraping of chairs, they got up and left, the ring leader blowing the trio a kiss on his way out.

Their plates were set down in front of them and the girls set about demolishing what might as well have been lunch given the lateness of the morning. A sound akin to ten hairdryers all going at once drowned out any conversation but they were too busy eating to care.

Patty was forking up the last of her beans when her face went red, then white and then red again. 'Oh my God, girls it's him. It's Lee Carter.' Her mind was racing and she wished she hadn't scoffed her food down so fast. Just as he'd waited for her outside work the night before he had to have come here seeking her out.

He stood in the entrance and scanned the room, his blue eyes alighting on her.

Sabrina saw several girls' heads turn towards him. She could see why Patty fancied him and she and Bernie tried to act nonchalant as he made his way over to their table with Bernie hissing at Patty to wipe the sauce off her chin. She flicked her a grateful glance and did so.

'Fancy meeting you here,' Lee said, flashing the dimple that made Patty's knees go weak.

'Fancy,' Bernie murmured, earning herself a kick in the shins under the table.

'Can I join youse?'

Patty seemed to have been struck dumb and so it was Bernie who intervened once more. 'Pull up a chair no one's stopping you.'

Lee went and got one of the recently vacated seats, eyeing the mess left behind on the table. 'Bit of a kip this place.'

Bernie bristled but kept her mouth shut as she didn't want to receive another boot.

He lifted the chair over and sat down on it backwards his arms folded and resting on the top of the back as he gazed at Patty in a manner that excluded the other two.

'I came to see if you fancy a run out in me Jag. When you're finished, like.'

Bernie's eyes widened at the mention of his car.

Patty had no intention of playing hard to get and she pushed her plate away. 'I'm done. I'll see you girls at home later.' She got up and he helped her into her coat, then slinging her bag over her shoulder and throwing an excited glance back at them she followed him out the door.

'I bet it's his dad's car,' Bernie muttered. 'What do you think of him? He's too smooth for my liking.'

Sabrina was apt to agree but didn't feel it was her place to pass judgment. She put her knife and fork down on her plate. She was full to the brim. 'That was gorgeous. Ta very much.'

Bernie agreed then glanced at her watch. 'I'm meeting my Don at The Palace in an hour. I can't ice skate to save meself but he likes it. The things we do for love.' She winked. 'You can come with us if you like?'

'No thanks.' Sabrina shook her head recalling her roller skating attempts with Florence, besides which she didn't want to gate crash their date. She'd try her luck down Bold Street again today and if the magic happened and she found her way back to her own time then Patty and Bernie would forget all about the strange girl who'd dossed down on their sofa. If she remained stuck here then she'd have to find a way of earning some money. She'd cross that bridge when she came to it.

Bernie drained her teacup. 'Worra you gonna do, Sabrina?'

'I'll head to Bold Street and keep looking.' She shrugged, 'Today could be the day I find her.'

'I didn't mean that although I hope you do. I meant you're here now and you've got no money.'

Sabrina opened her mouth to say she didn't plan on availing them of their hospitality for another night but Bernie had raised her hand.

'You'll stay with us. We won't see you on the street. You worked in a bridal shop you said.'

Sabrina nodded.

'You know your way around a sewing machine then?'

'I do, yeah.' Sabrina wasn't sure where this was heading.

'There's a machinist job going at the factory. You can come in with me on Monday and show Mrs Fraser in personnel what you can do. She'll be glad to be saved the job of interviewing.'

Sabrina stared at Bernie. For the second time since they'd met she could have kissed her. She really was proving to be her guardian angel. Then a thought occurred to her. 'Won't she want references?'

Bernie shook her head. 'No, I'll vouch for you. I'll say you're me cousin and that you've been working down in London. So long as you show her you're capable she'll be happy. She's always on about how hard it is to find good machinists.' Curiosity got the better of her and she blurted, 'Were you down in London?'

Sabrina stared at the dregs of tea in her cup. Bernie had been so very good to her. She deserved the truth. All Sabrina could do was tell her it. Whether she believed her or not would be up to Bernie.

She met Bernie's trusting brown eyes across the table and said, 'Bernie, there's something I should tell you about where it is I come from.'

Sabrina could tell Bernie was dubious when she'd finished talking. She didn't blame her but Bernie was by nature a trusting girl.

'I suppose it explains the odd clobber you were wearing yesterday.'

'Ta very much!'

'Sorry, but those jeans of yours and that sweater, they're not like anything I've seen in the shops. It's not the first time I've heard talk of strange goings on where Bold Street's concerned. One of the girls at work told me something odd like that happened to her cousin. I'm open minded me.' She laughed, 'I still believe there's fairies at the bottom of the garden.' Then she was quiet digesting everything, staring into her empty teacup before looking up suddenly. 'Tell me something from the future then.'

John Lennon's face swam in front of Sabrina's eyes. No, she'd not share that. It was too sad. There was John F Kennedy's assassination too and Martin Luther King Jr. *C'mon, Sabrina, think of something cheerful!* She played with the serviette twisting it in her hand as she tried to remember her history lessons from school. It was no good though because she'd daydreamed her way through most of them and then the obvious became clear and she gazed directly at Bernie. 'The Beatles go on to be the biggest band the world's ever known.'

Bernie's eyes saucered. 'The Beatles that play at the Cavern? I mean, they're boss like and they're going places but the biggest band in the world?'

'Yeah.' Sabrina nodded emphatically. 'In another year or so Beatlemania will sweep the world—watch this space.'

'Beatlemania,' Bernie echoed, wonder in her voice. 'What else?'

'Erm, well in my time we have a female prime minister, Margaret Thatcher. She's very tough, oh and Prince Charles marries Lady Diana Spencer in July nineteen eighty-one and their wedding is televised around the world. It was a huge event. She's fabulous, very pretty and a fashion plate who's always in the magazines. People love her. Erm...' She drummed her fingers racking her brains for more.

'Enough! Me head's spinning,' Bernie said, shaking it. 'I believe you. What reason would you have for making it up?'

'None.' Sabrina gave her a grateful smile.

Bernie checked the time and said, 'If you're going to Bold Street you'll need bus fare.' She dug around in her pockets. 'Here's a few bob to tide you over.'

'I'll pay you back, Bernie,' Sabrina said, taking the money gratefully.

Bernie waved her hand dismissively, explaining where she could hop on a bus to take her to that part of the city. They talked on for a few minutes until Bernie, with a glance at her wristwatch, shot up out of her seat announcing she'd have to run if she didn't want to be late meeting Don. As she wound her scarf around her neck before shooting out the door she said, 'Me and Pats, we'll help you, Sabrina. You're not alone, girl.'

Sabrina had watched her go, thankful the girl with the teased blonde hair had stopped to ask if she was alright as she'd huddled on the cold stone flags of St Luke's. She didn't know what she would have done otherwise. Catching a look from the harassed café owner and interpreting it to mean if she wasn't going to order anything else she could let someone else have her seat, Sabrina got to her feet. There was no point whiling away the day in here, tempting as it was with the toasty temperature. With a glance at the street outside, she donned her borrowed coat and stepped onto the pavement heading in the direction of where Bernie had said she could catch the bus.

Chapter Twenty-five

Patty watched as droplets of rain hit the windscreen of the immaculate blue Jag, Lee had parked outside the café. The wipers swished back and forth sporadically and the radio was softly playing something jazzy. The window on the driver's side was halfway open and Lee would flick the ash off the end of his cigarette out of it now and again as the car purred down the streets. It had been his suggestion they take a run out to the beach.

'It'll stop in a minute,' he said, turning off the road and parking near the sandy dunes of Crosby Beach. 'And we can go for a walk.'

He didn't sound very convinced of it, Patty thought, unconvinced herself as she glanced up at the gunmetal grey sky through the passenger window. The wind was whipping the dune grasses so that they were almost bent flat and, overhead, seagulls screeched. She didn't care though. It was a perfect day for a drive to the beach so far as she was concerned because she was sitting next to Lee.

At that moment, a white plop landed on the windscreen, sliding down in a gooey smear causing Lee to curse. Then, remembering who was sitting next to him, he threw her an apology.

'I wonder if it's good luck for a bird to poop on your windscreen.' Patty smiled, amused by whichever gull had had the audacity to bomb the Jag.

'Where did you get that from?' Lee stared at her.

'Well, it's supposed to be good luck for bird poo to land on your head.'

Lee shook his head. 'That's mad that is.'

She had to agree. She didn't think she'd count herself fortunate if it were to happen to her.

Lee flicked the butt out of the window and opened the glove box, rifling through its contents before pulling out a rag. He'd a frown on his face as he eyed the windscreen and the offending poo once more. 'I can't have that on there. Back in a jiffy, luv.' He got out of the car and wiped it off. Then, tossing the rag on the back seat, he clambered back in, closing the door and trapping a blast of fresh, salty air in the vehicle with them.

'Sorry about that.' He grinned.

'It's a gorgeous car. I can understand you wanting to keep it nice,' Patty said, hoping he wouldn't be the sort of lad who was more in love with his car than his girlfriend. One of the girls at work had a fella like that and she always moaning about him.

He studied her for a moment with those intensely blue eyes of his and in the end Patty squirmed in her seat. 'What?' Perhaps she still had sauce on her chin.

'I gorra tell you something.' Lee twisted toward her in his seat.

Patty met his gaze, uncertain as to what was coming and whether she wanted to hear it given the serious expression on his face.

'I don't tell birds this usually but this isn't me car. It's our kid's, like. He's older than me and earning good money working in a bank. Which me dad never lets me forget. Pete, that's me bruvver, he's ahright he is. He looks out for me. Makes it bearable at home, like.'

Patty fancied if she hadn't been a little in love with him already the boyishly sheepish look on his face after this admission made her fall head over heels. He'd wanted to impress her! Gone was the cocky lad who swaggered about the place. She thought she might just prefer this version.

'I don't mind. I don't want a fella who's forever polishing his car anyway.'

Lee gave her a grateful smile and then his voice softened. 'I don't think you're like most girls, are you Mysterious Margaux? That's why I told you the truth. I could tell it wouldn't impress you anyway.'

'No,' she agreed. 'It wouldn't. But you're right. I'm not like most girls.' He didn't know how true this was, though not in the sense he meant. She doubted many of the girls he'd gone out with had been abandoned by their father or had their brother snatched and sent to the other side of the world.

Patty kneaded her hands together in her lap and gazed out at the grasses valiantly fighting the wind. For a moment she imagined Davey running through that grass toward the stretch of sand that lay beyond. Unbidden, a tear rolled down her cheek. She wasn't aware it was there until she felt Lee's soft touch wiping it away.

'Have I said something to upset you? Pete says I'm always putting me foot in things.' He was bewildered.

Patty shook her head. 'No, it's not you. I meant it though, you know, when I said there's nothing mysterious about me.'

'You're like an exotic flower I saw once on a school trip to some gardens. Shy and beautiful.' There was no hint of the cheeky banter she'd heard from him previously. 'I've watched you coming and going from the factory and you stand out just like that flower did.'

'There's nothing exotic about me, Lee,' Patty said. 'Me mam died when I was ten and my brother Davey and I were sent to a children's home soon after because our dad didn't want us. You see, nothing mysterious or exotic in that.' She shrugged. 'That's how I know Bernie. We were both brought up at Strawberry Field Children's Home.'

'What was it like?'

'It was ahright, like. We weren't mistreated and I know there's other kids who had it far worse than we did at Strawberry Field. We had food in our stomachs and a bed at night. We even had summer parties. They were fun. But it wasn't ever a proper home, you know with a mam and dad who care about you. Me and Bernie became each other's family along with me brother Davey of course.'

Lee nodded slowly and they sat in silence, hearing only the soft patter of rain on the roof now the engine and radio were off. The roar of the sea was lost on the wind. 'Me dad didn't want me either. Mam died having me and he blamed me for that. He never came right out and said it or anything but he's different with our kid.'

'That's hardly fair.' Patty was indignant.

This time Lee shrugged, 'Nobody ever said life was meant to be fair.'

It was true, Patty thought, wishing she smoked as he fished his cigarettes out and tapped one out of the pack. As he lit it and drew it back he leaned his head back against the seat.

'Nothing I ever do is good enough for me dad. He thinks I've lost me marbles singing in a band and I'd be rich if he gave me a penny for every time he says how if I'd applied meself at school I wouldn't have wound up on a factory line. Just once I'd like him to say, "You've done well, son." Just once.' He smoked angrily for a few puffs and then blowing a stream of smoke out of the window said, 'I've never told anyone that before. You get it though, don't you?'

Patty nodded. She understood alright. She was angry at his father for making him feel anything less than the talented young man he was. She wondered if parents knew how much power they wielded when it came to wounding their children.

'As soon as I've got some money together I'm moving out. Our kid's engaged and once he marries Deborah they'll be moving into a place of their own. He says I can stay with them but I've got plans, you know.'

'What plans?' Patty was curious.

'The band's going places. Our manager was talking about us going to Germany. There's big demand for Brit bands over there. And then who knows, the world's me oyster.' He stared out at the wild scene spread before them. 'The music's everything. It's me ticket out of here.'

'It's everything to me too,' Patty said. 'It's my ticket to my brother.'

'Where's he then?' He flicked the cigarette out the window and wound it up.

Patty told him the story of how he'd been snatched from her when she was sick in hospital and sent to Australia. She couldn't help her hands balling into angry fists as she recounted her dad having signed the necessary paperwork for him to go and how keenly she'd felt the underhandedness of it all.

'That's tough.' He shook his head. 'I couldn't imagine losing Pete like that.'

Patty didn't say anything, instead, she watched a trickle of water slide down the windscreen just as the tear had her cheek.

'I haven't even heard you sing yet. Give us a song,' Lee said in an abrupt subject-change to lighten the sombre mood settling over them both.

'What?' Patty pulled herself back to the here and now.

'Give us a song.'

Patty wanted to show Lee Carter what she was capable of. She licked her lips and filled her lungs imagining she was singing to Davey as she gave a repeat performance of last night's song, Where the Boys Are. The Jag was steaming up by the time she'd reached the end.

She didn't look at him. She didn't want to see his face but as the silence stretched long Patty began to feel uncomfortable and self-doubt kicked in. Perhaps Bernie and Patty had been kind to her last night. Maybe it wasn't the song for her. She could have lost her touch. It had been a long time since she'd sung at church. Miss Ascot would be appalled if she knew how long it had been since she and Bernie had even attended church!

'That was bloody brilliant!' Lee finally said and she breathed out a sigh of relief.

'They're gonna go mad over you, Patty Hamilton. You just wait and see.'

Patty smiled and bit her lip then she remembered. 'It's not Patty Hamilton when I'm singing, Lee. Not anymore. It's Margaux. Just Margaux. None of that mysterious lark.' Her chin jutted out.

Lee looked at her with an earnestness in his eyes which usually danced and twinkled with hidden banter. 'You could go far with a voice like that but you've gorra want it. I mean more than anything. It's not enough to be pretty and talented you've gorra want success so bad you can taste it.'

'I do want it. It's all I ever wanted to do and I'm no good at anything else other than shorthand and typing and I'm not planning on doing that for the rest of my days.' She shuddered.

This time he was sceptical. 'You've gorra be prepared to give up everything for it though, Patty. If you want to make the big time you've gorra give up your old life.'

Patty hesitated, she'd never give up Bernie, and Davey, well, he came before anything else because he was her little brother and nothing could change that.

He picked up on her hesitation. 'Is it your bruvver holding you back?'

Patty nodded slowly. 'I don't feel as though my real life, the life that Davey's supposed to be part of, can begin until we're together again. Once I've my fare saved I'm going to get him and bring him home where he belongs.'

'With a voice like yours, babe, you'll be on the boat to Australia in no time but I hope you come back.'

Their eyes locked and her breath snagged knowing what was coming next as he leaned toward her.

Chapter Twenty-six

Sabrina knocked on the door of the flat. If neither of the girls was home she'd have to sit on the stairs and wait for them to come back. She counted to five and when there was no answer she went and sat down hoping their grumpy neighbour didn't decide to pop out between now and when whichever of the two got home first.

She pulled the Opal Fruits from the pocket of the pedal pushers, Bernie had loaned her. They'd been in the pocket of her jeans when she'd stepped back and she'd transferred them over. She popped an orange sweet in her mouth, the familiar fruity burst comforting.

Her afternoon had been spent searching the faces of the women passing her by hoping against hope she'd see the face she could only vaguely remember. She'd traversed the stretch of pavement outside Cripps to no avail and wandered down Wood Street to poke her head in the door of the Swan. Not much had changed inside the pub except the fella pulling pints had hair and a full set of teeth, unlike Mickey. She'd no money for a pint and so had found herself standing with her nose pressed to the window of Brides of Bold Street.

She didn't know how long she'd been stood there when she'd seen a familiar face heading down the street. For a moment, her breath caught and she blinked. He was younger and slimmer and Sabrina could see the outline of Adam's face in his as he whistled his way down Bold Street, hands thrust in the pockets of a blue suit. The confident aura he always exuded was firmly in place and he gave her a cursory glance as he came to a halt outside the shop.

'Ahright, luv?' Ray Taylor said holding the door open for her. 'You coming in?'

'Oh, no, ta. I'm just window shopping,' Sabrina said and he disappeared inside the shop. She felt a little like a voyeur standing there watching as her Aunt Evie appeared. She watched the scene unfurl curiously.

It was unnerving to see younger versions of people you knew, a little like watching a home film but without the annoying flickering.

She wondered what they were talking about.

Ray, despite being close in age to her aunt, would be married with a young son, she thought, trying to picture Adam as a little lad in short pants. He may take after his father a little in the looks department but he was a gentler personality altogether with a sensitive soul even if he reckoned he shared his father's gift of the gab! She wished she could take back that conversation at Beeston Castle. She'd give anything to push rewind and have a different outcome to that day.

There was no point dwelling on it. She couldn't make amends while she was stuck here.

Her Aunt Evelyn's gaze flicked past Ray Taylor to her and Sabrina quickly turned away to make her way back to the flat.

She was on her third Opal Fruit, having given up on the idea of stretching the packet out, when she heard the door bang down below. Footsteps sounded and then Bernie appeared, the tip of her nose red from the cold.

'Sabrina! Sorry. I hope you've not been sitting there long. Our housemother Miss Acton always said you get piles from sitting on the cold ground.'

Sabrina laughed, 'Aunt Evie says the same.'

Bernie rummaged around in her bag and pulled out the key, letting them both in.

It was half an hour later that Patty trudged up the stairs, back from her afternoon out with Lee, flushed and feeling as though she were floating up the stairs to the flat. She didn't even notice the mackerel odour still lingering. She couldn't wait to tell Bernie all about the way Lee's eyes had softened just before he closed them and kissed her. She wanted to relive the feel of the roughness of his chin on hers and breathe in the scent of ciggies, sea, and the faint smell of citrus and soap on his skin.

She flung the door to their flat open and announced theatrically, 'Bernie, I've so much to tell you! Hello, Sabrina.'

Bernie and Sabrina were sitting on the sofa deep in conversation. They hit pause on whatever it was they'd been talking about and Sabrina smiled her greeting while Bernie said, 'We've got a lot to tell you too.' She gave Sabrina a meaningful look.

Patty unwound the scarf from her neck and draped it over the hook on the back of the door asking, 'Well, who's going to go first?'

'You go first,' Sabrina said. She could see she was fit to burst.

Patty didn't need encouragement and she launched into every detail of her outing with Lee including the magical moment he'd kissed her.

Bernie had her hands steepled to her chin as she listened captivated and Sabrina thought longingly of Adam and how it felt when he kissed her. She wondered if she'd ever get the chance to kiss him again.

'It was the best kiss ever,' Patty declared, her eyes focusing once more on the two girls seated on the sofa. 'I want to pinch myself that all this is happening. Lee, singing tonight...' Her voice trailed off.

'It's happening ahright,' Bernie said, noting the sparkle in her friend's eyes; she was glowing! The way Patty had just gushed about Lee was exactly how she'd felt after her first date with Don. She'd not felt like that with any other fella and she knew in her heart, he was the one. She wondered if Lee was the one for Patty. She had mixed feelings about him but she'd never seen her friend walking on air like this before. She glanced at the dainty gold wristwatch Don had bought her for her birthday. 'We've another half hour and then you'd better get yourself ready for this evening.' She turned her head toward Sabrina expectantly.

Sabrina cleared her throat. 'Erm, Patty, this is going to sound rather unbelievable but believe me, every word of what I'm going to tell you is true.'

Patty could tell by the tone in Sabrina's voice and the graveness of Bernie's face she needed to listen and so she tucked Lee Carter away in a compartment of her mind while she gave their guest her full attention.

THE ONLY SOUNDS IN the chilly flat were the distant rumble of traffic on the street below and the grumbling of the old fridge when Sabrina finished telling her story.

Bernie took Patty's hand in hers. 'It's a lot to take in but I believe every word of what Sabrina's told us. You want to have heard some of the things she's told me about what happens in the future.'

Patty shook her head. It was too strange, too farfetched. She couldn't wrap her head around it. Sabrina was saying she was from the future, 1981 to be exact. That she'd stepped through some sort of time-slip portal and wound up here now, nineteen years earlier.

'Patty, listen,' Bernie urged. 'Sabrina says you go to Australia and find Davey. She said you get married there and have a daughter. And that she's seen your face on a record cover.'

'My bezzie mate, Flo. Her parents had one of your records,' Sabrina explained softly, hoping Patty didn't decide she was some sort of lunatic and ask her to leave the flat.

'Is it really true?'

Sabrina reached forward and took Patty's hand. 'I promise you, it's true, all of it.'

'I will see Davey again,' Patty breathed, wanting to believe this with every ounce of her being. She looked from one to the other. Sabrina nodded and Bernie wrapped her friend-sister in an embrace. 'And there's all the other wonderful things coming your way, too, Pats.'

Patty couldn't speak. Her throat had tightened and a lump had formed which she swallowed down.

'Sabrina's coming to work with me on Monday morning to see about a job. I've told her she can stay here with us for as long as it takes until she can, you know...'

'Go forward in time,' Patty said slowly, beginning to understand.

'Yeah, back to her own time,' Bernie elaborated.

'Nineteen eighty-one when a girl called Nicole who's my daughter comes into your shop to look for a wedding dress.'

Sabrina nodded her stomach clenching as she added, '*If* I can get back to the right time.'

Patty mulled it over a few seconds longer and then said, 'You must have been frightened.'

'I was and I still am. I don't know why or how this all works I just know I'm here now and meeting you two has helped but the need to find my mam's stronger than fear.'

'That's how I feel about Davey.'

They smiled at each other in mutual understanding.

'Like Bernie said, stay as long as you need to,' Patty said, and Sabrina smiled her gratitude.

Bernie took on her managerial role then, snapping to attention as she glanced at the time once more. 'Right now though, Pats, you've a performance to be getting ready for.'

Patty looked at Sabrina and Sabrina smiled. 'You need to listen to your bezzie mate.'

Chapter Twenty-seven

'I can't do it!' Patty wailed half turning as though she were about to push her way back through the excited crowd to the stairs and make a run for it.

Bernie could see, even in the dim light, that she was pale beneath the pancake make-up she'd insisted on helping her friend apply. Her eyes were enormous too, partly through fright and partly through the firmly glued eyelashes. She looked gorgeous though in her bold-patterned, shift dress with her hair curling beguilingly around her chin.

'Look at all these people. I'll make a fool of myself. I know it.' She was jiggling on the spot in definite flight mode.

Sabrina grabbed hold of her hand and gave it a squeeze. 'You're not going anywhere Patty and you won't. You're amazin' and they're all going to know it soon too. Remember what I told you this afternoon about seeing you on a record cover? Hold on to that, girl, because you're already a star. It happens for you so get on up there.'

Bernie however took a different tack from Sabrina's encouraging one. Her tone was laced with steel as she squared up to her friend. 'Now you listen to me, Margaux. You left Patty Hamilton from Strawberry Field behind at that door. Patty Hamilton was the girl left at that home, not Margaux, She's a born star and it's belting a tune out tonight that's go-

MICHELLE VERNAL

ing to get you to your Davey. When Lee calls you up, you're going to get up there and send this lot wild. Do you understand?'

Patty stared at her friend, unused to her taking a hard line with her. She was really quite intimidating. 'You sound just like Miss Acton,' she muttered. Bernie was taking her managerial role very seriously she thought. Her mouth formed an 'O' as she let the air out slowly through it and told herself she already had this in the bag. Her heartbeats per minute gradually slowed as she got her breathing under control. She couldn't do anything about her clammy palms though.

Bernie suddenly jumped and spun around as she felt hands span her waist. She wagged a finger playfully telling off the good-looking fella standing behind her for giving her a fright and then turned her attention to Sabrina who was watching the scene curiously.

'This is my Don. Don this is our new roommate, Sabrina.'

She knew Bernie had told Don her story but in the darkened club it was impossible to tell whether he thought she was a crackpot or not. His teeth flashed white against his smile however as he leaned n to ask, 'How're you, Sabrina?'

She was about to respond when deafening screams erupted and her attention was pulled towards the stage where the lads from Lee and the Sundials were piling out with a wave. Bernie let rip with a particularly piercing whistle as they took their places and picked up their waiting instruments.

If you can't beat them join them, Sabrina thought, giving it all she could. She hadn't let go of Patty's hand and she held it tighter just in case.

Patty sought to meet Lee's eyes as he gazed out at the throng and he locked eyes with her for a moment. It was all she needed and she felt bolstered by the wink her gave her before slinging his guitar around his neck.

The drummer began to beat out a tune to get the crowd going and it was bedlam as anticipation swept the tiny club.

Lee leaned into the microphone. 'Hello, and thanks for coming along to our little get-together,'

Sabrina looked around her at all the wringing of hands and starry-eyed looks. You'd have thought Jesus Himself had just spoken to the crowd. 'I'm Lee.' He grinned at his band-mates at the reception they were receiving. 'And on my left is Jimmy on bass guitar!'

Jimmy strummed a few chords and it was like he'd turned water into wine.

'And Joe on lead guitar.'

Joe hammed it up with his guitar egging the crowd on.

'And... Reggie on drums.'

Reggie held his sticks up in greeting.

'I've got a favour to ask you.' Lee was managing to make every person in the audience feel as though he were speaking to them personally. 'We're going to play a song Joe here wrote that you might have heard us play once or twice before.'

A chanting went up. 'Hey Girl, Hey Girl, Hey Girl.'

'He's got real stage presence,' Patty shouted proudly to Sabrina who had to agree with her. He was holding the crowd in the palm of his hand.

'I want you to stamp your feet and clap along. Ahright?'

A thunderous foot stomping began as Lee nodded at his bandmates and they dove straight into the catchy tune.

Patty's nerves were shelved as she lost herself in the rock 'n' roll rhythm and the sheer joy of moving to the music.

'They're brill!' she shouted over the din to Bernie who was jiving along with Don. Lee could really hold a tune, she thought, a shiver coursing through her as she remembered the unfamiliar sensations his mouth on hers earlier had invoked. He'd a voice like silk and she gave a particularly loud scream as the band launched into a new number.

The fourth song was winding down and Sabrina was fanning her face with her hands when Lee said, 'A little bird, a Liverbird to be exact, told me there's a songbird in the audience tonight. Are you out there, Margaux?' He put his hand to his forehead as though scanning a vast ocean vista and pretended to scan the crowd, knowing full well where Patty was standing.

Bernie nudged her pal, who was frozen to the spot, in the back before pointing down at her head. 'She's here, Lee!'

Club-goers swung around for a look and the crowd between Patty and the stage parted as Bernie gave her a firmer push this time and she made her way up to the stage. Lee took her hand and pulled her up next to him and Patty stood blinking at the bobbing heads spread out before her. She licked her lips which were paper dry and sent up a silent prayer that she wouldn't blow this opportunity.

'Oh my God, girl, I think I'm going to be sick,' Bernie said, covering her eyes with her hands and peeking through them. 'Give us one of those sweets of yours to chew on, it might help.'

Sabrina felt exactly the same way and she pulled the packet from her pocket passing it to Bernie who took one. Unwrapping it and popping it in her mouth she began to frantically chew. Sabrina did the same, offering one to Don who declined. The fruit burst did nothing to quell her nerves and from the way Bernie was jiggling about she was guessing it hadn't helped her either. It could have been the pair of them up there on that stage the way they were carrying on. Thank goodness it wasn't because she couldn't sing to save herself and she'd heard Bernie murdering an Everly Brothers number in the bathroom as she did her morning ablutions.

'What are you going to sing for us tonight, Margaux?' Lee gave her an appreciative once-over and Patty felt adrenalin surge. Up here under these glaring lights, she wasn't Patty Hamilton the little girl who'd not been loved enough by her father to be given a home with him and his new family. Oh no, here, right now, she was Margaux.

'Erm...' She held her index finger to her lips feigning deep thought before turning to look at Jimmy, Joe and Reggie one by one before turning her attention to Lee, 'How's about Little Eva, boys, Locomotion?'

Jimmy nodded and strummed a few bars of the tune.

'Yeah, I think we can play that one, lads. What do you think?' He addressed the eager throng who made it clear they thought it was a great song choice.

'Are you ready to learn a brand new dance with me?' Margaux asked coquettishly before tilting the microphone toward the audience. 'Was that a yes because I couldn't quite hear you?'

There was no doubt it was a yes and as Lee and the Sundials began to play the popular hit, Margaux began doing a chugging train motion with her arms, launching into the song. She sang like she'd never sung before.

Bernie and Sabrina stared at her and then at each other open mouthed and Don leaned in between them summing up what they and everyone else at the Cavern that night was thinking, 'She's flippin' amazin'.'

Chapter Twenty-eight

Two months later...

'How was work?' Patty asked, sliding a foot into her black kitten heel, the other shoe dangling from her hand as she stood in the doorway of her shared bedroom. The air was ripe with the heady scent of lily of the valley and jasmine thanks to the Diorissimo she'd sprayed liberally. Lee had bought the bottle of French perfume for her and she felt exotic and very grown-up each time she sprayed it. She'd never worn real French perfume before.

Bernie and Sabrina tumbled in the door full of moans as to slave labour and old bite supervisors. Sabrina kicked the door closed with practised ease using her heel and made a beeline for the kitchen, dumping her bag on the floor en route. She was greeted with a sink full of breakfast detritus and with a sigh she filled first the kettle and then the sink.

Patty had raced in the door twenty minutes earlier in order to change and freshen her make-up before she had to hare across town to the club she'd been unexpectedly booked to sing at. She'd only found out about the impromptu performance when Lee had come looking for her at lunchtime with the message from his manager, Alan.

Now, she glanced at her wristwatch. She'd have to get a move on she thought slipping her other shoe on before fluffing her hair.

'How do I look, girls?' She gave them a twirl and struck a pose.

Sabrina, whose head was buzzing with the thrumming of a hundred sewing machines, made admiring noises before rolling up her sleeves and sinking her hands into the sudsy water. Her friend looked every inch the performer and she'd a joie de vivre about her these days which was down to Lee.

He was good for her. She'd blossomed so much in confidence since she'd been getting about on his arm. He'd grown on Sabrina and Bernie too, who were now well used to his posturing. It didn't mean anything, it was all part of his pop singer persona and a mask Patty had confided in them, for the insecure young man who lurked beneath the surface.

She was gasping for a cuppa, Sabrina thought, eying the kettle and willing it to hurry up and whistle as she turned the cup she'd just washed upside down to drain. She tried to stretch the crick she seemed to permanently have from being hunched over a sewing machine for eight hours a day out by tilting her neck to the left and the right.

The initial shock as to the monotony of her machinist position where Bernie, true to her word had organised for her to be interviewed, had long since passed. She'd quickly learned to switch off and allow her mind to wander while she hemmed and stitched her daily quota. There was no chance of messing about or taking a break on their shifts because the supervisor was like an overweight panther with her preference for sombre black dresses as she prowled the factory floor. Like the big cat too, her eyes never missed a thing.

She was a fierce woman despite her short stature and Sabrina had felt like a five-year-old putting her hand up to ask if she could go to the lav on her first day. The glare she'd been on the receiving end of had seen her hold on the next time and she'd been knock-kneed by lunchtime.

It was the banter of the other girls during their breaks and the knowledge she'd be able to pay her way with Patty and Bernie, who'd been more than generous towards her, that spurred her on. She'd made a pact with herself in that first week of work that she'd never moan about her more demanding brides ever again after her taste of working at the factory.

She'd made all sorts of promises to Him upstairs too, all hinging on her getting back to her own time but He was obviously dubious as to the likelihood of her keeping them because that had been over eight weeks ago.

She was still here and Bold Street's timeslip was remaining stubbornly shut to her.

She'd lost count of how many times she'd stalked up and down the pavement outside Cripps hoping to blink and find herself returned to 1981. Back and forth she'd go until her feet ached and when she couldn't face another circuit she'd take herself off to Brides of Bold Street. There, she'd find herself an outsider looking in as she stared through the window at the world inside which was at once familiar and strange.

If her Aunt Evie noticed the young woman who came window shopping every other day she didn't make it known and eventually, Sabrina would make her way back to her new

home in Kensington on the verge of tears at the thought of
never seeing Adam, Flo, and the Aunt Evie she knew again
or at the very least, not for a very long time.

She was missing Adam terribly and couldn't shake the
hurt look she'd seen on his face that afternoon at the castle.
Seeing Patty and Bernie with their beaus only made her
yearning to see him more palpable. The bond between the
two friends whom she now counted as her own friends had
made her appreciate Flo all the more. Like Patty was Bernie's
friend-sister, so too was she Flo's and she desperately missed
her.

She'd not seen or heard a single thing to give her hope
of finding her mother nor had she gleaned any further clues.
The only good thing that had come from her wandering back
in time once more was meeting Bernie and Patty. She wiped
the last bowl and fished around for the spoons and knife in
the water before draining the sink just as the kettle sang out.

She realised Bernie, who'd discarded her coat and
flopped down on the sofa, was eyeballing Patty with a perplexed frown. 'Why are you heading out this early?' Her eyes
darted up and down the dress Patty was wearing. It wasn't
one she'd seen before. 'I didn't think you were due on stage
until nine? And where did you get the dress?' The questions
flew out in rapid-fire.

'Lee treated me. It's gorgeous, isn't it? He came and saw
me at lunchtime to say Alan got me an opening at the Iron
Door for six this evening. I'll go straight from there to the
Sink Club. Don't worry, I'll be on time.' Patty crossed the
room to grab her coat. 'The money for the Iron Door gig's
good.'

Her savings were looking much healthier since she'd begun singing regularly at various clubs about the city. The end goal was in sight. She had her plan. She and Bernie would go straight to the address of the children's home on the letter Davey had sent her. He could well be long gone from there but she would wring a forwarding address out of them one way or another. Come what may they'd not be leaving Australia without her brother.

Patty had never once wavered about going to Australia but her only hesitation now was leaving Lee. Even if everything went well and she managed to track Davey down without any trouble, she'd still be gone for months given the time it would take to sail there and back. Lee was a good-looking fella with plenty of girls who'd be more than happy to step in and take her place once she was out of the picture. There was no time for dwelling on that now though.

'Why's Alan Marsdon getting you gigs? I'm your manager.' Bernie was most put out.

'Of course, you are but it was down to a last-minute cancellation and Lee and the lads were already booked for the Cavern. Alan thought of me. He knows I need the extra money.'

'Alan should have come to me,' Bernie said in a sulky manner most unlike her. 'That's poaching that is.'

'I'm sorry, Bernie, it was all so quick there wasn't time for toing and froing just a quick yay or nay. You don't mind do you?' Patty dimpled, her hand already on the doorknob.

Bernie sighed. 'No, it's been a long day that's all. You go knock 'em dead like you always do. Me and Sabrina will see you later at the Sink Club.'

Patty flashed a grin at both of them and then was gone.

'She's never home anymore,' Bernie grumbled kicking her shoes off. She wished Don was on hand to give her a foot rub.

It was true Sabrina thought as she splashed boiling water over the teabags. Since the night Lee had pulled her on stage at the Cavern, 'Margaux' had been in hot demand.

Word of the newcomer who'd wowed the crowd with her strong voice and stage presence had spread and Bernie had been run off her feet working at the factory all day and taking bookings for her fledgeling star to sing with the various bands at different clubs around the city of an evening. There wasn't enough money coming in yet for either girl to give up their day jobs though and Bernie had confided to Sabrina just the other day while they were on their lunch break, Don was getting fed up with never spending time together just the two of them anymore.

'He has so little time off anyway and when he does I'm at the clubs working,' she'd lamented over her buttie.

Sabrina made the tea and carried Bernie's cup and the jam jar which she'd grown used to drinking out of over before joining her on the sofa. She knew every spring in the antwacky piece of furniture intimately these days! Not that she was complaining because Patty and Bernie had been brill letting her stay on the sofa the way they had and they'd not once complained over her quirks as she thought of her need to flick switches three times or go back and check the kettle was switched off even though she knew it was when she was halfway down the stairs. Bernie had asked her once what it was about and Sabrina had shrugged that she didn't really know. She just knew if she didn't complete her rituals she was left with a feeling of impending doom. They made her feel she had a modicum of control over the world in which she moved.

Now, she wriggled her toes inside her shoes. Her feet were killing her, being unused to the hard leather of the Mary Jane shoes she'd bought with her first pay and she happily freed them before massaging her heels where the blisters had only just healed.

'Ta, I need this.' Bernie took a sip of the hot brew and closed her eyes briefly. 'You make a good cuppa.'

Sabrina thought of Aunt Evie who always enjoyed her brews.

The duo sat in silence for a few minutes each unwinding from their day. It was Bernie who spoke up first, putting her tea down on the upturned crate that sufficed as their table as she said, 'Things aren't turning out the way I thought they would.'

'What do you mean?' Sabrina asked, eyeing her friend over the rim of her jar. 'I thought getting Patty's singing career underway was the plan and that's taking off. It won't be long before you'll both be able to afford the fare out to Australia.'

Bernie shrugged. 'It is but it's going to come at a cost and I never thought about what that might be when we used to daydream about Patty becoming famous.'

'I don't get what you mean.'

'Patty, I mean, Margaux, she made inverted commas with her fingers, 'is slipping away. She's moving in different circles these days.'

'Yes.' Sabrina pondered her reply. 'That's true but as her manager so are you.'

'I don't know if they're circles I want to move in though, Sabrina, and Patty needs more than what I can do for her. Look at tonight. If I was taken seriously as her manager it would have been me the Iron Door would have got hold of to fill the spot.'

'But she said it was a last-minute fill-in thing. It wasn't a case of tracking her down, Alan put her name forward.'

Bernie's lips tightened. She didn't want to be placated because while she was annoyed she didn't have to feel guilty. 'Alan Marsdon's a shark. He's got his eye on adding her to his books and you know Patty's blind where Lee's concerned. Watch this space, Sabrina, it's only a matter of time until I get shafted.' She put her tea down with a heavier hand than was necessary and a little slopped over the side.

'Patty wouldn't do that to you, Bernie.'

'No, you're right *Patty* wouldn't but Margaux would. Haven't you noticed how she talks like Lee these days going on as to how it's all about the music and that has to come before everything else?'

Sabrina had heard this many times but she shook her head, not wanting to believe that of Patsy.

'It's not me she needs anymore.'

'Ah, Bernie, that's not true you two are like sisters.'

'We were always a team, me and Pats, but I'm not going to be the one who's going to take her to where she wants to go.' She folded her arms across her chest sinking down low on the sofa.

Sabrina recalled the conversation that seemed ages ago now when she'd first landed on Patty and Bernie. She'd sensed then that the two girls might be going down different paths. She didn't say anything though waiting for Bernie to carry on.

'She needs someone who knows the ins and outs of the business. Someone who the club owners want to deal with and take seriously. Someone like Alan. Not me. I don't have a clue, not really. I'm winging it.'

'Well, you've done a good job so far.'

'Maybe, but the thing is, Sabrina, I didn't bank on what we both wanted changing. Patty wants to go to Australia and fetch her Davey. Although from what you said she stays there so I don't know where that leaves me, or Lee for that matter.' Bernie's voice cracked and Sabrina looked at her alarmed.

'I only know what Nicole told me. I can't fill in the blanks in between. Anything could happen, Bernie.' Sabrina studied her for a moment. She didn't have a shared history with her like Patty did but Bernie wore her heart on her sleeve and she knew there was something more than what she'd said on her mind. 'What's really bothering you?' She laid a hand on her forearm.

The gesture saw Bernie swallow hard and when she turned to look at Sabrina her brown eyes were overly bright. 'I always said I'd go with her to fetch Davey. I told her we were a family. I promised her I'd never let her down.'

'And you haven't, Bernie.'

'Not yet, but I'm going to.' It all came out in a flood then. 'I don't want to go to Australia. I don't want to leave Don and I don't want to spend my life trying to prove I'm something I'm not in a world where I don't belong. I don't want to be Margaux's manager. I want to be Don's wife and have a family of my own. A nice, simple, quiet life. Not all this music madness. He's getting serious too, Sabrina, and if he asks me to marry him I'm going to say yes. Do you see though? I can't be both. I can't be Margaux's manager and travel to Australia *and* Don's wife and I can't have one without losing the other.' She erupted in noisy sobs.

BERNIE PULLED HERSELF together after her second cup of tea and reassurances from Sabrina that she wasn't being selfish in wanting to settle down with Don. It was only natural and she managed to convince her that Patty would understand because she'd want her to be happy. Even as she'd said this though, Sabrina hoped it was true. Patty had tunnel vision when it came to Australia and Davey.

'You've got to tell her what you've told me, Bernie. It's only fair and you'll feel much better once you have. Tell her tonight when we get to the Sink Club. There's no point putting it off and then you'll both know where you stand.'

Bernie looked uncomfortable at the thought of coming clean but said, 'You're right and I will but what if I don't see her again, Sabrina? If she goes to Australia I mean and doesn't come back. I can't imagine not having her nearby.'

'You've just got to trust that things will work out the way they're supposed to, I suppose. It's all any of us can do.'

Chapter Twenty-nine

The two girls had eaten a hasty dinner of beans on toast before getting ready to go out for the evening.

They arrived at the Sink Club to find it humming and pushed their way through the smoky haze out the back to where Patty was waiting anxiously to go on stage.

Her face lit up seeing them both. 'I was hoping you'd make it before I go on. I always feel better when I know you're here.' Patty had come to the conclusion that Margaux didn't take over until she walked out onto the stage. Poor old Patty however had to put up with the pre-performance jitters that didn't seem to get any better no matter how many times she got up and sang in front of a crowd.

'I'm sorry I was off with you earlier,' Bernie offered up and Patty gave her a quick squeeze.

'I should have made Lee check with you first, you were right. You're my manager, not Alan Marsdon.'

'No, I wasn't right, Pats. I was behaving like a spoiled child made to share her toys. There wasn't time for Lee to talk to me. You did the right thing in going for it. How did it go anyway?'

'Ah, Bernie, it was amazin'. I had to go back on and do two more songs after my set finished.'

'That's great!' Bernie was genuinely happy for her friend. 'Pats, there's something I need to tell you—'

A flurry of activity interrupted Bernie mid-sentence as The Dukes exited the stage and the girls called out their greetings as they flattened themselves against the wall to let the popular band pass.

'Good crowd out there tonight, Margaux, luv,' Ken the drummer said, waving his sticks as he breezed past them.

The moment was lost and Bernie didn't know whether she was relieved or not.

BERNIE ARRIVED HOME after the others, she and Don had gone for a stroll after the clubs had closed wanting some time alone. She looked to where Patty and Sabrina were seated on the sofa, a cup of tea with a greasy film on it untouched on the crate. Patty had her head in her hands and Sabrina had a protective arm draped around her.

'What's going on?' Bernie asked alarmed as she moved to kneel on the floor in front of them by the heater. 'Patty?'

Sabrina spoke up. 'Alan came to see Patty after the show tonight and had a quiet word with her about calling it quits with Lee.'

'But why?'

Patty looked up then, her face a blotchy red mess streaked with black train tracks where her eye make-up had trickled down her cheeks. Her voice wobbled as she spoke, 'Because they're supposed to be going to Germany tomorrow and Lee's making noises about not going because he doesn't want to leave me.'

'What? When did that happen?' Bernie had heard no mention of Germany being on the cards.

'Weeks ago, apparently.'

'You knew then?'

Patty shook her head. 'Lee never breathed a word about it and he told the other lads not to, too. They've been offered a permanent gig in a top club over there. Alan said it's the break the band's been waiting for.'

'Why can't you go too?' Bernie thought this was the practical solution. Margaux would have no problem finding singing gigs over there, not if her popularity here was anything to go by.

'Alan says it's not good for either of our images and we're holding each other back. He says the Sundials have got what it takes to make it big if they play their cards right and so do I.'

Bernie's hand was making a fist and she interrupted, 'He has a lot to say for himself does Alan. Too much if you ask me.'

'It's true though, isn't it? What girl wants a heartthrob who's already spoken for?'

'Patty, you can't let Alan dictate how you and Lee should live your lives,' Sabrina said. 'What about keeping things going long distance. Lots of people have to manage that.'

'Don't you see though?' Patty's teary gaze swung from one to the other. 'I'd be a distraction. Alan says they have to give this their all and remember what Lee told me? The music's everything. You've got to want it bad enough, and he does. Nothing can get in its way and that means me too. I love him enough to let him go.'

It was true Sabrina and Bernie had heard Lee go on about how you'd got to want it bad enough if you were going to succeed in the music biz but in that moment they both thought Patty looked broken, utterly broken.

'You can't break it off with him, Patty, you love him and he loves you,' Bernie offered up lamely. 'That must mean something.'

'That's what I said to her too,' Sabrina added.

'And what sort of person would I be if I let him miss this opportunity because of me? It's his dream.' Patty shook her head. 'No, I've got to focus on Davey and getting to Australia. It was never in my plan to meet someone like Lee. Davey has to come first. We're so close now, Bernie. Another couple of weeks and we'll have enough in the kitty to go.' At the thought of her brother, she brushed the tears away and managed a watery smile.

Bernie avoided the look she knew Sabrina was giving her.

'Bernie?' Patty said, noticing her friend hadn't said anything.

Bernie took a deep breath and her hands twisted back and forth as she suddenly blurted, 'Pats, I'm not going with you and I'm not going to manage you anymore either.' She blinked as though surprised she'd said the words out loud. There was no going back now and she hurried on. 'I've got Don to think about. I need to put him first. And, listen Alan Marsdon clearly thinks you've got star quality. He'd make a much better manager than I ever could. I can't just drop everything and swan off to Australia either, not now. I love Don. It wouldn't be fair on him. You'll be okay, Pats, you're braver than me. You'll go there and find Davey. You don't need me but you do need Lee.' Her brown eyes implored her. 'Don't do what Alan's asking of you.'

Patty stared at Bernie not comprehending what she was being told for the second time that evening.

'Pats? Say something.'

'What is there to say? You've said it all.' She got up from the sofa and headed for the door pausing only to put her coat on.

'Where are you going?' Bernie asked clambering to her feet.

'I've got to go and see Lee.' Patty headed out the door Bernie and Sabrina following.

'Patty, don't go.' Bernie reached out catching hold of her friend's coat.

Patty shrugged her off. 'Bernie, leave me be. I want to be on my own.'

Bernie stood on the landing, watching her disappear down the stairs and Sabrina took her by the hand. 'Come on back inside. She'll be ahright. Give her some time by herself to think it all over, Bernie'

Bernie looked at Sabrina, her pallor pasty. 'What if I've lost her, Sabrina. What will I do?'

Chapter Thirty

Sabrina woke as daylight stole in through the crack in the curtains, puddling in patches where she and Bernie were curled up either end of the couch. She stretched, trying to unknot herself and it took a few beats for her to remember why Bernie was on the sofa with her and for the panic that she'd overslept to dissipate.

It was Saturday morning. Thank God it wasn't a weekday because she wouldn't be able to work. They'd held a vigil here on the sofa waiting for Patty to come home until the wee hours. She couldn't remember consciously deciding to go to sleep but they must have nodded off at some point. She couldn't remember Patty coming home either.

Bernie stirred as Sabrina pushed the blanket aside and got up to check in the bedroom. Perhaps Patty had slipped in after they'd both crashed out. She'd no idea what time they'd finally nodded off only that it was closer to morning than it was night.

The door creaked as she pushed it open and her heart sank seeing the bed was unslept in. She pushed the worrying thoughts beginning to vie for attention away. She hoped she hadn't gone through with breaking things off with Lee. There'd be other opportunities if he decided not to go to Germany. What the pair of them had was more important than their careers. Money and fame would not keep either of them warm at night.

She recalled echoing that sentiment to Bernie the night before and receiving a quizzical look by way of return before she'd said, 'You've never known what it is to be proper poor, Sabrina.'

It was true, she hadn't.

'Pats and I have. If you knew what it was like to go to bed hungry and listen to your parents tearing one another apart you might not be so quick to dismiss money and fame because there's something to be said for the security of knowing where your next meal's coming from.'

Chastened, Sabrina hadn't said any more on the subject.

She jumped as Bernie peered over her shoulder. She hadn't heard her get up.

'Do you think she's at Lee's?' Bernie asked, rubbing her eyes.

'Bound to be,' Sabrina said with a brightness she didn't feel. It wasn't likely at all given Lee still lived at home with his dad. She set to the task of making them a brew while Bernie disappeared into the bathroom.

Her tea was waiting on the crate when she emerged looking decidedly fresh for someone who'd been up half the night. Sabrina by comparison felt rumpled and finished her drink quickly certain a wash would work wonders for her too.

'Do you think we should call round to Lee's and see if Patty's there?' Sabrina asked a short while later as ready as she'd ever be to face the world.

Bernie chewed her bottom lip for a moment. 'She said she wanted to be left alone.'

'That was hours ago.'

'You're right. She's had plenty of time on her own.'

They were out the door and down the stairs within minutes, too preoccupied to pay attention to the grumblings of old man Timbs, who poked his head out of the door or to notice the smell of the morning's catch.

It was Sabrina who spotted her, catching hold of Bernie as she strode down the pavement. 'She's in there.'

Bernie peered in the window of Bill's Café and through the smear of small handprints saw Patty hunched over a table, her hands cupping a mug. 'C'mon.' She pulled Sabrina inside.

Patty didn't look up as the door jingled open and Bernie and Sabrina stepped into the bustling café. The murmuring conversations and comforting aromas of frying food and hot drinks on a cold day washed over them. 'I bet she hasn't eaten,' Sabrina said. 'I'll order for us. You go on over.'

Bernie did as she was told and Sabrina took her place in the line. Two women in front of her were having an in-depth discussion as to the mysterious reoccurrence of her Jack's boils and she tuned them out, watching Bernie pull out the chair opposite her friend.

Patty looked up then, the dark rings framing her eyes visible even from where Sabrina was standing.

She was so busy observing their exchange, trying to read what was being said, she wasn't aware she was at the front of the queue until Bill, looking more red-faced than usual, barked, 'What are you after, luv?'

Sabrina ordered bacon butties for them all and a pot of tea before heading over to join Bernie and Patty. 'There's three bacon butties on the way along with a brew,' she said, sitting down.

'Ta, Sabrina. I'll fix you up later. I forgot me purse.'

Sabrina flapped a hand. 'No, my treat.'

'Well, I for one am starvin' and I bet you've not eaten anything since yesterday either,' Bernie addressed Patty who mumbled she wasn't hungry anyway.

Sabrina and Bernie exchanged a look and Sabrina had to ask. 'Where you've been until now?' There'd been a lot of hours between Patty having left the flat and winding up here at Bill's Café which didn't open until eight on a Saturday.

Exhaustion was etched on Patty's fine features and the telltale smudges of make-up she'd tried to wipe away with the crumpled serviette on the table were still visible on her cheeks. She stared over at Sabrina and then dipped her head again so the girls had to strain to hear what she was saying. 'I went to see Lee and then I walked around for ages until I wound up here. I waited outside until it opened.'

'Oh, Pats, you'd have been frozen. Why didn't you come home?' Bernie was aghast at the thought of her wandering the streets for half the night.

She shrugged. 'I needed to clear my head.'

'What happened between you and Lee?' Bernie asked.

Patty's eyes glistened and her grip tightened on her mug. 'I finished it with him. He wouldn't listen at first but I told him he was holding me back. I said I have to make singing and Davey my priority and that there was no room in my life for him.' Her voice was flat and dull as she added, 'He'll be on the boat now. Gone.'

'Oh, Patty, I'm sorry.' Sabrina automatically reached over the table, uncaring as she knocked the pepper pot over to squeeze her friend's hand. She didn't know what else to say or do. She'd only been with Adam for a few months just like Patty had Lee but it was long enough to know she'd found something special with him. They'd both had to say goodbye to their fellas on bad terms and she knew what a chasm it left. Unlike Patty though, she had hope that she'd get back to him and that they could sort things out. She couldn't imagine not having that hope.

Bernie bounced her chair around the table until she was next to her friend. She pulled her into an embrace and when Patty didn't protest said, 'Pats, I'm so sorry I've let you down.'

Patty did pull away then and she swivelled to face Bernie, taking both her hands in hers. 'But you haven't let me down. You've always been there for me. That's what I was thinking about after I left Lee's. I could see it then. It's me who's been selfish. All I've thought about since they put Davey on that ship is what I want. I'm not that much of a selfish cow though that I don't want you to be happy and your Don's lu-vly. You've got to do what's right for you, Bernie. We'll always be friend-sisters no matter what. I promise.'

There were no dry eyes at their table as Bill, flustered by the sight of weepy-eyed women, banged their butties down. He even ignored the spilled pepper, quietly righting the pot and hurrying back to where he was comfortable behind the counter.

Chapter Thirty-one

Two weeks had passed since Lee and the Sundials had left for Germany and a lot had happened in between.

Patty had given notice at work and in just under two weeks she would be sailing on the *Ayrshire* to Freemantle in Australia. She was both terrified and excited at the prospect of the adventure that lay ahead but underscoring these emotions was a deep sadness at having lost Lee.

The only way she could survive the heartache which hit her afresh each morning when she woke was by focusing on her search for Davey. She'd no clue as to how she would get from Freemantle to Adelaide or whether Davey was even still in the South Australian city but she'd find him wherever he was. She knew this deep in her soul and she believed what Sabrina had told her about what lay in store for her.

Bernie, despite her dismay at Patty leaving so soon, was frothing with excitement because as she'd suspected Don had finally summoned the courage to get down on bended knee. That he had to choose to do it on Everton Brow overlooking the city on the coldest night of the year was beside the point. She'd said yes and was now sporting a sparkly ring on her engagement finger which she flashed around at any given opportunity. Her thrill at the prospect of becoming Mrs Don Cole was keeping her distracted from the fact her dearest friend was going to be travelling half a world away from her shortly.

For Sabrina's part, things were moving quickly for her friends and she was happy for them although she'd felt a tug upon hearing Don had proposed on Everton Brow. It was where she and Adam had had their first kiss. Nothing had changed for her though. She was still desperate to get back to her time but had no control over whatever mysterious forces were at work on that little pocket of Bold Street and until the portal or whatever it was opened, she had no choice but to get on with life here.

Bernie and Don had decided there was little point in waiting to get married. Neither wanted a big, flashy do, preferring to put all their money towards a deposit for their first home.

All Bernie really wanted on her wedding day was for Patty to be there and as such, she'd ignored her future mother-in-law's raised brow followed by a hard stare at Bernie's belly, and booked the registry office the day before Patty's sailing.

Another Saturday had rolled around and instead of languishing at Bill's Café, the girls had ventured into the city on a shopping excursion. There was Bernie's wedding dress to find, not to mention suitable clothes for Patty to wear on the ship and in Australia which was going to be considerably warmer than it was here in Liverpool.

They'd spent the morning canvassing shops for any sign of early spring fashions and were now laden with bags but one bag had been with Sabrina each and every time she'd ventured out to Bold Street. Patty cast a glance at it slung over her arm and had to ask, 'Why do you cart that lot with you whenever you go out?'

Sabrina glanced at the bag in which she had her Calvin Klein's, bomber jacket, sweater, and boots. 'In here amongst the other clothes I was wearing when I stepped back to well, now, are my all-time favourite jeans. And in my time a favourite pair of jeans is like gold. They've got to mould to you just so and when you find a good pair you wear them until they need patching. Besides, they cost me a bleedin' fortune and I'm not leaving them behind.'

Patty and Bernie laughed.

They'd wandered under the enormous arch into Chinatown near the top end of Bold Street and Sabrina noticed a sign outside a restaurant advertising a cheap set-lunch menu and as the door opened spicy aromas tickled her nose and tastebuds. She realised she was starving. 'I think we've earned ourselves a spot of lunch before we go to Brides of Bold Street, don't you?' It was a given that Bernie would buy her dress from Sabrina's Aunt Evie even if she didn't know she was Sabrina's aunt so to speak. It would be a whole year before Sabrina would come into Evelyn's life as a lost little three-year-old in 1963.

'Definitely,' Patty concurred. She'd lost weight in the days after Lee had left but her appetite was slowly returning and she was determined to keep her strength up for the voyage that lay ahead. Six weeks on a ship!

'I'm starvin.' Bernie put Sabrina's thoughts into words.

Sabrina held open the door to the restaurant with its swirling red and gold dragon overhead and Bernie and Patty felt very avant-garde trying something foreign.

'My Don won't eat Chinese,' Bernie whispered across the table after they'd ordered. 'You know on account of the moggies disappearing, like. He says places like this help keep Liverpool's stray cat population down.'

'Bernie!' Patty paused with her glass of water raised halfway to her lips and stared at her friend in horror.

'That's an old wives' tale, that is,' Sabrina said shutting the topic down. All the same, she wished she'd ordered a beef dish instead of the chicken on rice special they were all having.

Patty was all for moving the conversation on and brought up the matter of Bernie's mysterious disappearance as she and Sabrina had flicked through a rack of dresses at C&A's earlier. She'd called back over her shoulder that she'd meet them in half an hour under Dickie outside Lewis's and had hurried off before either of them could question her as to where she was going. With this in mind, she pinned her friend under her gaze and asked, 'Where did you get to earlier then? Scurrying off like that with no explanation.'

Bernie grinned and retrieved her handbag which she plopped down on the table. Opening it with a flourish, she retrieved two black velvet jewellery boxes and slid them across the table to her friends. 'There's one for youse both.'

Patty and Sabrina looked at one another and then back at Bernie curiously.

'G'won, open them.'

They snapped the boxes open and stared at their contents. Inside each box was an identical delicate silver chain with a dainty silver medal dangling from it. Sabrina held hers up to the light and exclaimed over how gorgeous it was.

Patty was stroking the medal as she looked questioningly at Bernie as to its significance.

'It's a St Christopher's medal. He's the patron saint of travellers. I want you both to promise me you'll never take them off because if you're wearing your medals then I'll know he's watching over you.'

Sabrina was touched by the gesture and she blinked back tears. 'Thank you, Bernie. I'll treasure it.'

'You've got to promise.'

'And I promise never to take it off.'

'You too, Pats.' Bernie swung her attention to her friend whose eyes were also suspiciously bright.

'I promise I'll always wear it. It will be like having you with me, Bernie.'

Bernie got up then and did the honours fastening the chains around their necks and then sitting down to admire them, satisfied her dear pals would be safe on their travels now.

Half an hour later, stuffed full of chicken and rice which they all agreed had been tasty and most definitely chicken, they rolled back out onto the street and made their way to Sabrina's stomping ground—Bold Street.

'I've always liked Bold Street, me,' Bernie said. 'It feels special, posh like, but now knowing what I know about it I shall be avoiding Cripps and that part of the street like the plague.'

'Me too,' said Patty. She couldn't be doing with disappearing in time, not now she was so close to setting off for Australia.

'Is it very much changed, you know, in your time?' Bernie asked as they strolled along, Patty in the middle, their arms linked companionably as bags slapped against their sides.

Sabrina gazed at the buildings. They hadn't changed, though the shops and cafés below the businesses and flats housed upstairs had. In 1981, there were empty shops with To Let signs in the windows which Aunt Evie often lamented was a by-product of the country under Thatcher. The ports were in decline and the shipbuilding was all but ancient history then.

The upmarket, exclusive feel of the street on which she now walked with Bernie and Patty had been replaced with an artier, quirkier air in 1981 and where now the shop frontages gleamed, a good portion in her time were in need of tender loving care. The people who shopped here had changed too. It was more diverse in her era.

She wondered what the girls would make of the punks who hung around outside the record shops or the women in their corporate suits with shoulder pads so sharp they'd take an eye out. She glimpsed a woman with a headscarf knotted under her chin as she hurried down the street. That was something that hadn't changed!

She relayed all this to Bernie and Patty who were goggle-eyed at the thought of girls with studded dog collars around their necks and tartan miniskirts or fellas whose heads were adorned with rainbow-coloured spikes and safety pins through their ears.

They reached Brides of Bold Street and Sabrina hesitated for a moment. Today, for the first time since she'd stepped back into 1962, she had a legitimate reason to go inside the shop. Butterflies beat their wings in her tummy as she pushed the door open.

She could hear the familiar thrumming of the Singer machine out the back and as they rang the silver bell on the counter the sound came to a halt.

'I'll be right with you,' came Aunt Evie's familiar voice and a smile spread across Sabrina's face hearing it. She swept the shop, absorbing the creams, whites, champagne and oyster shades along with the different textures of the fabrics. She itched to take up her position at the work table out the back, a cup of tea in front of her, a garibaldi biscuit ready to dunk. She could do none of this though and she held her ground, feeling Patty's steadying grip on her arm.

Evelyn appeared a moment later, a younger version of herself in a powder blue shop coat with a pair of pinking shears peeking out of the front pocket. 'Good afternoon, ladies.' She beamed, spectacles on the bridge of her nose as she peered over the top of them. 'Now then, which one of you is the bride-to-be?'

'She is,' Patty and Sabrina chimed, pointing to Bernie.

Evelyn smiled at Bernie but then was compelled to take another look at the girl with the unusual whisky coloured eyes. She was familiar and Evelyn was certain their paths had crossed before.

'Have you visited the shop before?' she asked, already convinced she must have. In fact, as she spoke she made the connection only it didn't make sense. The girl who'd sprung to mind had been distraught trying to convince her they knew one another. That was over thirty years ago and had been a most unsettling experience which was why it had stayed with her. If it was her, she hadn't aged a day and that was impossible. Evelyn shook her head. She was being fanciful. Everybody had a doppelganger or so they said.

'I have as it happens but you didn't know me and you won't know me now but one day in the future I promise it will all make sense. I'm Sabrina.'

Evelyn was unsure what to say. She didn't want to be rude but the girl was barking mad. She opted to say nothing and being a businesswoman first and foremost she focused on her bride-to-be taking herself over to the rack of ready-made gowns and ignoring the unsettled feeling those whisky coloured eyes had given her.

It was the third outfit Bernie tried on that left them all staring at her open mouthed.

'Oh my God, girl, you look amazin'!' Patty gushed.

'You're going to be a gorgeous bride, Bernie,' Sabrina said. 'Don will think he's the luckiest man alive.'

'I always think there's something particularly beautiful about a winter bride,' Evelyn said softly, her hands steepled beneath her chin. This was the magical moment when the perfect dress was found and an ordinary lass who worked on a factory floor became a Cinderella bride-to-be. She never tired of it. 'You need one more thing though.' She hurried off to a shelf and returned with a white faux-fur wrap which she draped around Bernie showing her how she should wear it. 'There, perfect'

Bernie blushed then beamed before slowly turning to admire every angle of her tea-length dress and stole in the mirror. The creamy undertones of the heavy satin fabric brought out the roses in her cheeks and the high neckline with its daisy embroidery added a pretty embellishment to an otherwise simple but elegant dress.

'Will you be wanting a veil or are you going to keep it simple with perhaps a tiara?' Evelyn asked.

Bernie looked to her friends and Sabrina answered with an emphatic, 'A tiara. Don should be able to see your pretty face the whole time.'

'And what flowers were you thinking of for your posy, sweetheart?' Evelyn asked. 'Delphinium would add a beautiful splash of colour and perhaps some liatris and hypericum berries.'

Sabrina was nodding her agreement. A winter posy needed some bright jewel colours. Bernie and Patty however looked at Evelyn as though she were talking in tongues.

'Erm, sounds lovely,' Bernie murmured. She'd leave it up to the florist.

It was with reluctance Bernie carefully stepped out of her dream dress and back into her civvies a short while later. She couldn't stop smiling as Evelyn wrapped her gown, stole, the satin pumps she'd selected and the finishing touch, the diamante tiara that shimmered under the lights. She'd slide it into her hair which she planned on wearing piled high on her head on the day she decided watching as the tissue paper-wrapped precious items were placed in a white bag with gold trim.

It had been a successful afternoon, Evelyn thought with a contented sigh, watching the girls walk out of her shop a moment later but that encounter with the girl they called Sabrina had been most unsettling. Most unsettling indeed.

'A cup of tea, girls?' Bernie asked as Patty pulled the shop door to behind them. She was on a high. Or shall we go and celebrate with a Babycham?'

'Ooh, let's have a Babycham, queen!' Patty grinned. 'What do you say, Sabrina?'

'You two go ahead. I'll join you in a little while.' Her head turned in the direction of Cripps and she felt a magnetic tug towards the patch of pavement she knew so well.

Bernie and Patty glanced at one another. 'Don't be too long or the bubbles will go flat. It's my treat,' Bernie said as Sabrina strode off in the opposite direction.

Part Three

Chapter Thirty-two

Present Day

Liverpool, 1981

Sabrina

The world seemed out of kilter and Sabrina felt a little like she'd stepped off a merry-go-round as she stared around her at the sights and sounds of Bold Street. The Christmas lights weren't on but they were there, strewn across the street ready to shine once it got dark. The traffic was heavier, the cars squarer or more rectangular than they'd been a second ago. She caught sight of someone waving an Everton scarf out of the window of a blue Ford Escort while the driver parped the horn and a group of lads wandering down the street gave a cheer.

Two girls passed by, barely older than Florence's sisters, with their arms linked just as she'd had hers through Bernie and Patty's earlier. They stared at her curiously and then giggled once past.

A woman around her own age with angry streaks of blusher down either cheek, black lipstick and magenta hair stopped mid-stride.

'You ahright there, queen? You look peaky, like.'

Sabrina blinked. 'Erm, yes I'm fine.'

'I like your outfit, proper sixties that is. There's a thrift shop down the road that has a black and silver sparkly cardi that would look gorgeous with that dress.' She held up a bag. 'I just got a tartan miniskirt.'

Sabrina only dimly registered her words as she asked, 'What year is it?'

The girl pulled a face and took a step away from her. 'Nineteen eighty-one and you want to stop smoking worrever it is you've been smoking, girl.' The magenta spikes wobbled as she shook her head and stalked off.

Sabrina's face stretched into a wide grin. She was back! She'd made it home. Her legs virtually cartwheeled up the street in her hurry to get to the shop. 'Sorry,' she tossed back over her shoulder as she received an 'Oi watch where you're going,' from a disgruntled fella.

'Aunt Evie, Aunt Evie!' she cried flinging the door to Brides of Bold Street open, uncaring whether there were any customers in the shop.

Evelyn who'd been about to turn the sign to closed nearly tumbled backwards as Sabrina flung her arms around her. She'd dimly registered her aunt was wearing her Saturday shop coat.

'Steady on, Sabrina, luv.' Evelyn laughed as she hugged her back tightly.

'I'm so sorry I left again without telling you,' Sabrina mumbled into her aunt's shoulder. 'You must have been worried when I didn't come home. I felt so bad. It wasn't fair of me but I'd fallen out with Adam and I—'

Evelyn shushed her patting her on the back just as she had when she was a little girl upset over something or other. 'You're home now, sweetheart, that's what matters.'

They stayed like that for a full minute both seeking reassurance that this was real. Sabrina needed to know she was home and Evelyn needed to know she was back.

It was Evelyn that released her tight hold.

'I expect you'll be wanting to know whether your young man's been asking after you?'

Sabrina held her breath. It was first and foremost on her mind.

'He's been ringing every night desperate to talk to you.'

'He has?' Maybe everything would be alright after all, Sabrina thought.

Evelyn nodded and her glasses slid down. She pushed them back up onto the bridge of her nose. 'He has and Florence too of course. I told them I suspected you'd gone off on a sabbatical once again and that I didn't know when you'd be home. They made me promise to get you to telephone them the minute you got back. We all refused to believe you wouldn't make it back.' Her voice wobbled at this and Sabrina picked up her aunt's hands. Her skin was soft and warm as she gave them a gentle squeeze.

'I'm so sorry, Aunt Evie.'

Evelyn regained her composure and in her usual brusque manner told her what was done was done and she was back now which was what mattered. She inspected the pink column dress Sabrina had bought for wearing to the clubs and which she'd decided would do for a girls' day out shopping before her eyes settled on the matching pink pumps. She still had the coat Bernie had loaned her on too and she could smell the heady Diorissimo, Patty had sprayed into the air and had them all walk into the droplets, on her hair.

'I take it from your clobber and hair, you've been on a jaunt back to the sixties then.'

Sabrina nodded. She'd forgotten about Bernie's bouffant backcombing efforts on her this morning. 'Nineteen sixty-two and, Aunt Evie, you won't believe everything that happened and who I saw.'

'Did you find her?' A part of Evelyn wanted Sabrina to be at peace and a part of her was terrified if she found her mother she might lose her.

Sabrina shook her head.

'I'm sorry, sweetheart.'

'So am I. I went back to nineteen sixty-two. If I'd been a year later then maybe—.' Her voice trailed off but then, too elated to be down for long, she asked, 'How long have I been gone?'

'A week.'

Sabrina shook her head. She'd spent months of her life in 1962 and yet only a week had passed here in the present day. There was no rhyme nor reason to the way time worked.

'What's that around your neck?' Evelyn peered closer.

Sabrina reached up and held the medal out to show her aunt. 'It's a St Christopher Medal. He's the patron saint of travellers. My friend Bernie gave it to me to keep me safe on my travels.'

'Travels?' Evelyn looked warily at the girl she thought of as her daughter. 'You're not planning on—'

Sabrina cut her off. 'Right now, Aunt Evie, I don't want to think about what the future holds.'

'Well, your Saint Christopher there brought you home to us, that's good enough for me. Now come on upstairs. I'll put the kettle on. You and I have got some catching up to do.'

Chapter Thirty-three

'Is that you, Sabrina? I've made scones, c'mon in,' Mrs Teesdale called out. She followed it up with a bellow aimed heavenward. 'Flo, Sabrina's here!'

A thudding sounded upstairs and Sabrina grinned to herself, knowing Florence had just rolled off her bed and would be stampeding down the stairs any second now. In the meantime, the lure of one of Mrs Teesdale's scones was too strong and she didn't wait for her pal to appear. Instead, she followed her nose through to the kitchen.

'G'won, help yourself. I've just finished buttering them.' Mrs Teesdale beamed as Sabrina appeared in the doorway.

Sabrina greeted the twins first before giving Mrs Teesdale a hug and kiss on the cheek. She spied the baking tray still sitting on top of the oven with the burnt bits of raisins she liked to pick off on it as she peered over the woman she thought of as her second mam's shoulder and releasing her, she hot-footed it over to that first.

'It's not fair, Mam! You always let Sabrina have the first scone.' Shona scowled from where she was intent on colouring-in at the kitchen table.

'I don't like the burnt bits anyway,' Tessa said, seeing Sabrina flick one off with the knife before snaffling it.

'Pipe down, youse two,' Mrs Teesdale ordered as Florence burst into the kitchen.

'Sabrina!'

Sabrina stuffed the raisin in her mouth and hugged her friend.

'It's so good to see you,' she managed to gasp out as Florence squeezed the breath out of her.

'Good grief. You'd think it had been months since you two saw each other.' Mrs Teesdale's smile was indulgent.

If only she knew, Sabrina thought, exchanging a glance with Florence.

The two girls took stock of one another. Florence's hair wasn't as white blonde as it had been a week ago. In fact, it had toned down to a golden blonde which suited her skin tone.

'She's been washing it every day using that special silver shampoo,' Mrs Teesdale supplied. 'Her father's over the shock of it all now although we think she shaved ten years off his life expectancy.'

Florence pulled a face at her mam.

'It suits you,' Sabrina said, and she meant it. 'Is it true then? Do blondes have more fun?'

'Not when their bezzie mate abandons them for a week.'

'Sorry,' Sabrina said.

'Did you get it finished then?' Mrs Teesdale asked, slapping Shona's hand as she tried to sneak away with two buttery scones. 'You won't eat your dinner, and wipe your hands down or you'll get grease all over your skirt.'

'Erm...' Sabrina wasn't sure what Florence had told her mam she'd been doing.

'The Princess Diana dress you've been busy making. Florence said it's been giving you nightmares.'

'Oh, yes, that. It was a sod of a thing but I got there in the end.'

'Glad to hear it. You can't have your brides-to-be disappointed. You'd better have one of these before those two over there polish them off.' She offered the plate to Sabrina. She was always intent on feeding her up and Sabrina loved it.

'One for each hand, luv,' Mrs Teesdale urged.

'That's not fair!' Shona and Tessa shrieked. 'Why's she allowed two?'

'And who's 'she' when she's at home?'

Florence inclined her head towards the door. 'C'mon, Sabs, let's go upstairs.' She turned and began to walk from the kitchen but Tessa pointed her red colouring-in pencil at her older sister's back.

'Flo's got an admirer, Sabrina,' she grinned.

'Shurrup you,' Florence growled, swinging back round to glare at her sister.

'It's true. He brought her flowers, look.'

Sabrina followed the jabbing pencil in the direction of the sideboard where a beautiful display of winter flowers brightened up the room. They made Sabrina think of Bernie and she hoped her wedding day had been perfect. She wished she could have been there but she wouldn't have swapped being back here now for anything.

Shona joined in. 'His trousers were so tight I thought he'd split them and Flo went all red in the face when he gave them to her.'

'That's enough, youse two,' Mrs Teesdale said, biting her lip in an effort not to smile.

Florence raised her chin haughtily. 'C'mon, Sabrina, let's leave the babies to their colouring-in.'

'Mam, tell her we're not babies.'

Florence and Sabrina raced upstairs. Only when Florence had closed her bedroom door and then opened it again a few seconds later to check her sisters weren't lurking in the hallway earwigging did she say, 'So c'mon on then, tell me everything.'

They flopped down on Florence's bed and Sabrina repeated the tale she'd told her Aunt Evie earlier beginning by telling her how Adam had fallen out with her and upset, she'd decided to see if whatever it was that happened on Bold Street to take her back in time, would happen again. Obviously, it had.

'He's been beside himself, Adam I mean. He was waiting for me outside work and everything the other day wanting to know what the chances were you'd want to hear from him if you managed to get back to us that was.'

Sabrina had telephoned Florence as soon as Aunt Evie had left to catch the bus for the Saturday match. Sabrina had been insistent she go. Half deafened from her pal's delighted scream down the telephone line, she'd changed into more appropriate clothes and headed straight around to the Teesdales' house.

When Sabrina had finished filling in the gaps as to where she'd been and what had happened while she was gone, Flo turned to face her, propping herself up on one elbow. 'You've got to telephone him.'

'I know and you're right I should ring him but I'm scared, Flo. He didn't want me to go back again but I did it anyway and I hurt him by turning my need to find me mam onto him.'

'I understood why you had to and I'm sure deep down he does too. His mam's obviously a sore spot which you can understand.'

'I should never have brought her into things. You should have seen the way he shut down, Flo.'

'I saw the way he looked when you were gone.'

'How did he look?' Sabrina wanted every detail.

Bernie looked woebegone but instead of tugging at Sabrina's heartstrings, it made her giggle.

'Ring him.'

'I will.'

'Now.'

'Five minutes and I promise I'll do it.'

'Let's see this necklace of yours then.'

Sabrina showed Florence the medal on the dainty chain.

'That's luvly that is. And I can't believe you saw John Lennon.'

'Me neither.' Sabrina felt the same searing sense of sadness as she'd felt seeing the musician across the crowded club but another thought sprang to mind and she sat upright. 'Oh my God, girl, I just remembered!'

'What?'

'I've got to check something.' She shot out of the room and was down the stairs in a flash with a bewildered Florence in hot pursuit. The front room was empty and she made her way over to the record player getting down on her knees to open the cabinet. She pulled the dozen or so records in there out and began going through them until she found what she was looking for only it wasn't what she expected.

'Flo, look.' She held it up for her friend to see.

'Margaux and Lee.' Florence read the name on the LP's cover.

'Yes, Margaux *and* Lee. Don't you see?'

Florence shook her head, she was lost as to what Sabrina was on about.

Sabrina laughed. 'I knew Margaux made a record because I saw the cover of it here but I only saw half of it. She and Lee, they must have made it back to each other.'

She hugged the record to her chest suddenly desperate to know the rest of Patty and Lee's story.

Chapter Thirty-four

'I'm sorry.' Adam and Sabrina spoke over one another and then exchanged self-conscious smiles. Adam got up and pulled a chair out for Sabrina. He'd been waiting for her at a table for two by the window of the bohemian styled Café Tabac on Bold Street. He'd come early, determined to take no chances of her arriving, him not being there, and her deciding to walk away.

They'd arranged to meet at the café during a rather stilted telephone conversation with Sabrina having rung him from Florence's while her friend sat on the floor in the hall next to her to make sure she didn't hang up before anyone could answer.

Sabrina had pressed the receiver to her ear, ignoring Florence and had half expected him to be at the match like Aunt Evie but he'd picked up after only a few rings and she'd heard the relief in his voice when she'd said hello.

There'd been an awkwardness between them that hadn't been there before though and as she'd ducked under the café's striped awning and in through the door moments ago, her stomach had been tying itself into complicated anxious knots as to how this would play out. Sitting down now, she doubted it would be worth her ordering anything other than a coffee. She'd not be able to swallow a bite to eat despite the delicious smells permeating the air.

Adam sat back down and looked at her with eyes that seemed even darker than she remembered. His gaze made her body feel warm. 'I missed you.'

There was no point playing coy. 'I missed you more. It's the strangest thing, Adam,' she rushed on. 'For you, I've been gone a week but I spent months in nineteen sixty-two.' Sabrina reached her hand out and he took it. The dry heat of his touch was both exciting and reassuring and they sat like that for a moment as the chatter and clinking of cutlery in the busy bistro café dissipated. They could have been the only two people in the café as a current of something neither of them properly understood rippled between them.

'We're getting the look from Rita,' Sabrina said, feeling the café proprietor's eyes upon them break the spell. Everyone knew she wasn't shy in coming forward if you took up space in her café without ordering anything.

Adam cleared his throat and flicked his hair, which was borderline shaggy, out of his eyes, 'I'll order.' He pushed his seat back. 'What do you fancy? I can never go past their sausage and apple sauce sandwiches.'

You, Sabrina thought. *I fancy you.*

'Sabrina?'

'Erm, just a coffee, ta.'

She watched him go to the counter, not wanting to let him out of her sight and tracked his return a minute or two later.

'I'm sorry I left without seeing you first,' Sabrina said as he sat back down.

'I behaved like an idiot.'

'No, you didn't. I get so caught up in this, this...' she tried to find the right words, 'need, I suppose to find answers as to what happened the day me mam and I were separated that I lose sight of what matters right here and now.'

'And I'm terrified of losing anyone I care about the way I lost me mam.'

Their hands reached out for each other again.

'We're a right pair aren't we?' Sabrina said.

Adam nodded. 'I haven't met anyone else who understands what it's like to lose your mam.'

Sabrina tilted her head to one side hoping he'd continue to talk.

'Dad tuned out when mam was sick. He couldn't deal with it. It's like he thought if he pretended none of it was happening then she'd be alright. She needed him though and there were times when I wanted to shout at him and...' His voice broke and his jaw tightened before he licked his lips and relaxed a little. 'I wanted him to acknowledge what was going on. In the end, it came down to me. Someone had to take care of her but it leaves scars watching someone you love fade away.'

Sabrina could sense how alone he'd felt, along with the complicated gamut of emotions where his father was concerned broiling beneath the surface. A surge of anger towards Ray Taylor for having put his teenage son through so much fired through her. 'You weren't the adult though. It shouldn't have fallen to you.'

He shrugged. 'It's in the past.' His voice was quiet as he added. 'I've never told anyone any of this stuff before but I can talk to you.' He wouldn't meet her eye across the table and then, looking embarrassed as though he'd said more than he wanted, he raised his head. 'Tell me about what happened. You said you were in nineteen sixty-two?'

Sabrina knew he'd say no more on the subject of his parents and so she opened her mouth to talk but their coffees and his sandwich arrived. She waited until he'd tipped a sachet of sugar into his coffee, taking a sip of her own while he did, before she settled down to tell him everything.

When she'd finished Adam shook his head, his sandwich untouched on the plate in front of him. 'I can't believe you saw John Lennon.'

Sabrina nodded. 'It was sad seeing him young and so full of life.'

'Yeah, flippin' tragic that was. But he did more with the time he had than lots of people do with a whole lifetime.' He paused. 'I wish you'd found her, Sabrina, because then you'd have your answers and I wouldn't have to face losing you again.'

Sabrina was quiet.

'I'm not going to ask you to make promises you can't keep.' Adam shifted awkwardly in his seat. 'I care about you, Sabrina. A lot.'

Before she could answer, he'd raised himself in his seat, his hands were planted on the table as he leaned across it. She tilted her head up to meet him and their noses bumped. They laughed, nuzzling one another for a split second before their lips found each other. Sabrina was aware of the leather smell from his jacket and the apple scent of his shampoo as her eyes fluttered closed and her mouth began to move to the ever-demanding rhythm of his. She'd completely forgotten where she was until a loud clearing of the throat from behind the counter saw them break apart, flushed and breathing fast.

They sat back in their seats.

'I'm glad you're back,' Adam said.

'Me too.'

Chapter Thirty-five

'What time did Nicole say she was calling in?' Evelyn asked overtop of the Singer.

'Ten thirty,' Sabrina said, looking up from the pattern she was cutting out for a new client to where her aunt was attaching the right sleeve to Nicole's dress. It would be finished once she'd snipped the thread off and Nicole was coming in to try her gown on one last time before taking it home.

The pips on the radio signalled it was ten o'clock now.

'Turn it up, Sabrina.'

Sabrina put her scissors down and did as she was told. They carried on with their tasks while listening to the news, Evelyn tutting about what the world was coming to as the newsreader mentioned a car bombing in Iraq.

'They've never got anything cheerful to report,' Sabrina moaned, leaving the volume where it was as John Lennon's (Just Like) Starting Over began to play. Hearing his voice jarred her and she listened to the words properly, feeling her eyes well up. She wasn't aware her aunt had stopped sewing until her arm squeezed her shoulder.

'C'mon now, luv. You've a bride-to-be coming in shortly you don't want to be all maudlin.'

Sabrina sniffed. Aunt Evie was right she had to be professional. 'I'll just go and give my face a splash with some cold water.'

'Blow your nose and put the kettle on while you're at it,' Evelyn called after her.

Sabrina took herself off upstairs and when she returned, feeling much more composed thanks to the two garibaldi biscuits she'd nibbled on while she'd waited for the tea to brew, she nearly dropped the tray she was carrying.

She couldn't believe her eyes.

There, clustered around the worktable, were Nicole, Bernie, Patty, Lee and a fella she didn't recognise.

'I'll take them off you before you spill them.' Evelyn was all business as she put her china cup and saucer down alongside her machine. She found a clear space for the mug on the work table, a safe distance away from Nicole's dress and the pattern Sabrina was in the middle of cutting out.

'I can't believe it.' Sabrina's mouth kept opening and closing.

'Sabrina, stop that, you look gormless,' Evelyn said but her smile softened the words. 'C'mon, girl, pull yourself together. You've got visitors. They didn't come here to see a goldfish. Now, can I offer you a cup of tea?'

'Oh, no ta, we've drunk enough to tea to sink a ship since we've been back.' Patty smiled before moving toward Sabrina who managed to close her mouth as she was wrapped up in a Diorissimo-scented embrace. Bernie was next and then Lee gave her a quick squeeze.

She was still in shock and Nicole, seeing her pale face, pulled out the stool she'd sat on the last time she'd called into the shop. She recalled sitting on it and listening to Evelyn tell her Sabrina had vanished. They'd tried to make sense of the fact that it was highly likely she was back in the sixties with Nicole's mother. Now, she patted it and said, 'Why don't you sit down for a bit, Sabrina.'

'Ta,' Sabrina said sinking down gratefully.

'I'll let you all catch up while I go and try the dress on shall I?' Nicole looked hopefully at Evelyn.

'That sounds a very good idea indeed,' Evelyn replied scooping the dress up carefully and draping it over her arm to carry it through to the fitting room. Nicole hurried after her.

'Now tell us cos me and Pats are dying to know. Did you make it up with your Adam?' Bernie asked.

Sabrina nodded and gazed at the familiar faces that age had tweaked. People's eyes didn't change though, she thought, seeing the warmth in Bernie's brown ones and the twinkling in Patty's blue eyes so similar to her daughter's. Lee's too still had a cheeky glint.

'Are you Davey?' she asked, finding her voice as her attention settled on the one person in the room she didn't recognise. He didn't look much like Patty although on closer inspection they had the same nose.

'I am, luv. It's nice to meet you. The girls have told me all about you.' He shook his head. 'It's a mad story.' His voice had an Australian twang with Liverpudlian undertones.

'It is but it's all true,' Sabrina replied. 'I'm so glad you and Patty found one another again.'

Sabrina smiled and looked at Patty who flashed a reassuring smile back at her. 'It's really us, Sabrina. And look at you, not changed. You're even wearing that sweater.'

'You are too, queen. I remember you sitting shivering outside St Luke's.' Bernie shook her head.

She was no longer blonde, Sabrina noticed, taking in the conker-nut coloured hair. She glanced down at her top with its diamond pattern set against the soft white wool and saw it was indeed the one she'd been wearing when she'd first met Bernie and Patty.

She gazed at her two friends not knowing where to begin and in the end, all she could come up with was, 'What happened after I left?'

'Well,' Bernie said, diving in first. 'When you didn't come back after we bought my wedding dress here we figured out what had happened. We were sad, Pats and me, that you'd gone but we hoped you'd managed to get back to the right time.'

'I did,' Sabrina nodded. 'I would have loved to have been at your wedding Bernie but—'

'I understood. It was a brilliant wedding, wasn't it, Patty?'

Patty nodded confirmation.

'Don and I have two boys. One's a year younger than Nicole and the other's sixteen, still at school. I've peeped in the window, you know.' Bernie gestured out toward the shop. 'I've kept an eye on you over the years but there was no point in me coming in until I knew you'd know who I was.'

Sabrina stared at her in wonder. 'And you and Patty have kept in touch?'

'Course. Don and I have taken the boys out to Australia twice. They think of Nicole as a sister and Patty and Davey came back years ago to lay old ghosts to rest.'

'We went to see our dad,' Patty spoke up. 'I had to find it in my heart to forgive him for leaving us the way he did or I knew I'd never make peace with myself.'

'That was brave of you both,' Sabrina murmured and Bernie nodded her agreement.

'He was sorry for the choices he'd made but in the end, all that anger I'd held onto disappeared and I was left feeling sorry for him. I don't think he'd had an easy life with that wife of his. We keep in touch with our half-sister, Amelia, though. That was something good that came out of it all. She'll be at our kid's wedding. Not me dad or Sheelagh though. I've forgiven him and her but I'm not a flippin' saint!'

Sabrina listened to this and then picked up her tea with a shaking hand, hoping the hot liquid would help her over the shock she still felt at seeing her old friends so unexpectedly.

Patty carried on with her story. 'I made it to Adelaide. It was quite the journey let me tell you and I had a few hairy moments along the way but it was worth it because I found our Davey. He'd left the home he'd been placed in by then of course being nineteen and he was working as a builder. Poor luv hadn't had a good time of it. They used those kids at the home as slave labour. It still makes my blood boil.'

Davey reached over and patted his sister's arm. 'It's history, Pats.'

Patty shook her head. 'It's wrong is what it is. All them years you and I missed out on each other.' She turned to Sabrina once more. 'One day soon it will all come out the way he and all the others were put on those ships and sent so far away.'

Bernie murmured her agreement. 'It will, Pats. Wrongs like that can't remain tucked away out of sight.'

'Like her with our dad, I had to put it behind me. You can't let bitterness rule your life or you have no life,' Davey said, giving his sister a meaningful glance.

'I won't rest until there's an apology from those behind it all,' Patty said, her lips compressing as she folded her arms across her chest.

A sombreness settled on the room but it was short-lived when Evelyn, marching in, told them all to close their eyes.

They did as they were told and when she said they could open them, there was Nicole every inch the beautiful bride, standing in the entrance to the workroom shyly waiting to hear what everyone had to say.

Patty unfolded her arms and her hands were clasped prayer-like as she raised them to her mouth before turning to Lee, 'Look at her, Lee, just look.'

Lee left his wife's side and kissed his daughter on her cheek telling her how her Andy was a lucky fella. Davey did the same, and Bernie fussed around her getting tearful as she said it was like looking at her mam all over again and how she hadn't been able to attend her wedding but she'd not be missing her daughter's.

Patty was the last to come up to her and with a trembling bottom lip, she said, 'I'll never forget right here, right now. You're a stunner, our Nic.'

Nicole hugged her mum and then announced, 'I don't want to get out of it.'

'I'm afraid you'll have to, luv,' Evelyn said. 'You might get some funny looks on your way home otherwise.'

'At least I don't have to wait long until I can wear it again. We're getting married next Sunday morning in Aigburth at St Michael's. It's Andy's mum's church and then it's back to the pub to celebrate. I'm hoping you and Evelyn, and your fella, of course, Sabrina, will come as our guests?'

Evelyn and Sabrina looked at one another in delight. They rarely got to see the brides whose dresses they'd toiled over on their big day.

'We'd love to wouldn't we, Aunt Evie.'

'We would, indeed.'

Nicole beamed and then found herself being herded back to the fitting room by Evelyn.

Sabrina turned her attention to Patty once more. 'Do you remember how I told you I'd seen a record cover with you, or rather Margaux on it, Patty?'

Patty nodded.

'Well, when I got back I dug it out and realised I'd only seen half the cover and Lee was on it too. You were a duo. Tell me how you met up again? When I left you were in Germany, Lee, and, Patty, you were about to leave for Australia.'

'Lee, you tell her,' Patty said.

Sabrina listened as Lee told her how he'd not been able to stop thinking about Patty and that the lads from the band were fed up with his mooning after her. His manager, Alan, had come clean as to the advice he'd given Patty about breaking things off for the sake of both their careers. 'I couldn't leave it and so I came back to Liverpool.'

'What about the band?' Sabrina asked.

'Joe the guitarist took over vocals. He'd always had his eye on being the lead singer so it suited him and the rest of the lads. They did the rounds in Germany for a few years and then got fed up and came home. Last I heard, Joe's an estate agent, Reggie's a plumber, and Jimmy's a record producer. When I got back here to Liverpool I wrangled it out of Bernie where Patty was and I got on the next sailing to Australia.'

'All that way,' Sabrina breathed.

'She was worth it. We got married in sixty-three.'

Patty and he exchanged a look. It was the sort of look Sabrina hoped she'd be lucky to exchange with her husband after eighteen years of marriage. She did the maths because something didn't add up.

'I'm glad he did come out because our Nicole was about to be born by the time he got to Adelaide.'

'You were pregnant when you left Liverpool?'

'I hadn't a clue until I was nearly five months. I put all the changes down to the stress of travelling over. Davey looked after me though, didn't you, our kid?'

Davey nodded and smiled.

'I couldn't believe my eyes when Lee turned up on the doorstep.'

'Just in the nick of time I was. She went into labour three days later.'

They laughed recalling the drama of it all.

'They stayed in Adelaide with me and then the three of them went to Sydney for a while. Nicole was tiny. I missed them when they left but I didn't want to go. Adelaide was home,' Davey interjected. 'I'd bought me own place and for the first time had a proper home of me own.'

'We wanted to pick up again with our music and Sydney had a vibrant club scene. It wasn't easy with Nicole being a baby but we managed. We did well too.'

The cocky Lee of old appeared then, posturing as he told Sabrina about the album he and Margaux had made that had topped the charts around the world.

'But then the record company wanted us to start touring and the reality of what our lives would be like if we wanted to say in the charts hit. I was missing Davey. I hadn't come all that way not to be near to him and the parts of me that had been missing had been filled. I'd found me brother, married Lee, and we had a child of our own. The dream had changed.'

'For me too,' Lee said. 'It wasn't what I wanted anymore and I always said—'

'You've got to want it more than anything,' Patty, Bernie and Sabrina chimed.

Lee grinned. 'Exactly, and I didn't. I'm a high school music teacher these days and Pats still sings don't you, luv?'

'In a choir, yes.'

Sabrina marvelled over it all.

'And guess what our Davey's got in his garden,' Patty said.

Sabrina turned to look at Davey.

'An orange tree. I got my oranges and sunshine in the end.'

Chapter Thirty-six

The day of Nicole's wedding, it snowed. Sabrina sat on the cold pew in St Michael's with her body pressed up against Adam's. It had been strange seeing him without his leather jacket on but he scrubbed up well in his suit. Evelyn was on her right-hand side and was wearing a hat with an annoying long green feather in it that kept tickling Sabrina's nose making her want to sneeze. On the front row sat a tiny woman with a lemon suit and a wide-brimmed navy hat with a white bow. She must be Andy's mam, Sabrina thought, watching as she retrieved a handkerchief from her handbag.

It made Sabrina's eyes smart to think she wouldn't be around to be part of Andy and Nicole's married life together. She thought of Adam's mam and her own mam before banishing such sad thoughts on what was such a happy day. Andy's mam was here now seeing them wed and that was what mattered.

All eyes swivelled to the entrance then as the fanfare of music announced the arrival of Nicole. There was to be no wedding march though.

Nicole glided down the aisle on her father's arm while her mam sang Frankie Valli's 'Can't Take My Eyes Off You'.

'Isn't she beautiful,' Sabrina whispered to Evelyn who was dabbing her eyes with a tissue, as she glided past. Evelyn always cried at weddings. The simple posy Nicole was carrying of winter honeysuckle and an early flowering Christmas rose gave off a sweet scent that mingled with the hint of Christian Dior's Diorissimo hanging on the air.

Later, when the vows had been exchanged and there wasn't a dry eye in the church, the congregation filed outside to where the new Mr and Mrs Littlewood were waiting. Nicole turned away from the gathering on the church steps, a gentle drift of snowflakes falling around her as she tossed her posy high into the air. Sabrina closed her eyes and reached skyward.

She caught it.

The End

THANK YOU SO MUCH FOR reading Book 2 in my Liverpool Brides series. I hope the story made you smile. A book review is the best present you can give an author and if you have time to leave one, I'd so appreciate it.

The next instalment in this twisty, time slip tale, The Spring Posy will take Sabrina back to the 1940's and wartime in Liverpool. It's out in paperback on August 26, 2021 and available for e-book pre-order now through Michelle Vernal's Amazon page!

Printed in Great Britain
by Amazon

26722602R00175